also by

Janet Wallach

DESERT QUEEN: THE EXTRAORDINARY LIFE OF
GERTRUDE BELL

CHANEL: HER STYLE AND HER LIFE

. . . . .

with John Wallach

STILL SMALL VOICES: THE REAL HEROES OF THE
ARAB-ISRAELI CONFLICT

ARAFAT: IN THE EYES OF THE BEHOLDER

THE NEW PALESTINIANS

Nan A. Talese
d o u b l e d a y

New York
London
Toronto
Sydney
Auckland

Seraglio

Janet
Wallach

PUBLISHED BY NAN A. TALESE

AN IMPRINT OF DOUBLEDAY

a division of Random House, Inc.

DOUBLEDAY is a registered trademark of Random House, Inc.

This book is a work of fiction. Although many of the names, characters, places, and incidents are based on historical research, the work is a historical novel drawn from the author's imagination. Any resemblance to actual living persons is entirely coincidental.

BOOK DESIGN BY TERRY KARYDES

TITLE PAGE PHOTOGRAPH: LORNA OWEN

Library of Congress Cataloging-in-Publication Data
Wallach, Janet, 1942–
Seraglio / Janet Wallach.—1st ed.
p. cm.
1. Du Buc de Rivery, Aimée, 1776–1817—Fiction. 2. Selim III, Sultan of the Turks, 1761–1808—Fiction. 3. Mahmut II, Sultan of the Turks, 1784–1839—Fiction. 4. Turkey—History—Abdul Hamid I, 1774–1789—Fiction. 5. Turkey—History—Selim III, 1789–1808—Fiction. 6. Turkey—History—Mahmud II, 1808–1839—Fiction. 7. West Indians—Turkey—Fiction. 8. Kidnapping victims—Fiction. 9. Women—Turkey—Fiction. 10. Harem—Fiction. I. Title.
PS3623.A444 S47 2003
813'.6—dc21
2002028698

ISBN 0-385-49046-1

PRINTED IN THE UNITED STATES OF AMERICA

February 2003

FIRST EDITION

1 3 5 7 9 10 8 6 4 2

To John,
forever

This book is based on the life of Aimée du Buc de Rivery, the eighteenth-century girl from Martinique, and cousin of the Empress Josephine, who was seized by pirates and sent to the sultan's harem in Istanbul. There, at Topkapi Palace, she became the wife of one Turkish sultan and the mother of another. Her rise from lowly slave to valide sultan, and her influence over her son, Sultan Mahmud II, one of the great reformers of the Ottoman Empire and a ruler who turned Turkey toward the West, has intigued generations of writers and scholars.

The story has always been controversial. Was Aimée, in fact, the same person as the harem woman called Nakshidil? If so, when did she arrive in Istanbul, what was her relationship with Selim, and was she the real mother of Mahmud? After several years of research, visits to Topkapi and to the impressive turbe where she is buried, and with the help of Ottoman scholars who combed the Topkapi Palace archives, I had to concede that little specific information exists about Aimée/Nakshidil or, for that matter, any of the women in the Ottoman sultan's harem. No journals or diaries were permitted inside the imperial harem, no contact was allowed with the world outside; the women's pasts were deliberately erased, their futures defined by the palace.

It was Father Chrysostome, the Jesuit priest, who told of the last rites given to Nakshidil on her deathbed. That the sultan's mother was born a Christian was not unusual; it was her wish to die as a Christian, and her son's acceptance of it, that set her apart. It was harder to prove that she was the missing daughter of the Martinique plantation family du Buc de Rivery, yet many students of Turkish history believe it to be true. And when Sultan Abdul Aziz journeyed to France in 1867, he was greeted with great enthusiasm by Napoleon III, who told the press that their grandmothers were related. What's more, the sultan brought with him a miniature of Nakshidil that had a likeness to an earlier portrait of Aimée, and while in France Abdul Aziz sent out word that he was looking for members of Aimée's family.

I began this book as a biography and ended writing it as a historical novel. It will not end the debate over the origins of the Valide Sultan Nakshidil. But I hope it will provide a glimpse of her mysterious life in the seraglio two centuries ago. Perhaps too it will shed some light on the Muslim world today, whether it be a handful of rulers ensnared in plots for power and succession or the millions of women who still live cloaked behind the veil of the harem.

Seraglio

•••••

From the

JOURNAL DE FRANCE,

JULY 10, 1867

Sultan Abdul Aziz arrived in Paris this week for a State Visit. As the first Ottoman Emperor to visit France, he was given a warm welcome by the Goverment, which provided him with a huge suite at the Elysée Palace, and a staff to assist his own vast retinue of servants. Among the Sultan's wishes were hardboiled eggs at breakfast, Napoleon pastries at lunch, chocolates in the evening, and private performances in his suite by the girls from the Folies Bergère. When asked why he had invited Sultan Abdul Aziz to Paris, Emperor Louis Napoleon replied he was most curious to meet Sultan Abdul Aziz because "we are related through our grandmothers."

Prologue
· · · · ·

Father Chrysostome knelt before the crucifix in his cell, his thoughts disturbed by a knock at the door. "One moment," the Jesuit called, pushing away the vision of the woman he had glimpsed in the park: the sultry eyes, the delicate wrist, the musk scent wafting through the air. She was part of the sultan's harem, yet hadn't he noticed a frisson of flirtation when she caught his glance; and, he had to admit, hadn't he returned it?

Vowing to speak of this at morning confession, he said a quick prayer, wondering as he did so who could possibly be visiting him at such an hour. He lifted himself off the floor, smoothed his brown robes, and opened the door. Father George stood in front of him, a surprised look on his face; behind the good man stood two Janissaries, their towering turbans mocking the small round priest.

1

"They wish to see you," Father George said nervously, rolling his eyes up to indicate the sultan's soldiers. "They have come from the palace with a message. It is urgent." The priest's heart pounded. Had the eunuch who escorted the harem woman noticed the look in his eye this morning? No man, not even a priest, dared cast a glance at a sultan's female slaves. Were they here to put him in prison, or worse?

One of the special soldiers pushed an envelope into Father Chrysostome's hand. He opened it hastily and read the brief message: "It is imperative that you obey the Janissaries and come at once." He looked for a signature, but the note gave no hint of its author.

"One moment, please," he said, looking up uneasily at the men. "I am your most humble servant. I must find my cape."

As soon as the Jesuit had arranged his wool cloak over his shoulders and blown out the candle in his room, he followed the Janissaries. It had been raining and the summer downpour caused a thick fog, but, with no one else on the streets, they hastened down the hill from Pera to the Galata dock where a caïque bobbed between the waves. The priest counted the ten pairs of oarsmen and knew that the boat belonged to a high official of the palace.

Having settled himself on the floor cushions, Father Chrysostome tried to glean information on who had called for him, but each time he started to speak, the sultan's soldiers glared fiercely and told him to hush. "You will find out soon enough," one of the Janissaries said, twisting his drooping mustache as he spoke. The oarsmen rowed swiftly in the dark and the priest could soon make out the European side of the Bosphorus and the Palace of Beshiktash. The boat had hardly reached the dock when the Janissaries jumped ashore and yanked the priest off with them.

Inside the palace Father Chrysostome wanted to stop and soak in the richness of the chambers, each more ornate than the last, but the soldiers rushed him through the gilded rooms. Finally they reached a heavy, painted door where a black eunuch stood on guard. "We brought him as fast as we could," the older Janissary whispered. The flabby eunuch raised a finger, indicating they were to wait, while he disappeared inside. Almost at once he was back at the door, waving in the Jesuit priest. Was this where he was to be called to task?

Father Chrysostome stepped warily inside. The pungent smell of sandalwood and incense filled the air, fighting off the stench of sickness. He looked around, noticed the silk tapestries hanging on the walls, and walked across the patterned rugs to the bed, where a Greek physician in attendance beckoned him closer. Under the netting a woman lay motionless. Peeking at her face he saw at once that she was ghostly pale. He guessed her to be somewhere past forty, but even at her advanced age and in her terminal illness, he noted her delicate features and cheeks like shrunken peaches and knew that she had been a great beauty in her day. Surely she was not the reason for the visit.

As he peered through the white mesh he heard a stifled cough, and only then did he glimpse the shadowed figure of a bearded young man. It took only a moment before the priest realized who had called for him, and he tried to hide his fear, twisting the cord of his belt around his fingers tighter and tighter. He had been in the presence of powerful figures before, but no one as awesome as this man.

"You are here on my orders," the sultan said, and the priest bowed as much in terror as in respect. And then, as though the priest had been given a choice, the ruler put his hand over his heart and added, "Thank you for coming. I promised my mother that she could die as she wished. Please," he whispered, nodding toward the bed, "give her the last rites." With that, the sultan stepped out of the room and indicated to the others that they were to follow.

Father Chrysostome breathed a sigh of relief, took off his cloak, and placed it carefully on a chair; it was then that he noticed the black eunuch hovering in the corner. The priest eyed him anxiously—his feminine face, his thick neck and curvaceous paunch—but saying nothing, he pulled a chair to the bed and sat down beside the Queen Mother. He knew that for the past eight years this woman, only now so fragile, had been the most influential female in the empire: the trusted adviser to her son Sultan Mahmud II, and the public face of the private ruler. The Ottomans called her Valide Sultan Nakshidil, and they called her son their padishah, God's shadow on earth, the caliph, leader of all Muslims. Now, she wanted *him*, a Jesuit priest, at her side.

"Valide Sultan Nakshidil," he whispered in a calming voice, "I am here for you, and for as long as you like. Please, let us begin with a prayer."

"Oh Father, I have so much on my mind," she answered feebly. "You must know that I have not been a good Catholic. As soon as I arrived in the harem, I was forced to become a Muslim. I did what I could . . . secret prayers . . . Christ . . ." and then her voice trailed off.

The priest took her frail hand and held it while she gained her strength. When he saw that she was ready to speak again, he nodded with encouragement.

"The harem can be a terrible place . . ." she confided, "such intrigues . . . there was a red-haired woman, I . . ." her voice faded. The eunuch edged over to intervene. In a castrato's high-pitched voice he cautioned, "My dear, you are weak, and there are things you must not talk about. Even to a priest."

A while later the priest removed a small vial from his robes and anointed the woman with the oil. Kneeling beside her, he said,

"Through this holy anointing and His most loving mercy, may the Lord assist you by the grace of the Holy Spirit, so that, when you have been freed from your sins, He may save you and in His goodness raise you up."

Soon after he conferred the rites, granting her the remission of venial sins and making her inculpable for unconfessed mortal sins, he saw that the woman lay absolutely still. He felt her wrist, but any sign of a pulse had disap-

peared; he placed her arms over her chest and closed her
eyelids. He crossed the room to reach for his cape, but the
eunuch was clasping it to his breast as though it were a life-
line to the valide. Gently the priest touched the man's arm,
slipped on the coat, and followed the odd figure who limped
slightly out the door. Father Chrysostome looked around
for the Janissaries but they had vanished. "I will take you
back to your monastery," the chief black eunuch said, seeing
what was on his mind. "The caïque is waiting."

They rode in silence in the boat, and after it returned to
the dock at Pera and the two men were at the doors of the
Jesuit convent, Father Chrysostome invited the fellow inside. "Please," he insisted, "this has been a difficult night.
Join me in a cup of good, strong nectar. It will do us both
good." The proud eunuch, who, though of modest height
with one leg slightly shorter than the other, carried himself
with a princely air, answered that he rarely drank alcohol—
not because his religion forbade it, he said, but because it
went to his head. Nonetheless, he agreed, yes, this had, indeed, been a difficult night, and thank you, he would accept
the Jesuit's offer.

As the two men sipped their wine, the conversation,
which at first was spare and halting, turned friendlier.
Father Chrysostome told anecdotes about life in Pera with
the Franks and the visitor smiled at the amusing stories
about the Europeans, but being taciturn by nature, he revealed little about his own life in the palace. The priest
yearned to know what the eunuch had stopped the queen

mother from saying, and he prided himself on his ability to coax confessions, but he knew he had to approach the matter with extreme delicacy. He began by asking the usual questions, what was the fellow's name, how long had he been at the palace, what positions had he held, and tiptoed along. Finally, he asked, how did he rise to the powerful position of chief black eunuch?

"It was the Valide Sultan Nakshidil," came the reply from the eunuch, who was nicknamed Tulip.

The priest pressed on, telling stories about his own family, his sisters and brothers, and in particular, his mother. From there he segued back to the queen mother. "You knew her well?"

"That is a difficult question, Father. None of us are what we seem. We are, all of us, more than we wish others to know and less than we ourselves wish to believe."

"And yet?"

"Over the years we became close."

"You must be a special person to have been close to such a woman," he said, hoping the compliment would spur the fellow on.

The eunuch took another sip of the wine and rested the empty glass on the table. "She saved my life once, and I saved hers."

Father Chrysostome leaned over and as he refilled both their glasses, Tulip continued. "She was a good woman and she fought for what she believed in." His eyes began to water. "I will miss her deeply when she is gone." He stopped for a moment and, choking on the words, corrected himself. "*Now* that she is gone."

The Jesuit priest heard the anguish in his voice. "Please, my friend," he said softly, "I see you are filled with sadness. Sometimes it is better to talk. Tell me about the valide sultan. I know that the palace slaves must convert to Islam. How is it that the sultan allowed her to die a Catholic? Who was she and where did she come from?"

It had been a long time since the visitor had spoken to anyone about Valide Sultan Nakshidil, and though they had been close and he had learned many things over the years, he had never betrayed her confidence. "It would take me many nights to tell the story," he said.

"You are welcome to come back as often as you like," the priest replied. "I look forward to many evenings together."

The eunuch took another sip of the potent liquid, loosened his girdle, and in a teary soprano voice, began to pour out a strange tale.

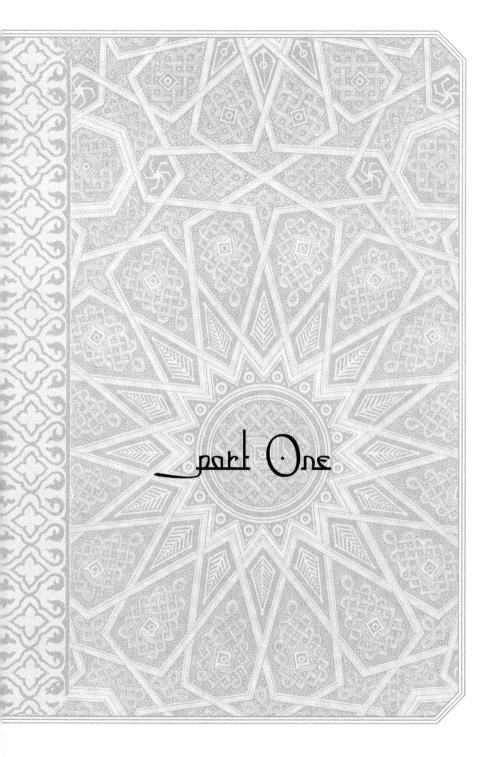

part One

1

· · · · ·

I first met Nakshidil on the day she arrived at Topkapi, in the summer of 1788, nearly thirty years ago. Several of us had been ordered to go to the seraglio pier: a corsair's ship belonging to the bey of Algiers had docked and word had been sent they had a gift on board for Sultan Abdul Hamid. We learned that three weeks before, the Algerian's pirates had captured a boat and presented the bey with the booty: along with gold, silver, and cargo, there were a dozen Christian men and a bud about to blossom. The bey scooped up the gold and silver, sold the goods, and enslaved the men. But when the Algerian saw the budding flower, he resisted the temptation to keep her for himself. Instead, he ordered her to be sent to Istanbul. The clever bey knew about the sultan's lust for young girls. She would be his oblation: the lecherous old Turk could do with her as he wished.

We took her gladly. She had an ethereal air, like a piece
of fluff that dances in the sky. Or a delicate lily; though I
suspected she had a steely gird. Looking her over, my col-
leagues made their round of predictable comments: "She's
too thin to be of any use," said one. Another asked, "Why
didn't God give *me* blond hair and blue eyes?" A third one
murmured, "Maybe she will learn to give me pleasure."

You look surprised, my friend. Of course we eunuchs
lack the private organs of a man, but we are not all as you
may think: some of us have the urges of a normal male; others prefer to be pleasured by men. I do not wish to speak of
my own sexual needs; it was survival inside the palace that
concerned me.

In any case, I promised myself I would wait to see what
the girl was like before I made any judgments on how to treat
her. One always has to be cautious in the palace: everyone
there is either an accomplice or an enemy; accomplices are
few; enemies are in abundance.

I could see she had been through an ordeal, and that the
pirates had treated her badly. She was numb and too confused to speak, but she held herself proudly and would not
budge; we had to drag her to the chief black eunuch.

The *kislar aghasi* was waiting in the entry hall to the harem,
that sacred world of females, forbidden to all men except the
sultan and his black eunuchs. He was drenched in attar of
roses, his face scowling, his giant figure cloaked in green silk
and thick sable, his cone-shaped turban towering over us all.
Satisfaction does not come easily to him, and we eunuchs

lived in fear of his discontent, demonstrated in his wretched temper. Although silence reigns supreme in the seraglio, I could see by the gleam in his black eyes and the twisted smile that appeared on his mouth that he was pleased by the bey's gift. A blond addition to the harem might win him praise from the sultan. But as always with a new odalisque, his first step was to examine her.

He brandished his leather whip and we followed his order, removing her torn dress and tattered petticoats that bore the shredded labels of a French maker. She stood with her head held high, but her eyes were dazed, shocked at the sight of the puissant eunuch and by her own nakedness.

The kislar aghasi studied her, moving his eyes slowly downward from her tangled hair, past her high forehead, her blue eyes, her slightly pointed, upturned nose, her cupid's lips. He pointed at me and ordered me to yank open her mouth and hold it wide so that he could check her teeth. At first I was afraid she might bite, but then I realized she was too frightened to move or make a sound. He ran his finger inside her mouth, counted her teeth and checked her gums, appraising her as he would a camel or a horse. When he had assured himself of her oral condition, he returned to inspect her flesh.

He ordered my colleague to lift her hair and his eyes grazed along her neck; he stopped for a moment, thinking he had spotted a mark, but it was only a tiny spider, and he continued, resting his eyes on her milky white breasts. He tweaked her nipples to make sure they held no liquid, and

she flinched, but he ignored her and ran his jeweled fingers
several times across her soft bosom. He glanced at her navel,
then continued his journey downwards, focusing on her triangle. He noticed the lack of pubic hair and smiled; she was
prepubescent.

He seemed pleased as he shifted his eyes to her well-
shaped legs and ankles and checked her toes to see if they
were straight. He cracked his whip again, made a circle in the
air with his finger to indicate that we should turn her
around, and started the whole procedure one more time.
He took another look at her long neck, stopped at what
might have been a mole on her back, and ordered one of us
to inspect it. It was a piece of dirt. He scrutinized the rest of
her back, followed her figure downwards until he reached
her buttocks and came to a halt. Then, cradling her round
bottom in one hand, he ran his other fingers over her
smooth pink flesh and pinched it slightly. He eyed her thighs
and legs and well-formed calves, and when he reached her
feet, he nodded, and I knew what was coming next.

We turned the girl around so that she was facing him. He
curved his hand around her knee and then inched it slowly
up her inner leg and northwards on her thigh until he
reached the place where the opening was and plunged two
fingers inside. The startled girl cried out, and I thought he
would slap her, but he didn't. Instead, he twisted his fingers
inside her, pulled them out and licked them. I saw her shud-
der and then her head dropped, and she wrapped her arms
around herself to cover her shame. Knowing she would be

worthless if she were not a virgin, we waited to see if the kislar aghasi would give us a sign to keep her. Slowly he tilted his head up and down, nodding in approval.

"Tulip, take charge of her," the chief black eunuch commanded. Pleased that he had confidence in me, though fearful if things went awry, I wrapped her dress around her, put my finger to my lips to let her know she could not speak, and took her to the baths, where I stayed with her in the dense heat until she was clean. It had been weeks since she had bathed, and she submitted readily when the slaves sat her on a marble slab, poured water over her from a silver ewer, and rubbed her hair and scalp. I could see the envy in the other girls' looks; they did not like her yellow hair or her azure eyes; or the patrician way she held herself; she was not a peasant from Russia or the Caucasus like most of them, and they did not take her strangeness well.

When she had adjusted to the swirling sulfurous vapors, she looked around with a saddened gaze: half a dozen young women lay languorously about, manes of black hair trailing down their backs, jet-black eyes glistening against their luminous white skin. Standing behind them were others, some white, some black, bare-breasted and thinly clad below the waist, grooming the girls like loving cats caring for their kittens. In a corner, two voluptuous figures were locked in an embrace. The girl did not say a word, but later she confided:

"I was humiliated and frightened; nothing seemed familiar. I did not know where I was or even when it was. After the pirates seized our ship I lost all sense of time; clocks and calendars are meaningless conceptions when they have no use. And as for place, in that first thick fog of the baths I watched the women fondling each other and thought I had entered Lesbos or the Limbo of Vanity."

When the bath was finished she motioned for her old frock and took something from the lining, but the dress was no longer hers to wear. Instead they wrapped her in a linen towel and slipped tortoise pattens around her feet. We use the wooden clogs to keep from falling on the slippery marble and to protect us from the heat steaming up from the floor, but though she moved with grace, she found the high heels too treacherous to walk in, and they had to help her into the cooling room of the baths where she seemed grateful for a cold sherbet. She drank the orange ices thirstily, hardly pausing to catch her breath.

In the dressing room next door, they gave her fresh clothes: she stepped into the thin *shalwar,* hesitant in the pantaloons gathered at her ankles; and then a gauzy blouse that let her breasts show, but she seemed glad for any kind of cover. Over that they slipped an *entari,* the long, tight-sleeved, silk dress scooped out to plump her bosom and buttoned only at her waist; and a simple linen girdle, without jewels, which she sashed at an angle around her hips. She sighed with relief when she realized she did not have to wear the tortoise pattens outside the bath; like all the others she was given embroidered slippers. Then I led her down the hallway to the mistress chamberlain.

Ordinarily, the queen mother rules the harem, but

Sultan Abdul Hamid had bid farewell to his mother long ago, and it was the *kahya kadin* who ruled us all. An aged virgin appointed by the sultan, who called her "Mother" now, the mistress chamberlain was privileged to carry a silver scepter and to have use of the imperial seal; the only others permitted to do so were the sultan and the grand vezir.

Charged with training hundreds of female slaves, it was her job to make certain that life in the harem ran smoothly: there was a staff of forty just for the padishah, to see to it that everything from his clothes and his jewels, his ablutions and his bath, his syrups and his coffee, his table and his laundry, his musicians and his storytellers were always ready and in perfect order. There was also a staff for the chief black eunuch, and staffs for each of the wives, the favorites—the concubines—and for the mistresses themselves.

Under the mistress chamberlain was a mistress for each area, all of them long past the age that could turn an eye: mistress of the Koran, the coffee service, the treasury, the sherbets, the pantry, the pitcher service, the scribes, the laundry, the wardrobe, the jewels, the embroidery, the coiffures, the ceremonies, the music, and the sick. Those mistresses, in turn, trained the younger women in their service. Lucky were the pretty girls chosen for the sultan's staffs; unlike their superiors who had never slept with a man, they had a good chance of being summoned by the sultan for an intimate rendezvous. If not, the fortunate ones might be chosen as wives for some important man outside the palace, a provincial governor, a pasha, or a military officer. Or if duty called, they might become palace mistresses themselves someday, enriched by material goods if not by matters of the heart.

I indicated to the girl that she should stand still and wait while I approached the silver chair; I bowed deeply and kissed the kahya kadin's sleeve. When I raised my head and saw the hint of a smile upon her face, I knew that she was pleased by the fair-haired virgin; the girl was young, but it was clear she was skilled in social graces and worth twice as much as any peasant we received.

Knowing I had a way with languages, she looked at me to translate; from the label on the dress, I assumed the girl spoke French.

"What is your name, how old are you, and where are you from?" I asked.

"My name is Aimée du Buc de Rivery," she answered in a quiet voice, making me strain to hear her. "I am thirteen, and I am French from Martinique."

"And how is it that you are here?"

"My father is the owner of a great sugar plantation. He sent me to school in Nantes. I had been there for three years when he ordered me home. But I never reached my destination. My ship was seized by pirates, I was taken to Algiers, and then brought here." Her voice was a little stronger now and I began to hear the melodic rhythm of the Creole. "My father is a rich man. He will pay you whatever you want to have me sent home." The head mistress ignored the offer.

"Have you any talents? Can you dance or sew? All the girls here must sew," I added.

She smiled a tiny smile and pulled a small embroidered cloth from inside her entari. "Here is something I hid when the pirates came on board my ship." She raised her head and I could see defiance in her eyes. "It is my favorite handkerchief and I keep it for luck. I sewed it myself at school."

She held it out but the mistress refused to touch it. Standing closer, I could see the stitches and knew the girl was able. "What about music? Do you play an instrument?"

"But, of course," she answered. Using her slender hands to show how she held a violin and a bow, she pretended to play. "Bach, Mozart," she said.

A few more words from the head mistress and the girl was dismissed, brushed off like a bothersome fly. Once again she was put in my charge, and I took her through a hallway, down a narrow flight of stairs, and into the dank basement where the novices slept. I opened the door of the windowless room, and when she saw the divans lining the walls, I could tell she wanted to sit, but I threw my head back, raised my eyebrows, and clucked my tongue to tell her no.

She grabbed my arm. Her voice was as sweet as a nightingale's. "I cannot tell you how pleased I was to hear you speak my language," she said. "It has been a long time since I have conversed with anyone, and my heart twinges at the thought."

"You are not to speak French any longer," I ordered. "You are to forget the name Aimée, and who your family is

19

and where you come from. You are in the harem now. You will learn Arabic and Turkish; you will study Islam; you will become a Muslim."

The mistress chamberlain had given me a slip of parchment and I pinned it to her breast. "This is your name now," I said. "Nakshidil."

She looked at me as if I had lost my mind.

"Nakshidil," I said again. "Repeat it after me."

She stood perfectly still, and though I said it several times, she refused to utter a sound.

. . . . .

Dusk was falling and the iron doors of the harem would soon be closed, the girls locked inside like pearls sealed inside their oyster shells. A black eunuch caught after dark could count his last breaths. I left, knowing that the hundred girls who slept in the long, narrow room were like stars crammed together in the cold dark night, warmed only by the coals of a brazier, kept under the watchful gaze of a dormitory mistress—one for every ten girls. What dreams those sad-eyed women once had, what expectations gone awry! Years later, one told me her heart grew heavier each time she watched the innocent girls who entered the harem; their dreamy eyes reflected her reveries; their ripe lips held hopes of kisses she would never taste. "I would never tell them of my despair, years of waiting, watching for signs from the sultan, empty years devoid of love," she had said.

"Was there never anyone?" I asked.

I could almost see her reaching back through memories as she winced. "I remember when Besmi first approached me, how I gave myself willingly, allowing her to explore my body in exchange for any kind of affection. Later there was Sesame, the eunuch, who offered his thick lips and satisfied me with his strange tools."

The mistress watched the girls, beauties every one, knowing that many had been rocked to sleep in their cradles with nursery songs about the glittering path to the palace. Again and again I heard their stories. None were Turks, for it is sinful for a Muslim to take a Muslim as a slave. Instead, they were from lands of the infidel—the Caucasus Mountains, the Greek islands, the Balkan Peninsula—and had come at the will of their parents, some as early as the age of eight or nine, some even at their own initiative, reminding themselves, as they made their way across the mountains and then by boat to Istanbul, that it was better to be the chattel of a rich man than the legal wife of a pauper.

Perhaps they were right: freedom may mean nothing if it is shadowed by hunger and cold; a slave girl in the harem has a better chance for a warm place to sleep and enough to eat than a hapless peasant at the mercy of Nature's whims. There is a kind of safety in this sequestered world of women slaves, where the only men allowed are the sultan and his black eunuchs. And unlike the peasant doomed to her miserable fate, the odalisque has the chance to improve her lot. The slave market may seem cruel and licentious to those who observe its auctions, but the girls, though thinly clad and intimately inspected, know their futures could be cloaked in layers of silver and gold, if only their beauty and their talents caught the sultan's eye.

It was different, of course, for Nakshidil. Her future had been rich with possibilities, yet here she was, lonely in the harsh swirl of foreign sounds and strange behaviors. That first night she followed the others and pulled cushions and pillows from the wall cupboards, dropped onto the thin divan, and drew the quilted covers over herself like a shroud.

That was the last I saw of her for a week. My duties were with the kahya kadin, and there were so many girls and so much to do that I nearly forgot about Nakshidil, until I received a message to come at once to the novices' room. When I arrived, the dormitory mistress was livid.

"The new one," she said. "She refuses to move; not even to get out of bed. One of the girls has been bringing her food; otherwise she would starve. They have tried to speak to her, but no one can understand a word. You are the only one who knows her tongue. Talk to her."

Silence prevailed in the rooms, as it did throughout the palace, and if the girls uttered any words at all, they were forced to say them in Turkish. If not, if they disobeyed, they were punished. Despite the risk of being hauled off to confinement, many dared to whisper together in their own languages, and once in a while you could hear the screams of a girl being beaten on the ears. Nakshidil risked the punishment and tried to speak to someone, only to be met with blank stares and dumb shrugs. The girls' tongues were a tower of Babel, a mix of Russian, Armenian, Georgian, Chechen, Circassian, Romanian, Bulgarian, Slovenian, Serbo-Croatian, and Greek.

Secretly, I was pleased to have another chance to practice my French, but I revealed only my anger when I approached Nakshidil. "You must do as you are told. This is not a place for spoiled children," I chided. "We work hard here, and you are no better than the rest. In fact, you are an odalisque, the lowest rank of slave. You may have been schooled in France, but you are inexperienced in the harem, a mere caterpillar in a world of butterflies. Be careful," I warned. "You can be punished for this behavior."

She looked at me blankly at first, and then a tear appeared on her cheek. Within a minute more tears were streaming down her face.

Save me from these theatrics, I thought.

"I don't want to be punished," the girl sobbed. "I just want to go home."

"You cannot go home," I said. I kept my face frozen in a frown, but something in her voice reminded me of how I first felt when I arrived in the palace, a young castrated boy, terrified, homesick, numbed by the loss of part of my body and stunned by my strange surroundings.

"I know that my parents will find me," she insisted. "They knew something was wrong when my ship did not arrive. I must get word to them that I am here."

"That will not happen," I snapped. "This is the seraglio,

the sultan's royal palace, his private world, and whether we are male or female, white eunuch or black, young page or soldier, vezir or holy man, wife or concubine, sister or mother, we exist to serve the Ottoman ruler. No matter who we are, the doors to our past are slammed shut."

"It cannot be," she argued. "I know the new opera by Mozart, *Abduction from the Seraglio*. Someone will save me, just as they do in the libretto."

"The only one who will save you is yourself," I advised. "You can refuse to cooperate and you will be punished and remain a lowly slave. Or you can work, study to become a Muslim, and learn how to please a man. Then you have a chance to become a favorite or even a wife." I pushed a strand of hair off her face and turned away.

The next morning I came by to check on her and saw that she had joined the others for the early meal, squatting on the floor around a large copper tray, eating in silence. She took a sip of the strong Russian tea, at once bitter and sweet, and nearly spat it out, and when she bit into the puffy bread, she frowned at the sesamed dough. She tried to scoop the feta cheese and preserves onto the bread, but using only her thumb and first two fingers of her right hand, she could not keep the food from sliding off. Frustrated, she stood up and, holding her head high in defiance, walked away.

I pulled her aside. "What's wrong with you?" I asked. "You must eat."

"I cannot," she said. "This food is for the others. Me,

I wish only for a cup of warm chocolate and some crusty bread."

"You will not find that here."

She sighed. "I still remember my last breakfast at the convent; my friends all hugged me and told me how much they would miss me and wished they were going home too. Now, there is no one to hug, no one even to speak to, and not even any chocolate to drink."

I suppose it was the loneliness that overtook her, and after a few more days she threw another tantrum, shouting in French at the girls and the mistress, storming off and taking to her bed. Again, I was called to speak to her. I entered the dank room, searched the perimeter of spare sofas, and saw her under the covers.

"What madness is this? What are you doing?" I scolded.

"I want to go home," she sobbed.

"It does not matter what you want. You must do as you are told."

"I am told almost never to speak. This place has an eerie silence, and the quiet penetrates my nerves the way cold penetrates the bones. When I am asked to say something, I must answer in this ugly language. I cannot. Why do they not speak French? Do they not know it is the only language that matters? French is the diplomatic tongue. And I am told to wear those ugly clothes. Why do they dress this way? My God, how they look!"

I glanced down at my tunic and gathered pants and recalled how foolish I felt when, instead of the simple cloth I wore in my father's house, I was ordered to wear these layers; yet, after a while, I looked forward to a few yards of silk for a bright new caftan or a pair of baggy trousers.

To be frank, I thought the clothing flattered the young female slaves, but I had to admit, in comparison to her, the girls looked plain. It wasn't just her lissome figure; there was something she did with the few pieces she had been given—the way she tied her sash or wrapped her tunic—that made her seem more stylish. I refrained from saying anything, but let her continue, hoping that if she finished all her complaints, she would be more willing to comply.

"Where is the wine? What sort of people do not drink wine?" she asked. "Imagine, here they drink water! Phui! And I am told to eat with my hands. This is barbaric. I am not some savage. And the beds. These are not beds at all; they have no mattresses, just wool stuffed into cloth. I come from France, the greatest civilization in the world. I do not belong here, and they have no right to keep me. I will leave at once."

I could not help but snicker. "I've told you before," I said. "That is impossible. This is the sultan's palace."

"Palace!" she cried. "This is no palace. From what I have seen it is nothing but four courtyards and a string of pavilions."

"Call it what you wish. You are here for the rest of your life." I paused for a moment, and added, "Like me."

She glowered at me. "I am not like you. How dare you

compare me to an ugly, limping eunuch?" I could feel her staring at my hairless face, and then her eyes dropped to my shorter leg. "I am not a freak," she said viciously. "I am a girl, a very pretty girl. People have always told me so."

My stomach turned as she spoke, and I slapped her hard across her cheek. Her face reddened and I could see the tears welling up in her eyes. She looked at me with contempt.

I lifted my hand to stop her from saying anything more. "Nakshidil," I said.

"I am not this name you call me. I am Aimée du Buc de Rivery. I am French. I am from Martinique. And I am going home soon."

I turned my back. I had had enough.

It was then that I saw the dormitory mistress and realized she had witnessed it all. As I left I could hear Nakshidil's screams and knew she had been given to another eunuch who slapped her ear ten times with a leather slipper. I walked back and peeked in the room: she lay in a crumpled ball on the floor, blood streaming from the side of her head.

She'll change now, I thought, wincing as I recalled the beatings I had received with the bastinado. It was soon after I arrived: they pulled my feet through wooden boards, tied them, and struck my bare soles with the wooden cane again and again, until I collapsed on the floor. For days I had to crawl to and from my bed because I could not walk. I wrapped gauze around my feet for weeks until finally the bleeding stopped. Every young eunuch is punished this way, not once, but many times; it is a method to make the novices compliant. We all learned quickly to obey. But not Nakshidil. At first I thought she had changed, but as I was to learn, it was her stubbornness that was to serve her so well in the years to come.

The next morning she followed the other girls: she rose from her bed, wrapped her bedclothes in a *bocha,* and put the cloth case back on the shelves. She pulled a prayer rug from the stack in the corner, found the white muslin cloth tucked inside, and placed it on her head. She followed the black eunuch imam who led them in prayer, and, kneeling on the carpet, she pressed her hands together in front of her eyes and tried to repeat the strange words, knowing nothing of what they meant. The words were not a request for her freedom, of that she could be certain. After she said the words out loud, she stayed for a moment, as if she were making a silent prayer.

Afterwards she dressed in the thin clothes she had been given and joined the others for the first meal of the day. When the Arabic lessons began, it was clear that only two of the other girls knew how to read a book or hold a pen. But the sultan insisted that everyone in Topkapi Palace be able to read and write, and all must memorize the basic tenets of Islam.

A true Muslim, she was told, knows the entire Koran by heart. She thought it inconceivable when she struggled so over Arabic. I must admit, Arabic is peculiar to read—not at all like French—but so much more beautiful to see, its script a curlicue that moves from right to left, its letters like chameleons changing shape as they change their location in a word.

As for speaking Ottoman Turkish, with its mix of Persian, Arabic, and Turkish, she found it nearly impossible: some of us have an ear for languages—I myself can imitate a Russian, a Greek, or a Persian and sound as if I were native to their soil—but for others, I know, it is not an easy task; the strange sounds, the stress on unexpected syllables, the verbs that trail like the last legs of a centipede, the words that had no connection to any they knew. If she must speak in such a language, she told me, then she would rather not speak at all. Whenever she saw me, she muttered something in French. I pretended not to hear, but it was always a gibe at the Turks: "They speak an unspeakable language," or "These people are no more than savages," she would say.

Unwilling to try hard, she could not be on intimate terms with any of the other slaves. She kept to herself, and did not understand their girlish chatter. At meals, the space on the floor grew wider between her and the rest. When the others giggled, she felt sure their laughter was at her.

Most of the time, she stayed apart and sulked, stubbornly insisting she would soon be rescued. She refused to respond when anyone called her by the name Nakshidil and refused to understand when anyone spoke to her in Turkish. I realized that if she did not start to conform, she might be shunned by the palace and sold at the slave market. I wasn't worried so much about her; I was concerned that the chief black eunuch would blame me for her failure.

And then, I remembered that one of the girls in the next room was of Romanian origin. The roots of their languages were the same and Nakshidil had studied Latin: with a little translation help from me, I thought, they could make themselves understood.

"Nakshidil," I said, bringing over a round-faced girl with wide brown eyes and a friendly smile. Her brown hair was plaited and wound around her head. "I want you to meet a girl who has been here a while. This is Perestu."

The girl introduced herself. "I am the one who brought you food when you first arrived and refused to leave your bed."

"You were kind," Nakshidil said. "But I am not sure I wanted anyone to save me."

"Ah, well," said Perestu, brushing aside her words, "that is just my way. I like to take care of anyone who is sick, and I always seem to be saving wounded animals." She smiled and two round dimples appeared on her cheeks.

"Perestu," said Nakshidil, "you have a funny name. What does it mean?"

"It is Persian for Little Swallow. What does your name mean?"

Nakshidil shrugged. "They tell me it is something like 'embroidered on the heart.'"

"It's rather pretty," Perestu said. And then she excused herself. "I must go but I'm sure we'll see each other soon."

In the baths, where all the girls spent time every day, I saw Perestu teach her to dye the tips of her fingers with henna and use a stick to apply black kohl around her eyes. But Nakshidil refused to paint her eyebrows and make them meet in the middle, and when I asked her why, she said,

"I know the others think I am stupid for not following the fashion, but I think it makes me look cruel."

In the hamam the girls had more freedom to speak, and they often gossiped about Sultan Abdul Hamid: they pranced around the cooling room, their eyes twinkling as they pretended what they would do if he called for them. But when Perestu told Nakshidil the ruler was old and lecherous, she shuddered at the very idea.

On a day when I brought the girls in the dormitory a second outfit and some cloth—their allotment for the year—Nakshidil talked about the yards of beautiful cloth she had bought in Nantes, gifts for her family upon her return to Martinique. There had been other presents too—special ointments and perfumes for her mother, pretty silver boxes for her sisters, a fine shaving brush for her father—all of them, along with the golden locket from her mother that she had worn around her neck, stolen by the pirates.

"If you do as you are told," Perestu said, "you will have far better things here: the sultan's favorites have an endless array of jewels and fabulous clothes and drink their coffee from pearl-encrusted gold cups. It is not so terrible to give yourself to a man who provides you with such gifts."

"I cannot think such things," Nakshidil said. "I spend my hours dreaming of François, the boy my father plans for me to marry. I only care about what our life will be like. I see myself, dressed in ribboned silks and panniers, proudly taking his arm as we walk down the street. I picture the two of us at home: me, reaching up to give him a kiss; he, bending down and smiling with his blue eyes, clasping a string of pearls around my neck."

"You'd better forget that picture," I said, "or there will be something else around your neck. The executioner uses a silken cord."

"You should be thinking about your work," Perestu advised. "What have you been assigned to do?"

"Nothing, of course," Nakshidil sniffed. "Why should I work?"

"Because you must," the girl said. "Everyone in the harem has some kind of task."

"Me, I am not everyone. I have never worked. And I do not intend to."

The Romanian shook her head.

"And what kind of work do you do?" Nakshidil asked, her curiosity clearly stirred.

"I am a musician," she said. "I play the ney."

"And I play the violin."

"You could learn a Turkish instrument, perhaps," Perestu said. "But you must do something. You will never amount to anything here if you do not obey."

"And what is there to amount to? Everyone is a slave."

"Ah, that is not so," answered Perestu. "There are slaves at the bottom of the ladder and there are slaves at the top. We are at the bottom, and we do not receive very much—a few outfits and a few piastres as our allowance, and little in the way of freedom. We cannot do as we please inside the palace nor can we leave the palace grounds; we are here only to serve the rest.

"In a year or two we will become novices and then we have the chance to better ourselves. Those who rise from novice to become concubines, and maybe even wives of the sultan, or those who, eventually, become mistresses of departments, all have enormous wardrobes, treasure chests of jewels, their own slaves, and more personal freedom; they can leave here to go on picnics or boat trips, and accompany the ruler to his summer residence. Once in a while they are even permitted to marry and leave the palace. A clever woman in the harem can accumulate great wealth and wield enormous power. That is my aim, and if you are smart, it will be yours."

"I do not expect to be here that long," Nakshidil answered. "My family will save me very soon."

"Really, Nakshidil," Perestu reproached her. "You must forget about your family. But then," she added wistfully, "isn't it strange, how my dream is your nightmare. I am so grateful to be here in Topkapi Palace. It is what my mother wished for me and what I was told to wish for myself. My poor mother, may God bless her. I thank the Lord she did what she did; if she had not sold me, my life would be like hers. Even in these bare surroundings, I am better off than I would have been in Romania."

"How is that?" Nakshidil's interest was roused.

"My family are peasants," she whispered. "They work in

the wheat fields ten hours a day. It is backbreaking work, and my poor mother is exhausted. But that is not all she must do. She scrapes together what little food there is, bread, potatoes, once in a while a scrap of meat; she tends to her husband and children and cares for them when they are sick; scrubs the hovel and keeps it orderly; and with it all, every year her belly is full with child. There were six of us when I left, all under the age of ten, and God knows how many more there are by now."

Nakshidil was quiet for a moment. "I'm glad for you, if this is where you wish to be," she said. "But I do not. I wish to be with my family, maman, papa, my two sisters, and François, and I will find some way to leave here soon; I shall not be detained for long."

I wanted to tell them about my own family, but as I began to speak I noticed the mistress coming through the door. The sight of her put an end to the conversation.

2
· · · · ·

Nakshidil scuffed her yellow slippers along the wood floor, scowling as I led her up a flight of stairs and along the labyrinth of corridors to the heavy inlaid door. I pushed it open, and we could see a group of girls seated cross-legged in a circle on the floor: in the center of the circle stood a carved wooden frame and stretched across it, a piece of saffron fabric. Overlooking it all was an older woman.

Nakshidil's handkerchief had impressed the head mistress, and she had been ordered to work in the embroidery room. The dour woman in charge of the sewing approached—thirty, perhaps, with sunken cheeks that once showed off chiseled bones but now were hollowed by rotted teeth. Resentment had put a chill in her eyes and pulled her mouth down into a permanent frown. Seeing her, the new girl scrambled to take a place next to the others on the floor.

A dozen slave girls were working on the heavy satin cloth. I watched their fingers fly across the fabric, a double running stitch in crimson to fill in the tulip here, or purple for the hyacinths there, silver or gold metallic for the outline, a satin stitch in green for the stems. They worked so skillfully it was impossible to tell the back of the cloth from the front. The piece was breathtaking with its ombrés and contrasts, its intricacy and detail, a robe everyone in the harem would covet. But this was not a robe for ordinary slaves: this was a caftan for Aysha, the first kadin, the sultan's most prominent wife. She was the mother of an heir to the throne, and as such, she held a place of great importance. One day she would become the valide sultan and would rule the entire harem. Everyone tried to please her.

Nakshidil was handed a needle and thread, and her fingers trembled. Her own small stitches, which had won praise at the Convent les Dames de la Visitation, were large and cumbersome in comparison to those of the harem girls. If she made a mistake here, if she took too big a stitch or put the needle through the wrong place, the consequences could be harrowing. It was difficult enough to sew through the silk warp, but could she handle the silver strips of the weft? What if her thread broke? I had cautioned her, she faced severe punishment if she did not do the work correctly.

She watched the others, knowing that to sew the metallic-wrapped threads or even the fine silk onto the heavy satin was far more difficult than embroidering a simple

handkerchief. She was given a plain cloth on which to practice, and threw it down in frustration.

"Here," I said, picking it up from the floor and nodding my head discreetly towards the mistress, "you must have dropped this."

She understood my warning and sewed some more. But that afternoon she brooded more than usual, and instead of joining the others at mealtime, she sat on her divan, nervously twisting a piece of cloth around her slender fingers. In the morning she told me she had tossed in bed all night, embroidering stitches in her mind. When she slept, she said, she dreamt of an old woman piercing her heart with a needle.

But after several days of practice she learned the technique well enough to join the others, and soon, challenged by the work, she felt relieved: she knew that far worse jobs could have befallen her. She might have been polishing braziers or carrying heavy food trays or washing laundry or cleaning the long pipes and the narghiles. Nevertheless, when she told Perestu that she liked her work, the girl gave a strange response.

"No good," she whispered, wagging her finger. "No good."

"But why?" Nakshidil asked, irritated by the answer. "I like to sew. I was one of the best at the convent. I can become one of the best here."

"You cannot admire a bird if it is hiding in a tree," was her reply.

I was pleased to see that Nakshidil ignored Perestu's remark and conformed to the daily routine. Rising early in the
morning to the wail of the palace muezzins and the musicians, she made her ablutions, covered her head, faced
toward Mecca, and followed the imam as he led the prayers.
For each one, she bowed from the hips, straightened her
back, slid to her knees, and lengthened her body to the
ground; lying prostrate, she touched her nose then her
forehead to the floor. With her palms together in front of
her face, and her eyes closed to shut out evil, she prayed,
sometimes in silence, sometimes out loud.

"Allahu akbar," God is most great, she said in Arabic. She
rose from the floor and stumbled over passages I was helping her learn from the Koran, repeating the five prayers.

Afterwards, she took her breakfast—she had grown accus-
tomed to the tea and the yogurt and the sesamed bread—and
went on to lessons in Arabic, trying hard to aspirate her *h*'s.
"Pretend you are blowing out a candle," I suggested, as I
stood behind her in the study room.

She was beginning to read the Koran, but when she came
to the line that read, "Men are in charge of women because
Allah hath made the one to excel over the other," she grimaced and said, "Allah did not make Turkish men to be in
charge of me." She hated having to memorize the history of
Islam, yet in spite of her infidel resistance, she was a good
student and had learned to recite the six doctrines: belief in
God; in His angels; in His book; in His prophets; in the
Last Day; in predestination. And she knew the five pillars of

Islam: there is one God and Muhammad is His Prophet; prayers five times a day; charity; fasting during the holy month of Ramadan; and if possible, pilgrimage to Mecca and Medina.

"You know," I said encouragingly, "you have been in the palace for six months and you are making good headway. It won't be long before you are ready to hold up your forefinger and say the words that will make you a Muslim: "'There is no God but Allah, and Muhammad is His messenger.'"

"If that is what I must do to survive here," she said, "so be it."

When the midday meal was brought from the kitchens, she squatted with the others and ate in silence: chicken and rice pilav, yogurt, eggplant, chickpeas, feta cheese, and beets. Once, when a plate of zucchinis and cucumbers appeared, Perestu giggled.

"Why are you laughing?" Nakshidil whispered.

"Do you know why these are sliced?"

"No," the girl replied.

"They are afraid that if they keep them whole, we will use them as a substitute for a man."

Nakshidil looked at her, mystified.

Later in the sewing room, the girls could not resist the urge to break the silence with gossip. Bits and pieces floated to Nakshidil's ears: Aysha was the mother of the middle prince, Mustafa; the eldest prince and heir to the throne was Selim; the youngest prince was Mahmud; the caftan had to be ready in three months; anyone who angered Aysha would be punished and dismissed from the room.

As Nakshidil worked, her restless mind returned again and again to Perestu, and she asked me several times about the meaning of her friend's words. I explained that if the old sultan saw a girl he found attractive, he might promote her to a new level, a concubine. This is what had happened to Aysha.

"Perhaps if the sultan saw me, he would show interest in my advancement," she murmured. She turned to the girl next to her.

"How long have you been assigned to the embroidery room?" she whispered.

"Soon it will be two years," the girl answered.

"That is a long time."

"It is. But some of the others have been here many years. The Turks consider it a great privilege to work on embroidery. It is one of the most important things a woman can do."

"Have you tried to leave, to do something else?"

"It is almost impossible. You are not given a choice. You must obey the sultan's wishes."

"But the sultan did not assign me here. It was decided by the head mistress."

"She is his representative in the harem. You must do what she says."

"Or else?"

"Or else," I interjected, "you can be thrown out of the palace and sold in the slave market."

"And have you ever seen the sultan?" asked Nakshidil.

The girl's eyes widened. "Once, at Ramadan, I saw him in the big celebration."

Nakshidil was quiet, and I supposed her thoughts had returned to Perestu. How could she be seen if she was secluded in the embroidery room? Like the bird in the tree, a girl who sewed would never come into view: her stitches would simply meld into the leaves.

For more than a week Nakshidil toiled carefully at her embroidery, laying out her plan. Only later I learned she was plotting an escape from the work. If it were to look deliberate, she knew she would be punished severely. Indeed, she sewed so well that her stitches even drew some admiring glances. But one afternoon she poked the needle through the wrong place in the cloth, and it wasn't until she had embroidered at least a dozen more stitches that the mistake became apparent. She looked helplessly at the mistress, who gently rebuked her.

"I am so sorry. Please forgive me. I will be more careful," Nakshidil apologized.

The following day she pricked her finger with a needle and a drop of blood fell on the cloth. The mistress glowered and scolded her more harshly.

"Stupid girl," she said, quickly wiping it off. "Watch what you are doing. We do not want your blood on the caftan.

You are lucky it fell on the red flower. Once more and you will be punished," she warned.

There was a gasp in the room when another girl's needle slipped, causing her also to make a mistake; the others shifted in their places, edging further away from Nakshidil. Someone whispered that the evil eye was upon her.

But as she embroidered the next afternoon, she could not ignore the flurry of whispers that rushed through the room. "What is it?" she asked. "Why is everyone suddenly so nervous?"

"Aysha is coming," one of the girls murmured. "She wants to see how work is progressing on her caftan."

Nakshidil peeked up from the satin cloth just as a fiery woman entered the room. She looked at me as if to say, so this was what a sultan's wife, a kadin, looked like! Red-haired, with flashing green eyes and a slant to her red mouth, the kadin sauntered around the room. She stopped to inspect each girl's work, swishing the hem of her skirt as each slave kissed it, and when she was not happy with what she saw, her head shook and the walnut-sized emerald she wore around her neck shivered with displeasure.

Nakshidil pretended to concentrate on her sewing. When she sensed Aysha standing just above her, she kissed the woman's skirt and kept her head down, embroidering the tip of the leaf. She jabbed her needle through the silk cloth and pushed it up again, and as she pulled the needle all the way out of the cloth, the thread snapped. Her eyes darted first to the mistress, then to Aysha, then back to the mistress, and from the expressions on their faces, she knew what was coming. She felt the hard slap of Aysha's hand against her cheek. The black eunuch haunched on guard in the corner pulled her up and dragged her from the room. As she went out, the mistress cursed her with contempt.

A few steps down the hallway, she was thrown into a small room. I followed and saw an old mistress waiting, a hard shoe in her hand. Nakshidil closed her eyes, clenched her fists, and drew in her breath, readying herself for the blows. The first smacks were bearable. But within a few minutes she could not even hear her own screams. The leather slipper seared her lobes and blood streamed from her ears. Dizzy, she huddled in the corner.

Later that day, I went to check on her. She was lying on her divan, and Perestu was at her side. "I heard that you were beaten," the girl whispered. "What went wrong?"

Nakshidil saw the mistress standing behind Perestu. One punishment was enough for the day. "It isn't so bad," she whispered. "I'll tell you about it tomorrow." Weak and tired, she folded herself into a tiny ball and tried to fall asleep.

The following morning when I arrived after breakfast, she was still on her mattress, her face swollen from the beating. "I've come to get you," I said.

"I'm not going anywhere." She spoke with difficulty but her attitude had not changed.

"I have my orders and you will follow me."

"I won't," she said, and as she turned her head I saw that her ears were covered with dried blood.

"You must come with me," I said. "You seem to forget your position. You are nothing but an odalisque, the lowest of slaves."

"I am the child of an important man." She spoke slowly, obviously in pain and barely able to move her jaw.

So am I, I wanted to say. I knew how she felt: snatched from a smooth and coddled world and tossed like jetsam into a turbulent sea. "You will be a great leader," my father had told me on my fifth birthday. His words filled me with pride and I looked forward to following in his footsteps.

Not long after, I was taken away, shackled, castrated, and condemned to a life of bondage. No longer a man amongst men, I was a slave who served at the whim of other slaves. At first I was filled with rage, and I felt betrayed by my father; then I became despondent, frustrated over my loss of freedom and my inability to flee. It was only after several years that I began to understand my captors, to see that circumstances forced them to behave as they did. And slowly, my anger turned to empathy, my coldness into cordiality; my bitter enemies became my friends, and eventually, I became one of them.

I looked at Nakshidil and saw my own early misery reflected in her eyes. This was not a girl like Perestu who sought to profit from her position. This was a child in pain.

"I can't go back there," she said.

"You won't," I promised.

"Then where are you taking me?"

"To the laundry. That is your punishment. To work there."

She followed me, holding her pounding head as I led her towards the room. But before we reached the laundry, she stopped and put her hand on my arm.

"No," I said sternly, thinking she wanted to return to the embroidery room. "No. You cannot go back to the sewing. The mistress does not want you there. Your poor work embarrassed her in front of Aysha, and she wanted you dismissed from the palace. But I insisted that you had been sent here as a special gift of the bey of Algiers and that you should be given another chance." I did not say that if she went, I would pay a price, and that if she stayed, I, too, would be given another chance. "You should be grateful. The laundry is far better than the slave market."

The girl listened and put her palms together as though she were praying. "Music," she whispered. Then she took her left arm and bent it up so that her hand almost touched her shoulder. Slowly she moved her right hand back and forth across the upper part of her left arm. Again, she put her palms together and made the praying motion, begging with her eyes. I understood. This is your last chance, I thought; you'd better make it succeed.

I turned down a different hallway and pushed open a painted door. I could see twenty slaves in the paneled room, some holding flutes, some lutes, others with the stringed kanun across their laps; one played the harp, others had

drums, and a few held tambourines. Perestu sat on the floor
with a ney. The nasal sound of Turkish folk songs filled the
air.

Twenty pairs of dark eyes followed us as we crossed the
room and I spoke to the mistress. I had known Fatima since
I first arrived at Topkapi; I had done her some small favors
in the past, and she listened begrudgingly as I pleaded with
her to take Nakshidil under her wing. Reluctantly, she
shoved a tambourine in the girl's hand.

But instead of accepting it gratefully, Nakshidil looked
around, spotted something on a cupboard shelf, and
pointed to it brazenly.

"What does she want with that old thing?" Fatima grum-
bled at me. "It was given to us as a gift years ago, and no one
has ever touched it."

But then, she ordered a slave to hand the instrument to
Nakshidil. I watched her take it. She fingered the long bow,
ran her hands across the wooden belly, and nestled the violin under her sore chin. As she turned the tuning pegs and
plucked the fingerboard, the pain from the beating seemed
to vanish, and her whole face brightened; I could see how
much the instrument was like an old friend.

She moved the bow across the strings and sweet sounds
emanated from the violin such as I had never heard; plaintive
strokes of melancholy floated into the room from another
world. But if it was Mozart she hoped to play in the palace,
she would be sadly disappointed. She would have to learn

Turkish music now: there would be no *Abduction from the Seraglio*.

Drawing solace from the violin, within weeks the girl became attuned to the rhythm of the harem. At breakfast she often took a second cup of tea and managed to scoop the yogurt onto the puffy bread. At meals she admired the way the older slaves ate with their hands, their fingers coiling and uncoiling like serpents dancing in the grass. She had to admit, she told me, she might never be able to eat with such grace.

Still, she had not given up all hope of escape. When she was home, she said, she would show her friends how the women danced sinuously with their hands. Nonetheless, in the music room she began to learn the Turkish songs. In the baths she gossiped more with the other girls and started to paint her eyebrows closer together. And when someone addressed her as Nakshidil, instead of ignoring them or waiting a while until she answered, she responded immediately to the name.

"You know, Tulip," she said one morning when no one else was around, "I am becoming used to the name Nakshidil. I even rather like it." She placed her hand on her heart. "Thank you, *chéri,* for giving it to me."

"It wasn't I who chose it. It was the head mistress."

"But you have helped me to appreciate it."

It wasn't often that girls in the harem expressed even a modicum of gratitude; most of them were hardened creatures, as tough as the mountain regions they came from and bent on their own ambitions; they tended to treat us black eunuchs with contempt, or ignore us, or pay attention only when they needed our intervention. To hear a word of thanks drop from her lips swelled my heart. I felt there was some softness in her, despite her temper and her strong will, some gentleness coming to the surface that touched me. And I saw that she was yielding more to life in the palace.

I suppose she found familiarity in the spare surroundings of the harem: the strict discipline, the studied routine, the austere mistresses, even the religious teachings. Cloistered in the damp quarters, living with other girls her age and supervised by the older virgins, it was not so different, she said, from the convent in Nantes. I hoped that her memories of the past, as they do for all of us in the seraglio, would recede further and further in her mind. But no, she still dreamed about François and marrying him.

Turkish rulers, I told her, choose their wives and their closest advisers, not from their own people, but from their slaves. "Don't you think you could learn to love a sultan?"

She was quiet for a moment. "You know, I feel so confused. Part of me would do anything to attract the sultan, and part of me is repelled by the very thought of him. He is more ancient than my grandfather. I cannot imagine being with him."

Sometimes the girl still exasperated me. "Of course you can. You must go to him if he calls. He is the sultan, the padishah, God's shadow on earth," I answered.

"I don't care who he is. He is an ancient despot who gains his power from enslaving everyone else. I know. I have read about it. Anyway, the sultan is not important where I come from."

"Where you are from does not matter anymore," I reminded her. "You are not the person you were. You are someone else. You must think of yourself as a chameleon: it is only who you are now and where you are now that matters. The sooner you accept this, the easier it will be to succeed here."

"You are wrong," she insisted. "Maybe you do not understand, but I am the daughter of an important man, a member of the Martinique Council."

"My father was also important, a man of great authority, second only to the tribal chief in Abyssinia," I retorted.

"Then why are you here?"

"The white men wanted me because they knew I came from a great heritage."

"And your father gave you away?" Her voice showed surprise.

"No. He did not give me away. He sold me. The men offered the tribal chief a good deal of gold. And the chief promised to share it with my father. He ordered my father to sell me."

"And your father agreed?"

I nodded my head in shame. "Yes, my father agreed. I was born with my right leg shorter than my left. He saw it as a bad omen. Besides, he never disobeyed the chief," I said quietly.

"I am sorry," she said. I thought I sensed a bit of sympathy, but she continued. "Perhaps that is the difference. My father would never sell his own child. And he would never answer to any chief. He is powerful in his own right."

She hesitated for a moment, as if there was something else she wanted to say, but then she seemed to change her mind. Instead, her jaw clenched and her voice grew louder. "They cannot make me a slave. I am a du Buc de Rivery."

I shook my head as much in sadness as in anger. Had she not understood? It did not matter who she was. The past was gone. Only the present was important. And at present, and for the rest of her life, she was and would be a slave.

. . . . .

I was in the dormitory when Nakshidil let out a cry for help. I put down the new cushions I had brought for the divans and hurried over. "What is it? What's the matter?" I asked.

"At first there was only a trickle, and then a gush," she sputtered; she was holding out a piece of cloth stained with dark red blood. I felt weak in the knees, and I could sense the color draining from my cheeks.

Seeing my face, she dropped the darkened cloth. "Tulip, what's wrong? You look as if you are going to faint."

"It's the blood," I replied. "I cannot look at it." I could not tell her why, and it was my good fortune that Perestu was rushing to her side. When the Romanian girl heard what had happened, she laughed. "Congratulations, Nakshidil," she said. "You're a woman."

"But what does that mean?" Nakshidil was almost in tears. "Of course I am a woman. I have always been a woman."

"No, no, you have been a girl. Now you are a woman." Perestu handed her a clean wad of cloth and continued. "You can have babies now," she answered, her cheeks dimpling with a smile.

Instinctively my hand dropped to the mutilated place between my legs. I recalled the way my own ability to have children had been removed, and I let out a groan.

"What's the matter?" Nakshidil asked again.

"Nothing," I said. "I just remembered something important. You must stay away from the baths whenever you are menstruating. It is unlawful to bathe when you are pregnant or sick, or when you are bleeding."

"Yes, fine," Nakshidil brushed me off, returning to Perestu, "but we all know that in order to have a baby you must somehow be with a man."

I felt sick again, but said nothing. Man. Woman. Only eunuchs know the agony of those words. I am tormented day and night by my invalidity as either man or woman. Instead I am half man, half woman, with the sexual longings of both but the physical looks of neither; a creature with the thick neck, broad chest, and shoulders of a man, and the hairless face, flabby belly, and high-pitched voice of a woman; a freak, as Nakshidil once called me. Once when a physician came to the palace to see the valide sultan, I stopped him on his way out. "My good Doctor," I begged, "you heal so many sick people. Is there not something you can do for me?" He looked at me and shook his head. "I am so sorry," he whispered. "So sorry." I could see tears in his eyes.

"You must learn to love the sultan," Perestu answered.

"But are there not younger men in line for the throne?" I nodded yes.

"Perhaps kismet will bring me one," Nakshidil said. She looked at me and smiled.

.....

Outdoors in the garden on an early spring afternoon, I watched her pluck a chrysanthemum and pull at its petals.

"What are you wishing for?" I asked.

"Oh, Tulip," she answered wistfully. "My scheme worked. I am out of the embroidery room, and, thanks to you, I am playing music. But even so, I am part of a large group. I am not one of the privileged girls who wait on the sultan. How will I ever draw his attention?"

"Have you ever danced?" I asked.

"Of course. In school we learned all kinds of dances—the minuet, the contredanse." She took a few delicate steps to show me. "Hold my arm," she said, and before I could protest, she skipped me around the garden.

I stopped to catch my breath. "I have something different in mind," I said. "Come. Follow me."

3
. . . . .

The ulema had announced that Ramadan was coming in two months, and, as always, on the evening of its arrival there would be entertainment for the entire harem. The head mistress requested that those with the most promising talent be taught to dance. Nakshidil moved with a pleasing grace, and I was sure she could be one of the dancers.

Ten girls were gathered in the large room where Safieh, the dance mistress, was about to demonstrate her talents. Curtains covered the stained glass windows and the rugs had been rolled up to reveal the polished wood floor. Standing with her feet spread slightly apart, Safieh bent her knees and thrust out her chest. She gave the signal for the musicians to start, and as they played the wailing chiftetelli music and clicked their castanets, she stretched out her arms, twisting her hands and wrists. She kept her shoulders stationary and swayed her hips from side to side, lifting them slowly, first the left, then the right, and as the bottom half of her body shifted, she drew her arms up and crossed them just below her eyes, then glided them gracefully down her sides, undulating so sultrily she could have made marble melt.

Perestu copied the teacher's movements, but when Nakshidil tried to imitate the teacher, she found it nearly impossible to isolate her belly from her hips. Of course, in France she had learned to do court dances, and she had told me that as a child in Martinique she had danced with the African slaves, but these movements were as different as a tulip from a turban. Told to sway her chest in one direction and her bottom in the other, she covered her mouth and giggled.

"I feel foolish," she said.

"Think of your body as a snake," I advised. "You must make the snake wriggle, and as it does, you must coil your arms as though they were serpents too."

Nakshidil practiced until she discovered muscles she never knew she had. She learned to make the top of her body yield to the right and the bottom yield to the left. She learned to do the kashlimar, stepping forward, then back on one foot, stepping in place with the other. She wound her hands and arms in and out as though she were luring her prey, and she circled her hips, shifting them, lifting them one at a time. Perestu taught her to squeeze her muscles so that the place between her legs tightened. Slowly she tilted her pelvis and swirled her hips, made her navel wriggle and bobbed her tiny breasts up and down. It wasn't long before she moved like a serpent, and the others watched, envying the talent I had been certain of all along.

.....

It was soon after this that the holy men declared they could distinguish the white thread from the black thread in the first crescent of the moon: Ramadan would begin. That night we were to have the entertainment. The slaves were as excited as children at a shadow puppet show. Skipping through the corridors, they whispered stories about the sultan, discussed what they would wear, and practiced what they would do. Perestu begged one of the slave girls who had performed for Abdul Hamid once before to describe him.

"I was so nervous I could hardly see," she said. "But I do remember the lecherous look in his beady eyes."

"I'll never forget his dark beard," another said. "It was dyed black to make him look young. But instead it looked like a cloak of evil hanging down his chin."

"It certainly did not help him with Roxana," another girl interrupted.

"What do you mean?" Nakshidil asked.

"Don't you know the story?" Nakshidil shook her head. "The sultan, for all his power, could not control the one woman in the harem he really wanted. Every time he called her to his bed, she found some excuse not to come. The more she refused, the more he wanted her. The padishah sent her letter after letter, each one more frenzied than the last."

"How do you know about this?" Nakshidil asked. The girl looked at me, and I turned my head.

"The eunuchs, naturally. They carried the letters to her from the sultan. And they spread the stories as quickly as the Janissaries spread their fires. That sloe-eyed Russian was jealous of the other wives and tried to make a fool of the sultan. When we heard about the letters, we were astounded; I even memorized them."

"What did they say?"

"The first one said: 'I am on my knees, begging your pardon. Please let me see you tonight. If you wish, kill me. I will surrender, but please do not disregard my cry, or I'll die. I throw myself at your feet.'"

Nakshidil listened with disbelief. "Surely, if a sultan is as important as everyone says, he would not write such things to a slave."

"I promise you he did."

"Tulip, is this true?"

I nodded sheepishly.

"How did she respond?"

"Roxana was brazen," someone piped in.

"No, clever," said another girl.

"Well, not clever enough," the storyteller continued. "To spite him, she refused his desires again. She told him it was the time of month when she could not come to his bed.

To ensure his belief, she bribed a eunuch to supply a drop of pigeon blood."

"Then what happened?"

"He sent her another letter. That one said, 'Do not let me suffer any more. Last night I could hardly control myself. Let me kiss your feet. Please let me be your slave. You are my master.'"

"And of course she went to him?"

"No. She refused. So to avenge himself, night after night the sultan took a different girl."

"Some nights he took three and four together," someone reminded her.

Nakshidil cringed.

"Not only that, with his ravenous appetite he has fathered twenty-six children. Unfortunately, most of them have died."

"And did he forget about Roxana?"

"Yes, but only after he put her in prison."

"And now, does he have a favorite girl?"

"A European girl was made his most recent wife. Her name was the same as yours: Nakshidil."

"What happened to her?"

"She died from typhus just before you came."

I recalled hearing how the sultan felt beleaguered when his seventh wife, a European who had borne him a son, had suddenly taken ill. Every day for two weeks he asked the chief black eunuch for news, and every day the news grew worse.

Finally the sultan could stand it no longer, and against the orders of the palace physician, he visited the kadin.

Treading softly into her sick chamber, he was overcome by the rotting fumes of disease. The poor girl lay pale and limp, and though her bedclothes hid them from view, he knew that rose-colored spots dotted her stomach and her chest. He could see only too easily how the typhus had drained the life from her beautiful body. Decimated by fever and diarrhea, she could not speak or even nod her head. At the sight of the great padishah, she struggled to blink her eyes in recognition. He left her rooms in tears; twenty-four hours later she was dead.

Nakshidil looked troubled by the story. "Tulip," she whispered and beckoned me away from the others.

"If I have been given the name of the sultan's late wife, perhaps I too will be called to his bed. What if he *does* call? What if he is so old and ugly, I cannot do as he wants?"

"You will," I said.

"And what if I don't. Will I be punished? Will he put me in prison like Roxana?"

"He might. Or, if you are lucky, he'll banish you to the Palace of Tears."

"What is that?"

"The Old Palace. It's a shabby place in disrepair. They call it the Palace of Tears because it is so gloomy, filled with women who have lost their men, or women who have never had a man to love at all. They say the only sounds you hear are the sounds of women weeping. I dread the thought of it."

"Oh, Tulip. This is awful. Who can I bribe to bring me pigeon's blood?"

"No one," I said. "If he were caught, the punishment would be too great."

.....

Before the evening of entertainment, the girls spent the entire day in the baths, with us, the black eunuchs, in attendance. Nakshidil lay back on the marble bench, soaking in the steamy heat while one of the slaves massaged her, kneading and pounding so hard that by the time the woman was finished, she could barely lift herself off the slab. "How will I ever be able to dance," she moaned.

More slaves splashed her body and scrubbed her with the loofah until every inch of her skin was new and pink, then soaped her and splashed her some more, rubbing her with rose petals so that the heavy scent saturated her hair, her scalp, and her skin.

They smoothed her face with a masque of almond and egg yolks, and bleached it with a jasmine and almond mix. Now that she was a woman she was examined for even the tiniest evidence of body hair—forbidden to Muslim females—but there was none. The air bristled with excitement. Some of the naked girls were playful and teasing, tossing their manes of black hair, kissing, nuzzling, fondling one another's breasts.

Wrapped in an embroidered linen towel and walking easily on the high-heeled pattens, Nakshidil moved to the next room where her fingernails and toenails were painted with henna. She smiled at her dark toes peeking out of her mother-of-pearl sandals and at the henna tulip tattooed on her ankle. Her blond hair was smoothed with butter and dressed with pearls, then pinned on one side with a jeweled cap. Her eyes were outlined with kohl, her eyebrows drawn close together with india ink, her lips dotted with cinnabar. A slave girl passed around a tray of sherbets and another offered coffee, but Nakshidil waved the second one away.

Each girl was given a choice of outfits for the evening. "What do you think, Tulip?" she asked, as she licked the last bit of sherbet from her spoon. She looked the clothes over carefully, smoothing her hands across the delicate silks and lush satins, sifting through the chest of jewels: blood-red rubies, dark green emeralds, sapphires as blue as the sea. She stepped into a pair of billowing red-and-gold-striped shalwar in a silk as thin as tissue; over her head she slipped a low-cut filmy dress, and over that a finely embroidered yellow tunic that buttoned well below the swell of her small breasts.

"Perfect," I said, as she slung a wide cashmere sash covered with colorful stones and sequins around her hips. From an array of gems, she chose pearl-and-ruby clusters that dangled from her ears, ropes of pearls to glisten her neck, gold rings and gold bangles encrusted with rubies, sapphires, and pearls, and bracelets of precious stones for her ankles.

Giggling with nervousness, the girls showed themselves off. One was complimented on her earrings, another on the color of her blouse. "Nakshidil," one girl remarked, "how is it that we all choose from the same clothes, yet your outfits always look smarter than ours?"

She shrugged. "It is so natural. Remember, I am French."

I reminded them how to act before the sultan, watched as they rehearsed making obeisance, and warned that they were to remain in absolute silence and never turn their back on the ruler. They had all learned the position of attendance, and once again Nakshidil practiced, drawing in her stomach and standing tall, shoulders back, arms crossed over her bare chest, left hand covering her right breast, right hand covering the left. She was to remain this way at all times in the presence of the sultan, except, of course, when they were performing.

The mistress came around with a hand mirror, and Nakshidil begged for a peek. Holding it to the light, she stared into the glass, blinking in disbelief. She hardly recognized herself. She touched her fingers to her bleached white skin, her darkened eyes, her reddened lips. As she looked, she seemed to enjoy the woman staring back, and slowly I saw her eyes begin to crinkle in a smile and her lips nearly press against the lips in the glass. I could almost see the thoughts going through her mind: she was falling in love with her new self.

And then she pulled back, as if to say that deep inside, she knew she would always be Aimée du Buc de Rivery. But the face returning her glance was no longer that of a little French girl, and the figure was not that of a child. Gone was any trace of her Creole youth or her innocent convent years. She was a full-blown woman now, with a woman's lust and a woman's desires. Transformed by the Topkapi sorceresses, she was, indeed, Nakshidil, the harem slave.

The transformation was like an aphrodisiac. Blood rushed to her cheeks, her pulse quickened at her temples, and her eyes flashed with ambition. I knew that she wanted all that a palace woman could have: the clothes, the jewels, the money, the power, and most importantly, the man. She was determined to be like Aysha: to have slave girls kissing her skirt, eunuchs carrying out her orders, a sultan calling her his wife. She hardly understood the meaning of such a thing, yet as surely as a tulip rises from the earth, she would rise to the top of the palace hierarchy. I knew the resistance she had shown until now had melted into the mirror. But I could hardly have guessed how much her life would change.

4
· · · · ·

A parade of peacocks, bejeweled princesses—the four sisters and six daughters of the sultan—followed by the five kadins, twenty-six concubines, and twenty mistresses—arabesqued into the Entertainment Hall of the harem. The twelve dancers came next, and we, the eunuchs, trailed behind like fancy horses' tails, sweeping into the vast salon, the most elaborate room in the private quarters of the sultan. Nakshidil looked around, wide-eyed at the gilded wood latticework, the brilliantly glazed tiles, the sculptured fountains, graceful Moorish arches, silvered Venetian mirrors, and the enormous Chinese porcelain vases. Gazing up in awe at the domed ceiling, intricately painted and rimmed with gilt calligraphy, she tripped, gasping as she nearly fell on the sprawling silk rug. I dreaded to think what might have happened.

The women, like Zubaydah in the *Arabian Nights,* so weighted down with jewels they could scarcely walk, arranged themselves by rank. First, the sultan's daughters and sisters, their dark hair flowing like rivulets down their backs, their smooth bodies robed in silk, their necks and arms glittering with chandelier diamonds and rubies as bulbous as radishes, stepped up to the platformed area along the side of the room and took their seats on the raised sofas behind the railing. The wives and concubines came next: sparkling with colored stones, they found their places on satin cushions on the floor.

Nakshidil spotted Aysha and saw her flaming red hair lit with jewels, her green eyes flashing against her porcelain skin. At the sight of the woman, dressed in the dreaded embroidered caftan that had caused her so much pain, Nakshidil turned away and touched her ears, as though, once again, she felt the stinging slaps of the leather slipper.

Along the opposite side of the room, a row of odalisques stood with their arms crossed, hands covering their bare breasts, while upstairs in the balcony the harem orchestra was preparing to play. She glanced up at the musicians with a wistful look and then surveyed the dancers standing beside her. Her face showed a smile of satisfaction, as though she was pleased by her decision to dance. She stayed close to the other performers as they made their way towards the columned and canopied throne where the sultan was soon to take his seat.

The pungent smells of incense and attar of roses wafted

through the air. A flourish of music sounded as the mistress chamberlain, tall and stern and bearing her silver cane, announced the sultan's arrival: at once, the women rose, their faces unconcealed for the one man allowed to see them. As they stood in attendance, arms crossed and hands folded on their breasts, a grand procession of eunuchs and princes led the fur-cloaked emperor into the room. Almost in unison, we all made obeisance, bowing down to the floor in respect for the man acknowledged as sultan, padishah, grand seigneur, caliph, king, emperor, and God's shadow on earth.

If butterflies fluttered in her stomach, no one could have discerned Nakshidil's fear. A serene expression on her face, she discreetly stole a glimpse of the sultan and shuddered. Undoubtedly, it was his eyes that disturbed her the most: set under high thin eyebrows arched with distrust, they were as small as beetles, sunken in dark circles of despair. His nose was large and hooked, the rest of his face long and thin, drooping into his thick black beard. His high, rectangular turban emphasized his long head; and pinned to his towering hat was a huge aigrette, a cluster of brilliant diamonds shooting upwards, topped with a plumed fan and long diamond ribs. Around his shoulders hung his red satin and sable cloak, and at his waist he wore a gold dagger sparkling with jewels. But despite his gorgeous accoutrements, the emperor bore a sorrowful air.

Disdain and despondency lined his ancient face. This man, who had spent most of his life isolated in the Princes'

Cage at the palace before coming to the throne in 1774, in-
herited an empire so vast it stretched from Baghdad and
Basra in the east to the edge of Venice in the west. But
though its holdings once swept eastward across the Caucasus
Mountains and down through the deserts of Syria, Egypt,
and Arabia as far south as Aden, and though its conquests
westward included the Balkan Peninsula, Bulgaria, Moldavia, Rumania, Hungary, and Greece, it had paid a great
price: it was weakened by war and deeply in debt.

Challenged now by Empress Catherine of Russia, who
showed a singular will to overthrow him, Sultan Abdul
Hamid had been forced to send his military into constant
battle. The Russian czarina hovered over his lands and insti-
gated rebellions against him, eager to grab whatever she
could of his empire. When her grandson was born, she
named him Constantine and nursed him on the milk of imperial ambition. Trained in everything Greek, he was her
hope to reconquer the Byzantine capital, Constantinople,
and install a Russian throne in that city where, three centuries before, Islamic Ottomans had routed the Orthodox
Christians.

Just two years earlier, in 1787, Abdul Hamid had summoned the French ambassador, advising him to send a
warning to France's allies. "Tell your Russian friends to return possession of the Crimean peninsula to Turkey," the
sultan said. The piece of land that jutted into the Black Sea
had been declared independent the year that Abdul Hamid
ascended the throne, but in 1783 Catherine annexed the

Crimea, threatening the safety of Turkish ships and the security of Turkish shores.

"So long as the Crimea remains in Russians hands," the sultan had warned, "Turkey is like a house with no doors that thieves can enter at will. You must send a message to the Czarina Catherine: If Russia does not disclaim the Crimea, Turkey will take the proper action."

Not long after, the sultan convened his Council of Ministers: the chief black eunuch, the chief white eunuch, the grand vezir, and the ten other vezirs. I was in attendance, assisting the chief interpreter, who had noticed my ear for language. At first my quick tongue had cost me numerous beatings; the chief black eunuch accused me of mimicry and ordered me beaten with the bastinado. But when the chief interpreter caught wind of my talents, he trained me in his skills. The opportunity was rare, and I was grateful to the good man.

"In the name of Allah, we cannot allow ourselves to be trampled on by these Russian maniacs," the sultan told his advisers. Seated on his jewel-studded throne, his small eyes burning with anger, his pale skin blanched against his black beard, he announced to his vezirs that the time had come. "The Russians have supported and supplied insurgencies throughout our empire. First they encouraged the revolt in Syria, then they armed the Albanians in the Morea, and after that they supported the Mamluks in Egypt. Our dauntless Admiral Hassan has staved them off, but an empire can be tested just so much. Do you agree that now is the time to declare war?" he asked, knowing that no man in the council dared object.

The very seat of the caliphate, the center of Islam, was being threatened. Not only was the power of the sultan under question, but the great Ottoman Empire itself. Since that meeting with the vezirs, the situation had only turned gloomier; the Turkish navy was destroyed by Russian forces as it entered the Black Sea. One never knew what Catherine might do next; there was talk she might aid Austria in its own war against the Turks.

But the sultan's problems came as much from inside his empire as from out: fires intentionally set in the city by his very own elite troops, the Janissaries, jangled his nerves; intimidation by his own admiralty chief challenged his authority; an assassination attempt against him by a vezir heightened his paranoia; unrequited love from his wife Roxana had increased his sense of impotence. The alchemy of desire and despair had brought on too many sleepless nights, and he had even been heard to cry, "God help the Sublime State!"

No amount of possessions, women, weapons, or heirs made him feel secure. The sultan who ruled an empire through a system of slaves was no more than a slave himself.

Was it the hashish bubbling next to him in his jeweled narghile that made him seem so impassive? Or was it opium? Some of the slaves sneaked opium pills into their rooms, and many sultans had made it a habit to chew on little gold pills. Perhaps he used the narcotic to dull his worries.

. . . . .

The music began and the girls started to dance, first performing the traditional Turkish dances: clicking tiny cymbals with their fingers, taking small steps around the room, they kneeled on their calves, bent on one knee, crossed their arms, and jumped in the air. Then came Nakshidil's favorite: prancing across the hall, they hopped around for the tavsan, the dance of the rabbit.

Out of the corner of my eye, I could see the three princes sitting on small thrones close to the sultan: the oldest one, Selim, son of the late Sultan Mustafa III and next in line to rule, was twenty-five, with intelligent eyes, soft lips and a gentle air; the other two were his cousins, both of them sons of Abdul Hamid. The elder of the brothers, nine-year-old Mustafa, had reddish hair, a mischievous smile, and a penchant to twist and turn in his seat; four-year-old Mahmud, with dark brown curls and large brown eyes, sat quietly on his chair. As the dance of the hares began, the little ones burst into laughter at the girl hares, and for an instant all three princes looked at Nakshidil. I saw her eyes make contact with the handsome Selim, but she quickly dropped her head.

The music from the gallery grew louder and faster, and

one of the dancing girls leaped into the air, her arms stretched high, trying to touch the huge chandelier. The boys watched with fascination as, one after another, the girls bounded up, aiming for the round crystal ball hanging from the center.

Coffee, candied fruits, and halvah, the sultan's favorite sweet made of sesame seeds and honey, were served to the guests, while the music quieted down; when it rose up again, the rhythm was slower and the girls formed a semicircle, shaking their tambourines and clicking their fingers as Perestu stepped to the center. The dancer began to twist her body, rotating her hips and plump breasts, moving this way and that like a ribald serpent. After a while another girl took her place, mesmerizing the audience as she shimmied to the nasal strains.

Then it was Nakshidil's turn. She took a deep breath and moved forward from the circle, thrusting out her tiny breasts like ripe melons. Slowly she threw back her head and slithered out her arms, twisting her wrists and hands as though they were serpents.

As the moaning music, slower now, flooded her ears, and the burning incense filled her nostrils, she lost herself in the dance. She had learned to control her body from the inside, drawing in her muscles and holding them for a long time, then releasing them, then holding them in again, and at the same time she moved her hips, gliding from one side to the other, lifting them slowly, the undulating motions rippling through her body.

Excited by her own sultry dancing, she stepped teasingly
in front of the honored guests, and offered her quivering
breasts, her hips, her thighs, even her jewel to the impassive
sultan. I watched, feeling the heat rise in the room like lava
rising in a volcano. Ever so slightly, I saw the emperor nod
his head and delicately drop a handkerchief on the floor.
Then the music changed, some of the eunuchs waved their
incense censers over the guests four times, and everyone
recognized that it was time to go. As we left the hall I tapped
Nakshidil on the shoulder.

"The sultan gave his signal," I whispered. "He dropped
his handkerchief when you danced. You will be called to his
bed tonight."

. . . . .

It was two in the morning when we were ordered to fetch
her. I dressed quickly in the dark of my cell, and as the gates
of the harem were locked from sundown to dawn, I took the
underground tunnel and rushed to her room. "Nakshidil,"
I whispered, but there was no need even to call her name.
She was sitting on her divan in the whitewashed dormitory,
wide-awake, still wearing her dancing clothes and her jewels,
her hair still perfectly dressed.

"What is it?" she asked jumpily.

"The sultan has asked for you at once."

Perestu overheard us talking. "*Allahu akbar*, God is great,"
she said. "*Mashallah*. Go safely."

With that I took her by the hand and led her through the secret passageway to the sultan's quarters. I walked as quickly as I could, and she put her hand on my shoulder to slow me down. "I must talk to you," she whispered nervously.

"Not now. We cannot be late for the sultan."

"But you must listen to me," she pleaded. "I'm scared, Tulip. I do not have any idea of what to do. And the girls have told me that if the sultan is not pleased, he banishes the offender. This will be the end of me."

It was true that the sultan punished incompetent girls with confinement, or worse, and Nakshidil had not had even a single lesson in how to please a man. More often than not, a slave was already accomplished in her work and knowledgeable in the art of erotic pleasure. But Abdul Hamid lacked patience; greedy and old, when he saw a beautiful girl, he demanded her at once.

"You'll be fine," I reassured her. "Remember to kiss the hem of the bedcover and crawl in. After that, just do as the sultan says." I could see tears brimming, and she seemed so vulnerable that I suddenly felt my heart go out to her. "Breathe deeply," I said; "imagine beautiful things, and carry on."

We had reached the door of the sultan's apartment. Outside two mute eunuchs stood on patrol, waiting for the morning: then, they would record the visitor's name and the date; if the girl were to claim later that she was pregnant, they could verify whether or not she had been fertilized by

the sultan. Hell to those who were discovered to be impregnated by someone else!

The eunuchs opened the door and she stepped inside. I
was not allowed to follow, but the mutes were friends, and
after the others had left, they saw the worried look on my
face and pointed to a tiny hole, no bigger than a round
pearl, at the base of the door. Those two scoundrels might
not be able to speak, but they certainly knew how to see. I
crouched down, closed one eye, and peeked in.

At first I blinked several times trying to adjust my blurry
eyes. And then I made out the furnishings, placed at such an
angle that I could see everything clearly. The padishah lay in
his gilt-canopied bed, propped up on silken pillows, his
satin and sable robe still wrapped around him. Without his
turban, his face looked paler against his dyed beard and hair,
and his whole body seemed shrunken. The scent of sandalwood was so strong it floated through the hole, and I saw
candles flickering with incense. But even they could not
smother the odor of his bad breath; "like the stench of a
lion's mouth"—I had remembered the poet Nizami's words
when the chief black eunuch took me to see the sultan—and
I was sure that Nakshidil would also be revolted by the smell.
She moved slowly, shakily towards him, but she was clever at
covering up her feelings, and I do not think Abdul Hamid
detected her revulsion.

I felt relieved that I had remembered to tell her to kneel,
lift the hem of the bedcover, and kiss it, and I watched as she

pulled it higher and slid in. But I had forgotten to tell her to kiss his feet; would she know to do that and to move slowly up his body? It seemed too soon that she was lying face to face with him, and I hoped the old man was not disappointed, or even angry with insult.

She closed her eyes, not out of passion I was sure, and the rogue reached over and kissed her on the lips. He pushed the covers aside, unbuttoned her tunic, and put his pudgy hands on her breasts, and as I watched, I wanted so much to feel the softness of her flesh. With no further ado, he mounted her and thrust himself inside. I could feel the passion rushing through me, the cruel pangs of yearning that could not be satisfied. She screamed and he covered her mouth with obvious delight. Then he rode her at a gallop, and after what seemed an eternity, he pulled himself out. I sighed, glad it was over, and then I gasped as I saw her face, ashen and still; not an eyelash fluttered, not a limb moved. She showed no sign of life. Was it possible? Had he killed her with his lust?

5
· · · · ·

The news of the death careered through the harem like a horse with its tail on fire. In the Grand Bazaar, where I was sent to purchase some potions and unguents, gusts of gossip swirled around. Have you heard? Have you heard? Turks repeated the news with both hope and dread. The funeral is today. Who's funeral? The sultan. The sultan's dead? How could he be? I saw him out the Friday before. He was mounted on his gray horse, his ten-year-old son on a white horse beside him. Did you see his diamond-ribbed umbrella? Well, of course, but he was surrounded by hundreds of Janissaries, on his way to the Mosque of Haghia Sophia. The caliph can't be dead; he seemed immortal. How did he die? He was in the Entertainment Hall, enjoying himself with the harem orchestra and the dancing girls. No! How true to form. Well, why shouldn't he? He was the sultan, after all. And did he die there? No, it was later that night; he keeled over and collapsed. The court physicians said he suffered a stroke. In any event, by morning he was dead.

I returned to the seraglio and saw dazed slaves walking about like shivering ghosts; others grieved together, mourning for their own lives as much as for the sultan's. Nakshidil sat on her divan, shaking from the events that had transpired.

"I must confess," she said to Perestu, "I was worried when Tulip said I might be called by the sultan. And then," she added, nodding in my direction, "when Tulip came for me, I was even more afraid. When I entered the room, I had no idea of what to do, except for the business of lifting the covers. Thank goodness, Tulip, you told me about that. But the moment I saw him, I thought I would die. Abdul Hamid was loathsome, and the thought of being near him revolted me."

"Tell us all the details, slowly," Perestu begged.

"I walked cautiously towards his bed, gathering my courage, hoping that my slow steps would not give away my disgust. He lay there, small and shriveled, hidden under his black beard, and I remembered that one of the girls called it 'his cloak of evil.'"

"Could you smell his breath?" I asked.

"Yes, of course. He was drenched in sandalwood, but as I came closer, I could not avoid the putrid smell; it took all my strength to keep going. I entered the bed and moved quickly to the top, and as soon as I did he put his wet mouth on mine. Ugh. The memory of it makes me sick."

The memory made me feel sick too, but I said not a word. I did not want her to know I had seen it all.

"But then what happened?" Perestu asked.

"He put his hands on my breasts—his skin was fat and wrinkled and covered with large brown spots—and I prayed that was all he would want, but before I could move, he was on top of me, breathing on me with his stinking breath." Nakshidil began to weep. "It was awful, just awful. First his heavy body on top of mine, and then I felt a shooting pain, and then pounding inside me. Finally it stopped, and I sensed his release, but I dared not move; he turned over on his side and went to sleep. He snored so loud I thought there were storms. I cried and cried, until I cried myself to sleep."

"And did you see him again?" asked Perestu.

"When I awakened in the morning he was gone. The guards told me he was on his way to bathe when he fell over and collapsed on the floor. They tried to save him, but it was impossible. He died a short while later. My God, Perestu, can you imagine, what if he had died in bed?" With that, tears poured down her face and she shook uncontrollably. Perestu rocked her in her arms.

"I can't get that old man out of my head; I was disgusted by him, and yet, for some strange reason I feel sorry for him; he was pathetic in his way," she said through her sobs.

"Nakshidil, you're being a fool. You must put it out of

your head. There is no point dwelling on the past. Forget about Abdul Hamid," Perestu said. "It is ourselves we must worry about."

"Yes, but if he had lived, I might have become a concubine in the harem. And then, perhaps, I would have been made a kadin. What is to become of me now?"

"We must think about the next in line. The only thing that matters is the new sultan on the throne."

"Selim?"

"Yes, Selim."

"You know," Nakshidil said, "I must admit when I caught a glimpse of him last night in the Entertainment Hall, I thought he was quite handsome."

"Not only that, he is highly intelligent," I added.

"But he will want his own harem now," Perestu said. "Unless, somehow, we can persuade him to let you remain here. Otherwise, you will be sent away."

"But what do you mean, *you* will be sent away?" Nakshidil looked at her friend suspiciously. "Won't you be sent away too?"

Perestu hesitated. "I don't know . . . I don't think so."

"But why not? Why only me?"

"Because you have been in the bed of Abdul Hamid. The new sultan will not want you in his harem."

"You mean to say that because I was called by Abdul Hamid I will be sent away, but because you were not you can stay here?"

Perestu looked at me for confirmation. I nodded quietly.

"But that is absurd," Nakshidil said, her face reddening in anger. "It was you both who convinced me to attract the sultan. You encouraged me to do everything I could to make him call for me. And now, because I succeeded, I will be sent away and you will stay." With that, she broke down in tears.

I felt ashamed that I had encouraged Nakshidil to lure the old sultan. "I was only thinking of your future," I said. "How could I know that he would die suddenly?"

"It won't be so bad," Perestu said. "There will be plenty of other girls going with you. Unless . . ."

"Unless what?"

"Unless the sultan changes his mind."

"It isn't likely," I said.

"Well, tell me, who will stay, and who will leave?" Nakshidil asked.

"Anyone who directly served the sultan will leave," Perestu replied. "Some of the old slaves will be freed. The dead sultan's sisters and daughters will lose their titles of sultana. They and the old sultan's wives who do not have sons will be given permission to marry."

"Who will marry them?"

"Most will be wed to provincial governors or high-ranking men outside the palace. They will be given documents declaring their freedom."

"And the rest?"

"The rest of the girls who attended the sultan—for instance, those who served him coffee or took care of his bath—"

"Or went to his bed," Nakshidil added.

"Or went to his bed, and the wives who have sons of the dead sultan, are to be sent to the Eski Saray, the Old Palace."

And what about the eunuchs, I wanted to say, but I knew it would never even enter her mind. Perestu was like most of the girls: they thought of the eunuchs as a tangle of weed in a flower garden.

Nakshidil heaved a sigh. Then she nodded in my direction. "What about the black eunuchs? What will happen to them?"

"Thank you for asking," I said, touching my heart. She seemed to be the only one of the girls who cared. I would have liked to tell her that the Old Palace is filled with eunuchs who also have never had the chance to love, but I held my tongue. Besides, I had heard that for a handful of lascivious eunuchs, the Old Palace was advantageous; with no one keeping a strict watch, they were able, in their way, to be intimate with some of the women.

"They'll go too," Perestu said with a shrug.

"Do you know why is it called the Old Palace?" I asked.

"No."

"It was the first palace built by the Ottomans in the fifteenth century when they conquered Constantinople from the Greeks," I explained. "It was in the center of the city, a huge, high-walled sanctuary with comfortable rooms, big baths, and orchards."

"Why didn't they stay?" Nakshidil asked.

"After Topkapi was erected on this beautiful site on the

Golden Horn, Sultan Mehmed moved, but the women stayed behind. It was only after one sultan's wife, Hurrem, insisted on joining her husband, Suleyman the Magnificent, that the harem moved here. Then, when the sultans died, their widows and female family members were sent back to the Old Palace. It became a place of disgrace, and the ruling sultans used it to punish women who fell out of favor."

"When will we be sent there?"

"Sooner than we would wish."

.....

The following day, the girls received the official information that they would be moving to the Old Palace. Nakshidil wrapped her scant belongings and readied herself for the trip to the Third Hill. There was little to do now but wait.

To keep her mind at rest she began stitching a piece of blue silk, embroidering a flower in red and silver thread. The needlework forced her to concentrate, and with her head down, studying the cloth, she hardly noticed when I appeared. When I called her name, she jumped.

"So much has happened since I first saw you, Tulip," she said with a deep sigh. "How quickly my life has changed, roiling from good to bad, and almost back again. But as soon as I began to make a path for myself in the palace, I found myself against a wall. Do you suppose it is my fate?"

"Nakshidil, come with me," I answered nervously.

81

"Already? I don't see the other girls leaving."

"Please, just come with me."

.....

I had been ordered to bring her to the chief black eunuch at once, but the reason had not been given. We walked quickly along the cobblestones to the quarters of the kislar aghasi, and when we entered the blue-tiled coffee room, I felt the warmth of logs burning in the fireplace. But the tall, thin chief black eunuch who met us was unfamiliar. Selim had already installed his own favorite. How soon we become obsolete, I thought. The new kislar aghasi, Bilal Agha, knew the sultan better than anyone except his own mother; he had been his nanny and tutor since Selim's youngest days, and he had the ruler's trust. His voice was firm.

"The sultan wishes me to speak with her."

Nakshidil moved forward, a worried look on her face. She knew better than to speak.

"The sultan watched your dancing in the Entertainment Hall," the chief black eunuch said.

I could see the fear in her eyes. We were aware that if the new sultan had caught her looking at him, her future was in question. For both of us, there was a fate worse than the Old Palace. I felt my throat tighten and ran my fingers around my neck.

"When the sultan asked about you, he was told that you

play the violin," said Bilal Agha. "Sultan Selim has a passion for Turkish music."

The violin was not a traditional instrument of Turkish music. And the first strains she had played were from Mozart: would that put her in even further danger? She looked at me with confusion. Why was he telling me this? her eyes asked. She must have remembered my earlier warnings: a woman who disobeys the rules of the harem can be punished severely or, worse, sewn up in a weighted sack and thrown into the sea. Lost in her thoughts, she did not hear the kislar aghasi.

"The sultan wishes to keep a handful of women from the old harem at Topkapi."

"Perestu," I saw her lips silently say.

"The sultan wishes you to remain here at Topkapi."

His words took her by such surprise that she did not respond.

"At the sultan's command," the chief black eunuch repeated, "you are to remain here at Topkapi."

I felt a knot in the pit of my stomach. I was happy for her, of course, but now, not only would I be sent to the Old Palace, I would be separated from the only slave girl who had ever really befriended me. I looked at Nakshidil and saw that her face had brightened, so much so that Bilal Agha was moved to comment:

"I can understand how Sultan Selim was taken by your beauty. Your smile lights up the room."

"Thank you, Excellency," she said, bowing her head modestly. "But what about Tulip?" she blurted. "Will he stay too?"

"He will join the others and move to the Eski Saray."

"Please," she said, turning towards me. "Tulip has been kind to me. I beg you, allow him to remain here."

Bilal Agha seemed taken aback by her words, and I wondered if he was angry that she had dared make such a request. Finally, he spoke. "That will be allowed," he said.

Leaving the quarters of the chief black eunuch, I wanted to shout with joy, but the rules of silence would not permit it. We arrived back at the novices' dormitory where the girls' bags had been piled, ready to be carried off. Perestu was saying goodbye to her friends. When she saw Nakshidil she threw her arms around her with congratulations. She had heard the news from one of the other eunuchs.

"Are there no secrets in the harem?" Nakshidil asked, laughing.

"Word travels fast here," Perestu said. "I suppose you already know."

"Know what?"

"Someone else is staying unexpectedly."

"Who else?" I asked. "Is it one of the other dancers?"

Perestu rolled her eyes. "No. I wish it were. At least they deserve it. You won't believe it. It is one of the wives."

"Which one?" Nakshidil asked.

"It is Aysha. She is staying here with her slaves."

Nakshidil's face dropped. "But how did that happen? I thought that all the wives were sent away."

"Usually they are. But she is a clever woman, and she convinced the chief black eunuch that since the new sultan wanted the two young princes to remain at Topkapi, as the mother of one of them she should live here too."

"When the feast is served, there must be lemon as well as honey," I said. But I was afraid that Aysha would serve up too much tartness for Nakshidil.

part Two

6

· · · · ·

The Black Winds shivered down from the Caucasus on an early April morning of 1789, but not even the bitter gusts from the Black Sea could stop the huge crowds from filling the streets of Istanbul. Wrapped in their thickest clothing, the men's heads topped with turbans—Armenians in violet, Greeks in black, Jews in blue, Turks in white—men, women, and children, envoys from the Ottoman provinces, and emissaries from the European capitals, all poured onto the cobblestones, struggling for a glimpse of the dazzling pageant: three days after the death of Abdul Hamid, Mirishah, the mother of Sultan Selim, was to be made valide sultan.

Unlike the quivering vezirs who shifted their favorites with the wind, or the Janissaries who jostled ruthlessly for might, or the rivaling princes who would kill each other to become the successor, the valide sultan's interests lay only with the sultan. Every padishah knew that his mother nurtured him in his early years, taught him whatever she could, became his confidante and remained so all her life. She shared his secrets when he was a child, and when he became the sultan, she not only continued to share his secrets, she even shared adjoining quarters with him in the harem. She wanted nothing more or less than to protect him, and if her son enjoyed the power of the throne, she too enjoyed that power. She would do anything for his cause, and, he could rest assured, she was the one and only person he could trust.

For her unquestioned loyalty, she was rewarded with unimaginable influence, prestige, and wealth, and she ruled the imperial harem, where female slaves and eunuchs served at her command. Her title, valide sultan, sounded alarms of authority over the entire harem, even over the entire empire. Her name inspired awe; her presence exacted obeisance; her word demanded respect.

Her stipend was the highest in the land, derived, in part, from income on land extending from Belgrade to Baghdad, and, in part, from tariffs on an array of goods: from crystal blown in Bucharest and carpets woven in Anatolia to wheat grown in Georgia and oranges grown in Damascus. Her rich treasury contained vast amounts of jewels: her diamonds, emeralds, sapphires, rubies, and pearls exceeded in size, quality, and quantity those of any queen.

Robed from head to toe in clothes made of silver, gold, silk, satin, ermine, and sable; attended by hundreds of slaves;

heeded by grand vezirs and head eunuchs; she was the only woman in the harem who spoke directly to the sultan and gave him counsel. And from her own cadre of slaves she even selected his concubines. Everyone, from pretty young girls to aging vezirs, Janissary chiefs to provincial governors, tried their best to befriend her. And in the seraglio, the sultan's palace where he carried out official duties and private pleasures, she held the highest status after her son.

. . . . .

The imperial procession for the valide sultan began on the Third Hill in this City of Seven Hills, at the Old Palace, where Mirishah had been forced to live after her husband's death, and the riot of costume and color soon stretched across the city. People ran in the streets, dashing from the Old Bazaar to the Blue Mosque in Stamboul, or from one European embassy gate to another in Pera, searching for the perfect spot from which to gaze on the parade.

I was ordered to accompany Nakshidil and I helped her don the warm cape she had been given, while I wrapped myself in the jewel-studded girdle the chief black eunuch had offered on loan.

"It's from the Valide Sultan Mirishah," he said, as he handed it to me. "She wishes everyone in the procession to wear the finest clothes. It sends a message to the people watching the pageant that our empire is as rich and glorious as ever." I was glad to help by putting on the sash, although I knew that while the pearls were embedded in cashmere, our empire was mired in corruption and muck.

We left early in the morning, along with Perestu and others, and were taken by ox-drawn cart to join the hundreds waiting at the Old Palace. Ceremonial events like this are carefully planned, but Abdul Hamid had died so suddenly that arrangements were made in haste, and we found things in confusion. Palace stewards were shouting "You go here" and "You go there," shoving people in every direction. I felt a hand on my shoulder, and before I knew what was happening, we were pushed into a large gilded carriage.

I walked behind Nakshidil. As she stepped inside, she turned her head back, and from the frozen look on her face, I knew that something was amiss. The moment I climbed in, I saw why. The two young princes, Mustafa and Mahmud, were seated on stacks of cushions, and in front of them, plumped on a bigger pile, was Aysha, an ugly black eunuch at her feet. I said nothing, but pointed to a place on the floor, next to Mahmud's nurse, for Nakshidil to sit, while I squeezed in behind her.

As the procession began, Aysha embraced her squirming son, ignoring everyone else, while four-year-old Mahmud asked question after question. Who was at the head of the parade, he wanted to know. Who was behind us, where were we going, why were we stopping? Nakshidil scooped him onto her lap and pulled back the silk curtain. Peeking out from behind the latticed window, we could see a long stream of people ahead of us.

"Look at the Janissaries leading the parade," she said, referring to the dozens of tall turbaned soldiers marching in front. "And just before us is Bilal Agha." The chief black eunuch practically pranced in his towering, cone-shaped white turban, his pleated tunic and his fur-trimmed cape. Behind us were the carriages of the princesses and the valide sultan, and more Janissaries on foot.

As the cavalcade moved slowly across the city, we could see the front of it wending its way along the Council Road, traveling past just a few of the properties—houses and commercial buildings—belonging to Mirishah, the new valide sultan. The procession stopped several times at military headquarters to pay homage to the Janissaries, and I explained to Mahmud that, as the sultan's elite army, they were essential to his success; if they gave him their support, he could stay in power a lifetime; if they withdrew their backing, he would be toppled from his throne.

At last the cortege approached the mosque of Haghia Sophia, and Mustafa cried out that he had been there two weeks before with his father, Abdul Hamid. Then, looming before us, were the great stone walls of the Imperial Gates. Riding through the tall arch, past the turrets and the high windows of the guards' rooms, I pulled Mahmud away from the window. I did not want him to see the display of freshly disembodied heads impaled on spikes that served as constant reminders it was best to be loyal to the sultan.

We entered the grounds of Topkapi and rode past the hospital to the middle of the First Courtyard where, in front of the royal bakeries, a thick circle of Janissaries, vezirs, and holy men were gathered around a dazzling figure astride a white horse. Wearing a crimson satin caftan embroidered with bold crescents, his long sleeves thrown over his shoulders, the new sultan Selim radiated strength; his face exuded youthful energy and his eyes shone with intelligence. Mounted on his caparisoned horse, the Ottoman sultan awaited his mother.

Nakshidil sighed with relief when she spotted Selim, her eyes brightening as though she were seeing an old friend. "He looks even more attractive than I remembered—so different from Abdul Hamid," she said to me, "even his beard is trim."

It was true that, though he had a stocky build and dark hair like his uncle Abdul Hamid, his youth, his warm face and sensitive eyes made him sympathetic. In spite of the ceremonial wrappings, he was almost accessible. But his short beard would soon change. "Now that he is sultan, he will not be allowed to shave again," I reminded her.

When the valide arrived, she stepped from her carriage, and I had my first glimpse of Mirishah. She was of medium height, with bleached white skin and almond-shaped eyes. She stood with her shoulders erect and though she was stocky, she walked with an easy grace.

The new padishah escorted his mother to her new home, and as they reached the sacred imperial harem, it was known that the Queen Mother Mirishah was the second most powerful person in the empire. Walking only a few yards behind her, we could practically feel the ground shake.

.....

Only weeks after Selim's installation at Topkapi, Nakshidil was summoned to the apartment of the new valide sultan. I was ordered to accompany her, and she followed me anxiously down an endless corridor to a large cobblestone courtyard. Threading our way through a portico of marble pillars, past a fountain and down another narrow passage, we reached a winding staircase, and when we climbed to the top, I heard her draw in her breath: the Hall of the Valide, ablaze with gilt and curlicues, was as rococo a chamber as any ever constructed in France. The coffered vaulted ceiling, the gilded boiserie, the lavishly painted landscape murals, the carved niches, and the gilded baroque fireplace reminded her so much of her past that she started to hum a Bach concerto.

Uneasy at the prospect of meeting the valide, Nakshidil paced the room nervously. She beckoned me to a corner where the large windows overlooked the Sea of Marmara below us, the Golden Horn in the middle, and farther up, the Bosphorus, flowing between the shores of Europe on the left and Asia on the right. Boats were sailing up and down the waters, like toys in the valide's private bath.

I suppose I broke Nakshidil's thoughts, but it was important for her to concentrate on where she was. "It is less than two months since Selim came to the throne, yet he has already created this room for his mother. Look at that place on the wall where the sultan's tugra is inscribed," I said, pointing to the Arabic calligraphy that proclaimed Selim's name and his special symbol. "That tugra will be used on all his official documents.

"Do you think Selim built this entire room?" she asked.

"Every sultan takes from the past and adds his own stamp. Some of this room must have already existed, but dozens of slaves worked day and night to finish this so quickly."

"He must care a great deal for his mother," she said.

"Look over there." I nodded, indicating a spot above a door. "It says, 'Mirishah, a sea of benevolence and a mine of constancy.' That tells us exactly how he feels."

With that, I gestured to the divan that ran along the perimeter of the room and motioned for Nakshidil to sit, but just as she did, Mirishah entered. She jumped up at once and paid obeisance, touching her lips and forehead to the valide's hand, bowing to the floor.

The valide sultan quickly seated herself on her silver throne, a black eunuch at each side. The traces of her beauty were easy to see. Though her youth was as distant as the Georgian mountains, she was still endowed with thick brown hair, hazel eyes, and strong cheekbones that swept across her broad Slavic face.

I had heard that she was sold in the slave market in Istanbul at the age of nine and, brought to the Sultan Mustafa III at

Topkapi in 1757, she bore the sultan numerous children; of these, two daughters and a son, Selim, still survived. After Mustafa's death in 1774, when Abdul Hamid took the throne, she was sent to the Palace of Tears, where she had lived for nearly fifteen years. Yet even in that dreadful place she retained the dignity of a prince's mother and the bearing of a woman who wears her authority as a habit.

Now, sitting on her throne, her head high and her back as straight as a halberdier's spear, she seemed intelligent and fierce. Woe to the female slaves, I thought, and shivered in my shoes. A eunuch handed her an amber pipe, and as he lit it with a heated charcoal, she drew in on the diamond-studded stem, let out the smoke, and spoke. Slowly, her demeanor changed: her hazel eyes began to sparkle, her disapproving mouth softened into a smile, and in measured tones, she explored the avenues of her curiosity.

"Tell me, my child," she said to Nakshidil, "I know that you were sent here by the bey of Algiers as a gift to Sultan Abdul Hamid, but how it is that you came into the bey's possession?"

Nakshidil stood before her, head bowed, hands clenched to hide their shaking. I stood by her side, ready to translate any time she needed my help. It was the first time since the girl arrived that she was allowed to speak freely of her childhood, and while she turned to me once in a while to interpret, the words rushed from her lips. Perhaps it was the older woman's curiosity after her long seclusion in the Eski Saray, or simply her interest in the outside world, but each answer that Nakshidil gave produced more questions from the valide.

"Oh, Majesty," the girl began, "it was only a few days before my ninth birthday in April 1785 when my parents announced they were sending me to study in France."

"Is that unusual?" the valide asked.

"It is done by every Creole family that can afford it. Our ancestors all came from France and most still have family there."

"I see." Mirishah drew in again on her pipe.

"The morning of my departure I ate my usual breakfast; I remember the taste of the fresh oranges, the bread, and warm chocolate. We left for the port. I can still picture the dock in Martinique, sailors rushing by, cargo of sugar, spices, and tobacco being carried on board, and my mother standing with a parasol under the hot son, her presence giving off the fragrant smell of jasmine.

"My papa, small in build but grand in stature in Martinique, surprised me and pulled a thin gold chain from his pocket; at the end of it dangled a locket belonging to my mother. As he leaned closer to fasten the chain around my neck, I smelled his aroma of tobacco sweetened with sugar cane. I kissed him on the cheek, and then gave Maman a kiss, and she said I should remember that her love was hidden inside the locket. I could see her lips trembling, and she turned her head to hide her tears. Papa always said I combined the best of the two of them: Maman's chiseled looks

and graceful manners and his own clever mind and firm re-
solve."

I noticed the valide staring at her pipe.

"And then you left?" I asked.

"The boat set sail that morning, and I left with my black
nanny. I felt afraid and confused, fearful of leaving my family, going off with Zinah. She was not much older than I, but
life had both aged and strengthened her; as we watched the
harbor disappear, she put her big arms around me, smiled
with her moon-shaped face, and said, "'We're going to have
a fine adventure.'"

"Where was the ship going and how long did it take?"
questioned the valide.

"The ship was headed to Bordeaux; from there we would
travel on to the Loire and the convent at Nantes. We made
the six-week trip across the Atlantic in fine spirits, and by
the end of July we reached Nantes."

"And then?"

"We soon found the rue Dugast-Mattifeux and the formidable arches of Les Dames de la Visitation. We settled into
place: Zinah was given a job as a gardener; I, like the other
girls my age, was called a 'young sister,' and was taught the
convent life. But I missed my family dearly, and each day as
I rose with the dawn, I reached for the locket around my
neck, patting it to make sure Maman's love was still inside."

"What is this convent life you speak about?" Mirishah
asked. "Is it like the harem?"

"In some ways, yes," Nakshidil said. "There were twenty girls my age, and we were overseen by the Visitandine nuns, women who had promised themselves to no man but God."

"And what was your day like?"

"Each morning I washed, dressed, and made my bed. Instead of the divans we have in the dormitory here, there was a row of hard cots placed exactly two and a half feet apart. Downstairs at breakfast, the crusty bread and the thick hot chocolate were daily reminders of home. Afterwards, I covered my head with a veil, joined the others for prayers, and then went immediately to class."

"What did you study?"

"My favorites were needlework, music, and dance."

"Like here," said the valide.

"Yes, like here. Only there were other subjects too. If I had my choice, I would have spent my days sewing, dancing, and playing the violin. But the nuns insisted that their convent emphasize academic education, and the strict curriculum included history, arithmetic, literature, Latin, spelling, penmanship, deportment, and, of course, catechism. Every night we had long assignments to memorize—oh, how I dreaded them!—and every morning we had to recite them back to the nuns."

"How strange," said Mirishah, "women memorizing history, arithmetic, and literature. And this catechism, you mention. What is that?"

"It is questions and answers we must learn about Catholicism."

"I assume you have put that knowledge aside," the valide said with a frown. "Islam is the highest religion of all. Jesus is one of our prophets, like Moses and others, but that is all. You have learned that, of course?"

The girl nodded and said nothing.

The valide continued. "But what about learning to be a woman? Did they teach you how to please a man?"

"Oh, Majesty, we were taught that too. We learned to uphold our familial duties, follow the wishes of our husbands, take good care of our children, and, above all, act as good Christians. We heeded the words of Madame de Maintenon. A wife 'must learn to obey,' she told her students, 'for you will obey forever.'"

"How wise of this madame," the valide murmured. "And did you become a wife?"

Nakshidil shook her head no. "I stayed at the convent for more than three years. And then in June 1788 our family celebrated a wedding in France, not my marriage, but that of a cousin. A few days later Zinah and I boarded a sailing vessel on our way back home, barely escaping a hailstorm. Little did we know we faced a storm of far greater proportions."

"What do you mean?"

"Our boat was seized by pirates and all of us on board were brought to Algiers—the men were taken on land in irons. I was taken to the bey, who ordered his corsairs to bring me here. It was not how I expected my life to be. It has all been a great shock."

"Yes, I see," Mirishah said, nodding sympathetically.

"Well, one thing I have learned. The more life seems predictable, the more radically it is bound to change." With that she warned Nakshidil not to speak with the other girls about her past, and to give her attention to her future.

"The sultan Selim has found you attractive. You are *gozde*," the valide said. "You are 'in the eye' of my son. You will be moved to larger quarters and taught to do the things that please a man—not just obey him, but give him pleasure. If you learn these well, you may be called to his bed. And from there, you may become a favored one, a concubine."

7
· · · · ·

Nakshidil's new room was closer to the valide's quarters. The large space held places for five girls, an improvement over the crowded novices' dormitory, with small windows overlooking a courtyard, but, still, only a brazier to keep them warm. Once again, there were plain walls, bare wood floors, and narrow divans lining the perimeter, and here and there a cupboard to hold their things. Nakshidil would continue her embroidery, music, and dance, but, as Mirishah mentioned, she was also to have instruction in the art of life.

At Mirishah's orders, the chief black eunuch assigned me to keep an eye on the girl during her daily lessons. The instructions began at once. Much of the time was spent improving her Turkish so that she could converse with ease. She knew enough words to communicate her basic needs, but to speak with elegance required hard work: she still made her r's rise from the back of her throat instead of trilling them off her tongue; she still pronounced her words through puckered lips instead of keeping them flat; and she often emphasized the wrong syllable. In addition, she practiced her writing in Ottoman Turkish, but the mix of Arabic script and Turkish words (along with some Persian and Arabic), confused her to no end.

There were other skills to improve as well. In the private kitchen of the valide, she learned to prepare certain foods. Her teacher was a slave who had never been called by the sultan but had risen in the palace hierarchy; she was now in charge of cuisine for the valide. Though her name, Gulbahar, meant "rose of spring," years of celibacy had caused the poor woman to wilt. The chance to teach the eager Nakshidil, however, was like a dose of sunshine, and she brightened each time she saw the girl.

Coffee was at the heart of Ottoman life, she said, repeating the well-known saying "A cup of coffee commits one to forty years of friendship."

"Yes," Nakshidil agreed, "but you know, for me it is still difficult. I cannot get used to the strong taste."

Gulbahar was surprised. "Why is that?" she asked. "Everyone here drinks coffee."

"As a child I drank only chocolate," she said. "And now I drink only tea."

"Never mind that," the woman said and waved the words away with her hand.

"At any time the sultan might wish to sip a frothy cup of

the black drink. You'd better know how to prepare the brew," Gulbahar said.

The girl learned to pound the dark beans, mix them with cold water and sugar, and boil the liquid with cardamom; most importantly, she became adept at holding the steaming kettle high above the small cup and pouring it into a thick froth.

"Take a sip," Gulbahar urged, holding out the porcelain cup in its filigreed holder. Nakshidil put her mouth to the cup, sipped the foam, and then grimaced as she tasted the coffee.

"You'll get used to it," I said.

Gulbahar nodded in agreement. "The sultan will wish you to drink coffee with him, and it would be impolite for you to refuse. It will not be long before you acquire the taste."

After a while, when Nakshidil became adept at coffee making, the teacher announced it was time for the next lesson.

"You must learn to prepare one or two dishes that will truly make a man happy. It is not so important whether the recipes are easy or complicated, but you must do them well, so that they bring a smile to his lips."

"What do you suggest?" asked Nakshidil, intent on pleasing the new sultan.

Gulbahar recommended dishes that Nakshidil might enjoy herself. "That way your enthusiasm will add relish to the food," she said. And then she added, "I must remind you that the sultan always eats alone. Your role is to prepare the food and then watch him take pleasure in it."

They decided upon a smoky aubergine dish, as the eggplant is considered even better than caviar, and a honeyed pastry. "The love of sweet things springs from faith; true believers are sweet and infidels sour," the teacher quoted from the Koran.

The recipe for phyllo dough and walnuts demanded enormous patience. We watched Gulbahar roll out the phyllo until it was paper-thin. It was important, she cautioned, not to let it become too dry, because the dough would break, nor to sprinkle it with too much water, because it would become too gummy. After she stretched it out as far as possible, she handed Nakshidil a feather. The girl dipped it in melted butter and brushed it onto a sheet of the dough, then spread the dough with a layer of chopped walnuts. Repeating this six times, she cut the layers into small squares, sprinkled them with water, and let them bake. When they were done, she drizzled them with a mixture of rose water and honey and set it to cool.

"This baklava reminds me of the *mille-feuilles* that the cooks in Martinique used to make," said Nakshidil, breathing in the sweet, baked smell. "I would stand in the big kitchen house watching them work the dough. Of course the best part was tasting it as soon as it came out of the oven." With that she popped a piece of baklava into my mouth.

"Is it good?" she asked.

"Delicious," I said. "The work of a true believer."

Flooded with memories of her childhood, she recalled another dessert the cooks prepared. Beating sugar and egg yolks together, she squeezed an orange and added the juice. "The most important part is the liquor," she said wistfully. "I realize it's against the rules of Islam. Where will we ever find some?"

I knew that the palace hospital used liquor to numb the pain of its patients; indeed, more than a few Topkapi residents feigned illness in order to enjoy the drink. I saw a twinkle in Gulbahar's eye and wondered if she had that in mind. "I've been cooking with Mirishah for many years," she said. "You must swear yourself to secrecy."

"I do," Nakshidil said.

She looked at me. "You too, Tulip."

"I do," I said. Was she about to suggest we all descend on the sick? But she had something better up her sleeve. Gulbahar reached way back into one of the cupboards.

"We always keep some flavored liqueur in the pantry. Even in the Palace of Tears we managed to hide some."

With that she pulled out a small bottle and held it up. We read the label, "Golden Water," and laughed as Nakshidil poured some of the alcoholic liquid into the bowl. Then she folded in the egg whites and, at Gulbahar's suggestion, added a touch of ambergris as an aphrodisiac before putting the whole mixture into the oven. After half an hour she held her breath and drew out the baked concoction.

I was about to clap with delight when I saw the lofty soufflé, but Nakshidil quickly grabbed both my hands to stop
me. "If you make any noise, it will fall," she warned.

We all took a bite of the warm soufflé. It was bitter and
sweet, and I had never tasted anything like the light crust and
soft spongy inside. "If nothing else works," I said, "this will
surely lift the spirits of the sultan."

In the afternoons the black eunuch Carnation gave
Nakshidil lessons in the erotic arts. His long frame and
round head fit the description of his name, and he fluttered
in, smelling of attar of roses. Nakshidil was apprehensive at
first, but Carnation's soft voice helped ease her over her
nervousness.

"You must always remember that sex is spiritual as well as
carnal," Carnation told her on the first day. "Your body is a
vessel meant to be filled with love. It is only when we learn to
enjoy the pleasures of our own bodies that we can give pleasure to our lovers."

Nakshidil looked at him askance, and I knew this was not
a lesson she had learned in the convent.

"It is written in *The Perfumed Garden* that Allah has granted
us the kiss on the mouth, the cheeks, and the neck, and also
the suckling of luscious lips." He ran his tongue across his
pink lips and continued: "As it says, 'He has given a woman
eyes that inspire love, and lashes as sharp as polished blades.
With admirable flanks and a delightful navel He has heightened the beauty of her gently domed belly.'"

Carnation pulled Nakshidil to her feet and smoothed his

hand along the tender flesh of her stomach and navel, then gently touched her cheeks. "God has given this object a mouth, a tongue, two lips, and a shape like unto the footprint of a gazelle on the sands of the desert," he said, tracing his finger across her face.

I could see Nakshidil warming to his words, her blue eyes following his every move, her head bent closer to his. Her mouth was open, as if ready to be kissed, but he continued.

"The words of the poet are beautiful and true," he said. "You cannot know how painful it is for me to say them. It is my punishment as well as my pleasure."

She gave him a curious look.

"I will tell you something," he confided, "but you must swear yourself to secrecy."

"Of course," she whispered, looking fearful of what she might hear.

"Even we who have been castrated, we who have lost our testicles or worse, can still feel the urge for sex." With that he heaved a sigh.

I wondered if he was telling her this to rouse her, or ease her apprehensions, or if he had been seduced himself by her innocence. Again she gave him an odd look, as though she, too, questioned why he made this admission. She glanced at me, but I said nothing. It was better to keep my thoughts and urges to myself.

"There are eunuchs who try to satisfy women and some who are even successful," he said. He, too, looked at me, but I kept my head down, staring at the floor.

"Of course," he went on, "we have our mouths to use and that can be most pleasing to a woman. And we have artificial means that we purchase in the bazaar."

I was curious if he was going to bring out any of these tools to show Nakshidil, but I realized, and so did he, that she was still not ready for the shock.

"You know," he said with a sigh, "some of the eunuchs have even married slave girls, and some of the girls have been happier than with any normal man. Then too, there are eunuchs who prefer the boys, just as some of the women prefer each other. Are you aware of this?"

Was he testing her? I wondered. I could see from the look on her face that Nakshidil was disgusted by the idea. "I've seen some of the women fondling each other in the baths," she said.

"And did it please you?" Carnation asked.

"It made me feel sick," she answered.

"Nothing about this should make you sick," he said. "There have been times in the past when sultans enjoyed watching women together. And there were times when sultans called for a man in their bed. All of this is natural."

The girls in the harem sometimes spoke of this, but I knew that Nakshidil found it difficult to listen. Now, she simply stared in horror at Carnation.

"These are the truths of life," he said, seeing the expression on her face. "You must not hide from them. As for Sultan Selim, you must know every inch of his body and how to love it."

One afternoon when we were sipping coffee, Nakshidil broached the subject of eunuchs with me. "Tulip," she said in a sweet voice that was almost flirtatious: "How is it that some eunuchs can have intercourse with a woman?"

"The most fortunate of my friends lost their testicles, but never lost their ability to penetrate a woman with their penis," I explained. "Others have seen their organ grow back. Naturally, they must hide this from the palace physicians during our yearly examinations. But for most eunuchs, the desire exists without the ability."

"I'm sorry," she whispered, and touched my arm.

In the days and weeks that followed, Carnation plied her with Persian manuals and books of erotic arts: *The Perfumed Garden* became her bible, the *Khama Sutra* her mantra. Using objects shaped in the form of a man's member, Carnation taught her how to make the sultan throb, how to stave off his pleasure, and how to bring him to ecstasy.

"You must play games," he advised her, "to keep the sultan interested."

"What sort of games?" she asked.

"Kissing games, to start with. Wager with him who will capture the other's lower lip, and using only your lips, see who can win. If you are the victor, take his lip between your teeth, but laugh and be gentle. Tell him you are the conqueror and if he tries to move, that you will bite. Tease him with your eyes."

"And if he wins?"

"Pretend to fight hard. Beat his chest with your fists and beg him for freedom with your eyes."

"Are there other games?" Nakshidil asked.

"You must make them up. It is important to think of new ways of lovemaking to rouse him each time."

Day after day she thought about little else, and just as she had learned to tease the sultan with her dancing, she learned how to please him with her love.

. . . . .

Six months went by before Nakshidil heard from Selim. At last a message arrived that the sultan wanted to see her. In the customary manner, she was taken to the valide's private bath where, for almost the entire day, she received assiduous care. The slaves massaged her to relax her limbs and calm her nerves, and spread almond and jasmine pastes to smooth and whiten her face. Once again they searched her arms and legs for any hairs, and as she had matured, I explained that the rituals of the bath would be expanded.

"It has an awful smell," I warned, as a slave appeared, holding a basin of odorous yellow cream. With quick strokes she smoothed a layer of lime and arsenic paste over Nakshidil's legs, examining her elsewhere, spreading it under her arms and even across the hair of her most private parts. The girl scrunched her nose at the strong smell.

"Don't think about it," I said, "just talk about other things."

"What will he be like?" she asked. "What have you heard about the sultan?"

"I am sure he will be kind," I said. "I have heard he is a sensitive man."

"My dream is that he will treat me as though he were the prince and I, the girl with the glass slipper." She looked down at her legs, inspecting the smelly paste. "More likely," she said, "he'll be like his uncle, Abdul Hamid. And then he will sweep me aside afterwards, like so much cinder."

Before I could reassure her, the old, black bath slave arrived and scraped off the burning cream with the sharp shell of a mussel, inspecting every inch of her to make certain not a hint of body hair remained.

More slaves came and soaked her skin and her long blond hair, rubbing her with hundreds of rose petals. They paid lavish attention to painting her eyebrows with india ink and encircling her eyes with kohl. She still disliked the way they made her eyebrows meet, but she agreed to do it when I told her that I had heard Selim liked the way it looked. She smiled, as always, when they tinted the nails on her fingers and toes with henna, and nodded yes when they asked if she wanted a tattoo.

The strong smell of eucalyptus wafted up as they dabbed it on her leg to open the pores. "I'd rather have that than the arsenic," she said with a laugh, and watched as one of the slaves mixed the henna powder with clove and the juice of a lemon. When the paste was thick as glue, the girl scooped it into a linen cone, and with the fine tip of the triangle, she drew a tulip on Nakshidil's ankle. After it was finished, she coated it lightly with syrup made from lemon and honey.

"Do you like it?" I asked. Nakshidil looked down at her ankle and smiled.

"Shouldn't we do the other leg?" she said.

As she let the henna dry and darken, they combed her waist-length blond tresses and sprayed them with diamonds. The mistress of the robes dressed her in filmy gauze and diaphanous silks perfumed with roses. The mistress of the jewels adorned her with glittering diamonds, creamy pearls, robust emeralds, rubies, and sapphires, and when she moved, her ears, her neck, her arms, her waist, her ankles, and her feet sparkled like an angel's.

8

· · · · ·

It was as if the eyes and ears of all the slaves were forced shut. The doors and windows of the slaves' rooms were closed and not a soul permitted in the hallways, as the chief black eunuch and I led Nakshidil through the passage between the valide's rooms and the sultan's.

"I can hear my heart thumping," she whispered. "I'm sure everyone in the palace can hear it too."

As we brought her closer to the padishah's private apartment, she stopped for a moment, and I could see a look of panic on her face. "Just remember that it will be silent, and he will be waiting in bed," I said. "You know what to do."

As we reached the eunuchs on guard at the door, we wished her good luck. Bilal Agha turned and left, but I stayed behind and watched as she stepped inside the royal chamber. I remembered the peephole at the bottom of

Abdul Hamid's door, and though Selim had chosen a different apartment, I was sure the eunuchs had done their work. I asked the two guards if I could take a look, promising them some gold coins in return. I was right. A quick bit of bargaining cost me more than I would have liked, but it did buy me good viewing.

Searching the room from my watching post, my eyes jumped from the glazed blue and red flowered tiles on the walls to the colored glass of the windows, from the tree-sized logs burning in the bronze fireplace to the fountain carved of painted marble.

"Come forward, my dear," I heard a man say.

Nakshidil was clearly startled by the sound of the deep voice, and so was I. Though I expected to see the sultan ensconced in his bed, I found him, instead, robed in red satin, seated on his canopied divan. As Nakshidil bowed and stepped across the Persian carpets, I could see that confusion clouded her mind. I felt badly: I had not prepared her for this.

Moving closer, she kissed the hem of his caftan and took her place on the floor. Her eyes fell on his soft hands covered with jeweled rings. Slowly she lifted her head but did not look in his eyes. "Do not be frightened," I heard him say.

"I confess, my sultan," she said in almost a whisper, "I am quite afraid."

"There is nothing to fear," he insisted. "My good

mother has told me of your Creole background and your education in France. I am most curious that you tell me more of your past."

"Oh Majesty, your words take me by surprise," she said in a honeyed voice. "I . . . I . . . thought you wanted other things."

I thought the same. Perhaps he was easing the way with conversation, preparing her for what was to come next. But it seemed he really had an interest in France.

"Thanks to my mother and my late uncle, Sultan Abdul Hamid, I have studied with numerous tutors and learned about things beyond Istanbul. I have read our envoy's reports of the court of Louis XV."

Nakshidil listened intently as he spoke, her eyes wide, as though every word he said was a pearl dropping from his lips.

"For the past three years I have been corresponding with King Louis XVI. I have read about French military power, and also French civilization—music, theater, science, and social customs. I wish to know if what I have read was correct. That is why I brought you here."

He raised a finger, and from my place I could see slave girls enter the room and pour coffee into diamond-studded cups, while others served pistachioed sweets piled onto plates of gold. Two more girls brought a narghile close to the sultan's side, and when all were dismissed, Selim puffed on his sweet tobacco and plied Nakshidil with questions.

"I would like to know more about your education," he said. "I am particularly interested in music. Tell me what they taught you at the convent."

"My padishah, I took many different classes," she said. "I learned the harmonic theories of Jean-Philippe Rameau, and how the Baroque composers used the contrasts of loud and soft, fast and slow, full chorus and solo to enrich their music."

"And was it only theory you learned?"

"At first. But when Sister Thérèse showed me how to play the violin, I took to it at once. She assigned me her favorite pieces to practice: sonatas, suites, and concerto grossi by Vivaldi and Bach."

"And why these composers?"

"Oh, my Glorious Sultan, their music is as sweet as the honey on baklava." She smiled, as if she held a secret. "I do think the fact that Bach was a choir director in a church and Vivaldi taught music in a Christian orphanage made them her idols."

"And were there any other composers she liked?"

"Yes, Majesty. Sister Thérèse taught me a violin concerto by Mozart; as a matter of fact, she called it his 'Turkish Concerto.' And when she heard a new opera that he composed, she thought it so sublime, she taught me to play some of the movements."

"And what was the opera called?"

"Forgive me, my sultan. But it was called *Abduction from the Seraglio.*"

"I see," said Selim, and he drew in deeply on the hookah.

Late into the night, after more questions and more coffee and sweets, he stopped and said with a solemn face, "This has been most interesting."

She nodded, certain, as I was, of what was coming next. She stole a glance at his hazel eyes and soft lips.

"I hope we can continue another time," he went on, his manner and tone detached, "I must have my sleep." He summoned one of his eunuchs.

She looked surprised as he turned his back, and I raced from my spot to hide, watching her leave with another eunuch to escort her back to her room.

That morning I saw her in the baths where, as always, the gossip was as steamy as the heat coming off the floor. I could not help but notice the nasty looks of those who were jealous, and the sneers of those who had already heard of her rejection. "I have failed miserably," Nakshidil said in a quivering voice, as she told me some of what had transpired.

I listened and tried to console her, but there was little I could do. She had been in the bed of Sultan Abdul Hamid, and, naturally, no other sultan would have her. I did not understand why Selim had asked her to stay in the palace, unless it really was her French background that intrigued him. Nevertheless, for a girl to be invited to the sultan's quarters and then turned away from his bed is the greatest rejection imaginable.

"Dear God, what's wrong with me? What did I do?" she asked me again and again. "Am I so ugly?" she said, inspecting herself in the mirror. Disgusted by her failure, she wrung her hands in despair. Even Perestu could not console her. "He'll call for you again, I'm sure," Perestu said, trying to comfort her, but Nakshidil shook her head and moved into the cooling room, only to encounter Aysha.

"Congratulations, Nakshidil. I heard the sultan invited you to his quarters. May I join you?" the redhead asked, seeing the girl hold out her hand for henna.

Eager for a friendly word, Nakshidil motioned for her to sit. "Perhaps she will know what to do," Nakshidil whispered to me. "She's already captured a sultan's heart."

As the bath slave began to stir the henna mix, Aysha started talking, her arms flying as she did, her elbow accidentally knocking the slave's hand. I watched in horror as the old woman dropped the pot, and the henna spilled, covering Nakshidil's hands and arms with the reddish-brown dye. "Can't you be more careful?" Aysha scolded the old slave. The black woman apologized profusely, but it took days for the color to wash out.

"The Fates are not on my side," Nakshidil told me.

"You must make your own fate," I said. "I have a suggestion. Why not visit the nursery? The sound of children's laughter will help drown out your grief."

.....

The following week she was called again by Selim. Once more the sultan plied her with questions, and once more, from my secret post, I heard her give a picture of life in France. When she was finished, he remarked that she had learned a great deal for one so young. "The nuns were stern and forced us to study hard," she said.

"And why was it that you left the convent?" the sultan wanted to know. "Were you going home to marry?"

"Oh Highest Excellency," she said, "it is true that my father had arranged for me to marry when my schooling was completed."

"And who was to be your husband?"

"I was to marry François, the son of the richest plantation owner in Martinique. He was not only rich, he was handsome," she said dreamily; "tall, and slim, with clear blue eyes and a noble nose. My future seemed so clearly laid out, as open as a fortune-teller's spread of cards: convent, marriage, family, a prosperous, if sometimes uneventful, life. But my stay at school was cut short."

"And why was that?"

"The thunder of discontent among the Third Estate in Paris rumbled westward. No great outbursts occurred on the streets of Nantes, but petitioners began distributing broadsides that boldly set down their complaints. Within a short time nearly a dozen pamphlets a day were being thrust at people."

"And what did the pamphlets say?"

"Their message demanded fair representation in the parliament."

"Where did they get their ideas?"

"They were spurred on by the American War of Independence. Someone said the city was 'inflamed in the cause of liberty.' But the flames were leaping too high. My family sensed the danger lurking and wished me to return to safety in Martinique."

"My dear," the sultan said, "I must tell you that I have received reports that confusion reigns in Paris. It is difficult to fathom the rebellious events occurring in France. It is not just fair representation that the people want. They are against religion, against the aristocracy, against the treasury."

He had grown tired and called for a eunuch. Once again she was escorted out.

Scowling and angry, she asked the black slave who led her, "Am I not a woman? What must I do to make him see me as a lover?"

But the eunuch was mute and could only stare ahead in silence.

This time, she withdrew to her room. Days went by and she languished, her spirits dark, her hopes of becoming a concubine clearly diminished. Was she to become another dried-up slave, she asked me, with only conversation as her memory?

"Of course not," I said. But, truth to tell, her future was bleak and impossible to prognosticate.

"Sometimes," she said wistfully, "I see the sultan's hazel

eyes and soft lips dance before me, and I think it's the devil's tease."

If the mood struck, she picked up her needlework and embroidered, only to throw it down in disgust. I suggested she play the violin, but her fingers found only sour notes. At Gulbahar's urging, she tried to distract herself with cooking; but what was the point, she said, if the sultan would never taste the food she prepared?

When I saw her again, two weeks had gone by and she looked sullen and sad. She had done everything she could, she said, everything she could think of to please him, but he had shown no interest.

"I despise him," she whispered angrily. "He has made a fool of me. I think of him, and his hazel eyes and sensuous lips smile at me devilishly through my tears."

The only thing that brightened her days was her visits to the nursery. She begged me to come along one afternoon and see the children: the two princes, Mahmud and Mustafa; the two young princesses, Hadice and Beyhan, sisters of Selim; and their half sisters, girls born outside the palace and given to them as playmates. Several other women were there, including Aysha, who spent her time with her son Mustafa. I noticed that Aysha also seemed to dote on twelve-year-old Princess Beyhan, whose mother had been married off to a provincial governor. Nakshidil played happily with Prince Mahmud, the little boy whose late mother had also been named Nakshidil. The five-year-old remembered riding with us in the imperial coach and singled her out from the other women.

"Nadil," he called her, unable to pronounce her name, "Nadil, come play with me." He threw her his rubber ball and laughed when she tried to catch it and it bounced away.

"Nadil, teach me this," he said, crinkling his upturned nose that resembled hers, looking up at her with his big brown eyes. He smiled as he brought her the checker game and she showed him how to move the wooden pieces across the board. And when his man reached the farthest row of squares and was crowned, he cried out gleefully, "Shah mate!"

One day when his older brother, Prince Mustafa, challenged him to a game, Nakshidil urged him to take the chance. I set up the board—Mahmud chose the white checkers, Mustafa the black—and as Nakshidil moved to the side, Mustafa's mother, Aysha, slid close behind her son.

"How amusing," she said, "seeing little Mahmud try to win against his big brother."

"Nakshidil," I said, "come close so you can watch the game."

The boys began to play. The game was even at first, and then Mahmud jumped one of his brother's men and pulled ahead. I saw Aysha bend over and whisper to her red-haired son, telling him where to move, but the clever Mahmud outmaneuvered him, jumping two more of Mustafa's pieces and scooping them off the board. Again Aysha leaned down and told Mustafa what to do, but this time Nakshidil protested.

The flame-haired woman glowered as her son lost another black piece. Mahmud went on to win the game, but I felt certain he and Nakshidil would pay a price for the victory.

. . . . .

Once more a call came from Selim, and this time Nakshidil steeled herself for rejection; when she arrived in his rooms, he pointed to a sable throw at his feet and told her to sit before him. He asked about books, and she spoke of the poetry of Shakespeare and Dante, and the ideas of Enlightenment expressed by the philosopher Voltaire.

"Enlightenment is a grand word," the sultan said. "Can you explain it in simple terms?"

"Oh my wise sultan," she answered, "it is a belief in scientific laws and an understanding that human beings are rational creatures. That we can think in wise ways and act in the interests of our fellow men. It is the simplest philosophy of all. It is merely the use of common sense."

"Indeed," he said. "That is the most illusive thing in the world. You call it common sense, but it is not common at all."

They talked some more about philosophy and then, again, about music; and he asked her to describe an opera. "What is this *Abduction from the Seraglio*?" he wanted to know.

She told him the story of Constanze, the captured Spanish girl, and the two men who come to rescue her;

Osman, the evil aide to the pasha; the chorus of Janissaries; and she noted his namesake, Pasha Selim, a kind and praise-worthy man.

Selim laughed at the idea that someone would come to save the girl. Silently, so did I.

"Ridiculous," he said. "And you can be sure, no Turk would return a girl from his harem. But," he went on, scratching his head, "you say they speak in song. Please, demonstrate one of these arias for me so that I can understand."

With that, she began to sing in such a high-pitched voice, I thought the precious cups in the room would rattle. The sultan smiled, and when she finished, he summoned a eunuch, whispering an order in his ear. A moment later he returned, carrying a violin.

"Play something," commanded Selim, and she did, making the bow dance across the strings as she poured her soul into the music of Mozart's *Seraglio*.

The moment has come, I told myself, as I watched his eyes light up. He will lead her to his bed.

But no sooner had this idea entered my head than the sultan said goodnight. With a boldness I could hardly believe, Nakshidil sputtered, "What is wrong with me, my great sultan? Why is it you do not want me?"

"To want carnally is one thing; to appreciate another. What I want has nothing to do with you or anyone else. What I admire is your intelligence, your talent, and your charm. I have many concubines, but few female companions. I wish you to be my friend."

"I desire only to obey His Majesty's wishes. The kind sultan has my friendship for life."

But in the morning she asked me, "Will friendship save me if I never enter the sultan's bed?"

"Let us believe it," I said. But I knew that friendship has its enemies in the palace, and that envy is a powerful force. I had heard too many times of those whose hearts were sworn to the sultan but whose heads were impaled on spikes. A concubine had a far better chance of survival than did a conversational friend. I hoped that the carnal needs of the padishah would overcome his inquiring mind and confirm her place in the harem.

. . . . .

On a starry winter night I led her again to the sultan's apartments, as always not quite certain what to expect. But whether the evening would be spent in conversation or conjugal bliss, her presence before the padishah required beforehand that she be prepared in the baths. Perfumed and ornamented, adorned from head to toe with an array of brilliantly colored jewels, her breasts transparent in silky gauze, her soft figure covered in pink and yellow satin, she appeared before him like a gilded gazelle.

Once more she bowed as she stepped silently into the room, and from my vantage point at the door, I saw a fire roaring in the fireplace. But this time the sultan's chair was empty.

Instead, the padishah was plumped against a pile of pillows, draped in fur, ensconced in his velvet bed. This was the moment she had waited for. As she dreamed of doing for so long, Nakshidil approached in silence, her figure swaying like a tulip in the wind. With perfect grace, she unleashed the swath of jewels around her hips and let the girdle fall to the floor. Then she raised her slender fingers, undid the diamond button at her neck, and removed her satin tunic. For just a moment she stood perfectly still, letting him enjoy the tease. Slowly, she released the pearl buttons on her filmy blouse, baring her milk-white breasts, her soft abdomen, her round navel. She turned her back for one quick moment, slid off her filmy trousers, and turned around again, standing before him like Eve. Folding her figure, she fell on her knees to the floor, lifted the hem of the sable cover, and touched it carefully to her forehead and her lips. After she kissed the sultan's feet, she crawled beneath the silk sheets and, as I knew Carnation had so carefully taught her, gently worked her way up, using her mouth and her hands to pleasure him.

When she reached the top of the bed, Selim drew her close and took her in his arms.

"Your eyes are like sapphires sparkling in the snow," he told her. "Your breasts are the ripest peaches topped with luscious berries."

He pressed his lips to hers, caressed her breasts, and took his tongue to her ears and her neck; throwing the covers back, he pinned her arms down with his hands and put his head to her thighs, lapping her cup of love. When he took her, I ached with yearning and turned my head.

After a while I heard him speak. "I did not wish to think of you only as a concubine," he said, stroking her hair with his jeweled fingers. "I wanted to be sure of your companionship; only then did I think it safe to have you in my bed."

I knew she would spend the night, and so I left, gratified that my efforts had come to fruition.

Later the next day she told me that when she awoke she found a note in the sultan's hand. "I am sure you have been told of the gifts that a concubine receives. I do not wish to disappoint you. Please take these presents and know that you mean more to me than any other odalisque."

"Next to the note," she said, "I saw a purse of gold coins taken from his pocket and with it, a pelisse lined in sable."

"That's very rare," I said. "Only the sultan and his highest advisers are allowed to wear sable."

"I know," she said. "I was so thrilled. I wrapped the cape around myself and stroked the fur, as though I were stroking him. I stood in front of the mirror for I don't know how long and admired his gorgeous gift, and then almost as if his spirit had taken over my body, I began to dance. I twirled dizzily around the room, enveloped in his love. Oh, Tulip, I am so happy. It's been two years since I came here. When I think of how afraid I was, and how you helped me, and then that awful time with Abdul Hamid . . . never did I believe it could be as beautiful as this."

Once she had washed, performed her prayers, and

dressed, I brought her to Mirishah. She was sitting in her reception room with a group of slaves in attendance. Nakshidil kissed her hand, and the valide sultan spoke.

"My son has made you a favorite," she announced. "Because you have been with another sultan, you will never be made a kadin. But my son wishes that you receive the privileges of a wife: your stipend will be raised; your food and clothing allotments will be increased; your living quarters will be enlarged. You will be given your own apartment and your own staff of slaves. But there is something else I wish to discuss with you."

Overwhelmed by the sudden rush of events, Nakshidil could hardly speak, but she quickly recovered her composure. Even with her new status, she knew she must not ask questions, but must show her gratitude to the valide.

"Oh Majesty," she said, "I wish only to see that the sultan is filled with happiness. And that his mother, the great Valide Sultan Mirishah, is content."

Mirishah nodded. "I have noticed your kind ways with the little Prince Mahmud. I watched you in the Entertainment Hall when you danced for Sultan Abdul Hamid, may God rest his soul, and tickled the fancy of the young princes. I heard from Mahmud's milk nurse when you rode in the carriage with the two young princes, and I have seen you play with him from time to time in the nursery."

Nakshidil kept her head bowed, but I could see her eyes smiling.

"You know that he has no mother—she died of typhus

when he was three, and indeed the poor child suffered the same disease. But God protected him, and by the will of Allah he survived. Now his nurse looks after him, but she is a mere peasant girl, chosen for the goodness flowing from her breasts. He has two sisters, but the princesses are too spoiled to give the boy the attention he deserves. The child is older now and he needs someone who can care for him as mother, sister, and friend. You are young, but I believe that you are able." With that, she motioned to her slaves, who brought out the small boy. He entered the room with his head bowed and walked nervously to the valide's side. As soon as he saw Nakshidil, he looked up at her and smiled.

"This is a great surprise and a great honor," Nakshidil said, and kissed the hand of Mirishah.

Outside, after the three of us left the valide's suite, Nakshidil clutched my arm. I could see she was overwhelmed by what had happened. "It's a tremendous privilege," I said, "to be the guardian of a prince."

"Yes," she said, half laughing, half crying as she looked at the curly-haired child, "and what a responsibility. How will I protect him? What if his older brother sees him as a threat? What if he thinks of him as his future rival for the throne?"

I looked down at the boy and I saw the way he looked at Nakshidil with his big brown eyes. "I think your love will protect him," I said.

"But what about Aysha?" she asked. "She is a real mother

and I am only a caretaker. She has the status of a kadin and I am only a concubine. Will we be rivals now? How wily is that woman? I remember Shakespeare's tale of Henry IV. 'Uneasy lies the head that wears the crown.' This *is* the Turkish court; will this be Amurath to Amurath?"

I asked her to explain this Amurath, and she told me how brother murders brother. I thought of the Turkish court of Murad III and how, when his son Mehmed was made the new king, he ordered his nineteen brothers killed. I, too, wondered what life would be like for her son Mahmud. And for her. How treacherous would it be for him, and for her, if Mustafa became king? Would they both survive?

"Of course not," I answered. "Think about all you can do. Think of what you can teach him."

"You are right, Tulip," she answered. "I will give Mahmud an education such as Aysha could never give Mustafa: I will teach him about the French as well as about the Turks; make him aware of Christianity as well as Islam; I will play beautiful music and tell him wonderful stories from my favorite books." She picked the boy up and hugged him in her arms. "You will be a great leader, Mahmud, a man of vision, of strength." She put him down, and with his small hand in hers, we walked to her new apartment.

9
· · · · ·

Like a bee drawn to a flower, Selim was drawn to Nakshidil. Beguiled by her charm, several nights each week the sultan ignored the required rotation of girls, and instead, summoned her to his rooms; and night after night she made love to him until he begged for release. He pleasured her too, turning her first sensations of joy into hours of ecstasy. And in between their lovemaking, she entertained him with dancing, the violin, and stories she remembered from books.

But the more time Selim spent with Nakshidil, the more the other girls were resentful. When she entered the hamam one afternoon, I saw the concubines give her a nasty look. Jealousy, that green-eyed monster in the harem, was on the rampage.

"It isn't right," I overheard one girl complain, "we are all supposed to have our turns, yet the sultan dismisses our names."

"It is the sultan's duty to produce heirs," another said, "but he isn't giving us the opportunity to provide him with sons."

"A woman should never give a man all that he wants," a sloe-eyed slave added, looking Nakshidil up and down. "She is overdoing it. He'll tire of her quickly."

Left to herself in the cooling room, Nakshidil looked forlorn. I was bringing her some sherbet and sweets, hoping to cheer her up, when Aysha approached. Smiling broadly, she sat down beside her, and said, "As the only mother of a prince, I would like to give you some advice."

Nakshidil seemed to welcome the redhead's company. Nodding at the older woman, she replied, "You have the wisdom of experience. I would appreciate your help."

"I believe we have much in common," Aysha said. Then, with her smile turning aslant, she added, "Of course, I am not a concubine of the sultan. My attentions are planted firmly on my son."

Nakshidil grimaced. "I, too, concentrate my efforts on the boy," she replied.

"Please understand that I am only looking out for your welfare," the woman continued. "You are still young and innocent. You know, of course, that, in order to ensure your attention to Mahmud, you will not be allowed another child. Even though Mahmud is not your son, and even though you are only a concubine, if you were to be impregnated by

Selim, you would surely face an abortion. And if, somehow, you were able to bring the baby into this world, it is certain that the head nurse would use her silken cord to strangle it at birth."

As Aysha spoke, I could see the hurt and rage welling inside Nakshidil. "My dear Aysha," she said, trying to control herself, "it is so kind of you to take an interest in my future. Most fortunately, however, I do not think you need be concerned." With that, she slipped on her pattens and left.

"You know, Tulip," Nakshidil told me later, "nothing would mean more to me than, as a result of our union, for the sultan's seed to sprout. Indeed, I am surprised that my menses has not already stopped. I have assumed that as surely as day follows night, Selim will want me to have his child. I am certain he will want me to bring into the world a baby who, I know, will be beautiful not only in its looks, but in its talents and goodness."

"Why would he not want this?" I responded, though I was not quite sure of the answer.

"But is Aysha questioning my loyalty to little Mahmud?"

"She couldn't possibly."

"Do you think she is jealous?"

"Perhaps. But it is ridiculous," I said. "She was the number one wife of the late Sultan Abdul Hamid, may he rest in glory. The woman is more than ten years older than you. She is nearly thirty now, and certainly not a candidate for Selim; her days as a sexual partner to the padishah are over."

"Then why did she say these things?"

"You know as well as I do that every emotion is known in the harem. It is true that there are a few women who are revolted by the idea of sex with the sultan and will do anything to worm their way out: they will bribe eunuchs, or sell their favors when their turn comes up on the list. But most are like you and would do anything to be called."

"I understand," she said, "and I do not even like to think of others in the sultan's bed. But how can a woman like Aysha be so filled with envy?"

"Think of the women in the past who scarred, or strangled, or pushed their rivals to death. You know, there was one kadin so jealous of her sultan's new lover that she prepared a special dish. When the ruler sat down to dine, she served him the head of his newest concubine, baked and stuffed with rice."

"Are you trying to scare me about Aysha?"

"Of course not. But I do think you ought to be wary of this woman."

.....

Such comfort did Nakshidil offer Selim that he continued to share his thoughts with her. "Another concubine may satisfy my flesh," he told her, running his finger along the nape of her neck; "but only you nourish my mind and my soul. Each time I lift a veil, I find another intriguing layer. I cherish our moments together."

With the noise of rushing water muffling the sound of

his words, he confided his fears. "Corruption and debt have left the empire in a precarious position," he said in anguish; "serious changes must be made. I am ready to content myself with dry bread, for the state is breaking up." He stood near the room's fountain as he spoke, knowing that palace spies eavesdropped at the walls.

It had been a year since the start of his reign in 1789, when, with no time to waste, he had taken a risk no ruler had taken before. Leaving behind the trappings of his coronation, Selim had convened a meeting of his closest advisers and asked each man for a list of ideas. Within weeks the suggestions arrived: they ranged from changing the system of taxation to replacing the corrupt Janissaries with a new army; although the sultan dismissed the drastic notion of doing away with the special soldiers, he did implement some of these reforms.

But his rash of laws caused consternation in the streets, and the enthusiasm he had inspired soon turned into malaise. Months later he was still submerged in a sea of troubles. The war with Russia had gone badly, and as had been feared, the czarina had sent her favorite general to assist her allies, the Austrians. To counter, Selim called on his best military leader, Admiral Hassan, who had served the sultan well in the past.

Hoping that he could repeat his successes and staunch the combined offensive against Bosnia, Serbia, and Moldavia, Selim promoted Hassan to commander in chief of the army and grand vezir. But even Hassan was not clever enough for the formidable Russians, and his troops were soon in disarray. So horrendous was the defeat that the Ottoman public demanded Hassan's death. Against his own wishes, Selim was forced to bow to public pressure and order the executioner's cord. Tears filled the sultan's eyes as he described the stress of acceding to the people. "One does not rule alone," he said to Nakshidil. "The problems are overwhelming, and the public is always watching. I must escape from time to time if only to see more clearly."

On occasion Selim's escape was a visit to her comfortable rooms. Each time, as the silver hobnails of the sultan's shoes proclaimed his presence in the hallways, slave girls scurried into their cells, eunuchs hid behind closed doors, and everyone but Nakshidil was kept from witnessing his arrival.

His visits were more like family get-togethers than official calls, moments for the sultan to act as father to Mahmud, much as Abdul Hamid had done with Selim. He cherished his young cousins, the only Ottoman heirs, as he would his own offspring, and spent time with them both, though Mustafa was slow and tested his patience, while Mahmud delighted him with his cleverness.

Once in a while Nakshidil allowed me to stay when she entertained the sultan. Her two rooms were simple, but hers alone; somehow, with a few yards of fabric she had managed to turn them into a French abode. A small room for sleeping had divans done up with ruffled covers and pastel swags; the plain walls were hung with pretty embroideries, and the cupboards for storage were lined with cloth. A second room, warmed by a fireplace, was used for entertaining, eating, and prayers. Glazed blue and white patterned tiles lined two of the walls of the visiting room, and satin cushions in the same azure blue, embroidered in silver by Nakshidil, covered the divans along the perimeter. Turkish carpets covered most of the floor, but she had added curtains with tassels and swags, and here and there were tapestries and cloths she had stitched.

On a damp day, as logs crackled in the fireplace, the sultan sat on a rug, playing draughts and dominoes with Mahmud; I saw how pleased he was by the boy's keen mind.

"You are quick to figure out what I am holding," Selim told him, smiling as he looked at the chain of ivory bones the boy had strung together. "A sultan must know what his opponent has in his hand. You will do well when you are on the throne."

Every Ottoman ruler is taught one artistic skill, but Selim was accomplished at several: calligraphy, poetry, and music were his passions. He wrote poems under the name Ilhami, and sometimes read them aloud to Nakshidil and Mahmud; he played the ney, and delighted them both by performing his own exquisite compositions on the wooden flute. Handing the boy the slim instrument, he taught him how to finger the holes and blow with his mouth to make music.

At times Selim and Nakshidil played duets together, he on the flute, she on the violin, while Mahmud listened quietly, watching the sunlight dance through the windows' wooden grille; sometimes they encouraged the boy to play along with them and helped him compose his own small pieces, some in the European style, some in the Turkish.

When Selim was in the mood he asked Nakshidil to dance, and she performed the sultry Oriental moves or showed him the court dances she had been taught at school. She convinced him to hire a French dance master, and a few of the odalisques began to learn the minuet and the contredanse.

Selim showed them how he wrote his tugra, his sultan's emblem, in ornamental Arabic script. Dipping a pointed reed in ink, he drew three thick black lines slanting upwards, and made two circles on the left that swirled through the three vertical lines; then he drew three intersecting strokes dancing downwards and put a series of elegant squiggles at the bottom. In smaller letters he wrote his name: "Selim, khan, son of Mustafa, always victorious," the tugra read.

"The reed is a magical instrument," he said as he gave Mahmud the thin brown stick. "It can sing beautiful music and write beautiful words."

The sultan helped the boy dip the sharpened nib into the dark ink, and the young prince slowly drew the curving Arabic letters of his own name. "When you are older," Selim promised, "you will have lessons from Muhammad Rakim, my own calligraphy teacher."

Selim quizzed Mahmud on his religious studies, and, holding the Koran and the diamond-studded set of Koranic verses that the boy had received on his fifth birthday, he made him recite the lines.

"The sultan is caliph," he said to Mahmud, "the highest religious ruler, and you must know the words of the Prophet and the laws of Islam. Now tell me, who did the Prophet say will taste the sweetness of faith?"

The boy thought for a moment and recalling the words from memory, answered: "First, the one to whom Allah and His apostles becomes dearer than anything else. Second, the one who loves a person and loves him only for Allah's sake. Third, the one who hates to revert to disbelief after Allah has saved him from it, as he hates to be thrown in fire."

I thought I saw Nakshidil gulp, but I made no mention of it and smiled as Selim gently tweaked the long, dark, braided lock of hair that hung down Mahmud's back. "Remember," he said, "these are the last strands of your childhood. When you reach the age of circumcision, they will be cut away and you will be a man."

In the Ottoman tradition, almost as soon as he could walk, the agile prince learned to ride, to hunt, and to shoot with a bow and arrow. At the age of six, Selim presented the wide-eyed boy with a pony, and day after day the child mounted his horse, honing his skills with his equestrian coach. Sometimes he rode with his brother, and the two raced across the flat fields as if they were warrior Turks on the northern steppes.

One summer day the brothers went out riding together,

but when Mahmud returned to Nakshidil's apartment, she saw that the boy was shaken. What happened? she asked, holding him in her arms. The boy explained that Mustafa's horse had raced in front of his, blocking Mahmud and forcing his Arabian steed to veer sharply. The younger boy was tossed to the ground.

"Did he apologize?" Nakshidil asked.

"Of course," Mahmud replied. "He said, 'My brother, please forgive me,' and stopped his horse to help me."

"And what did you say?" I asked.

"I told him not to worry and waved him away."

"I am certain it was not an accident," I said later, when she related the story. "I wonder if Mustafa is jealous."

"I do not like to think such things," she replied. "You know, Tulip, it is such a great honor that the sultan spends so much time with Mahmud."

"It is with good reason that Selim pays more attention to Mahmud," I said. "He is bright and able. And with your guidance, he will be a great ruler someday."

A few days later, Selim invited the boys to play cirit. In the early times of the empire it had been used to keep the cavalrymen well trained when they were not at war. Now it was a game of horsemanship, a test of their agility and skill.

In a distant garden pavilion, Nakshidil and Aysha were seated on piles of cushions, while Aysha's eunuch, the hare-lipped Narcissus, and I stood behind them. We watched from the latticed windows as the sultan took his place in a pavilion closer to the field, and then the princes and the palace pages chose up sides: Mahmud was on the "Okra" team; Mustafa on the "Cabbage." The seven players on each team, each astride a swift horse and with a wooden spear in hand, lined up on opposite ends of the long field and faced each other.

Instantly, the grass was furious with riders as the young centaurs raced across the field, hurling their spears, hoping to hit their opponents. Nakshidil cheered as Mahmud's spear sailed through the air, causing an enemy's horse to turn off course, and scoring three points for the Okras. I heard Narcissus mumble something, but I could not understand his words, only the nasty tone of a gibe.

Then a Cabbage's spear whizzed by, landing directly on an opponent, and even Nakshidil could not help but admire the page's elegant form, although his powerful stroke meant six points for his team.

"I'm so nervous, I can hardly watch," she whispered to me, taking a violet sherbet from the tray of refreshments. "I know that Mahmud is still young and has plenty of time to learn. Still, I would like to see my little boy win."

Suddenly a spear zinged towards Mahmud, and we saw him nearly fall from his steed. Nakshidil cringed at the embarrassment to the boy, and almost dropped the dish of sherbet. Ottoman soldiers are at one with their horses, and a prince who may have to lead his men to war is expected to keep his balance, no matter what the circumstances. But even more upsetting, the spear had come from Mustafa.

I glanced at Narcissus and he gave me a sneer. I looked at

Aysha, but no words of apology came from her lips. Worse, I thought I saw a smirk. I wanted to say something, but it was not my place. I wondered if the saying was true that redheads are born with the power to cast the evil eye.

Thankfully, with childish innocence, Mahmud recouped himself. Horses whirled by again, spears whizzed back and forth, and after two pages from his team scored points, the Okras were declared the winners. As Selim stepped forward from his viewing pavilion to congratulate the team, Nakshidil beamed.

"I knew they could do it!" she said, clapping.

I turned to look at Aysha, but she had already left.

.....

Selim's visits to her rooms were an excuse for Nakshidil to prepare the baklava and soufflés she knew he loved, and after a nod of approval from his head taster, the sultan sat, cross-legged on the carpeted floor, savoring the sweets and praising her talents to the skies.

"Your touch could squeeze honey out of lemons," he said one day, licking his fingers, sticky from the sweet, flaky cakes.

Nakshidil's slave girls brought out coffee, and I slid the narghile next to him, but Selim surprised us by pointing to something he had brought along. "Open it," he said, and there was such a loud pop I thought a firecracker had exploded. But Nakshidil knew exactly what it was.

"Champagne!" she said excitedly. "Where on earth did you find it?"

"Many years ago the French ambassador brought a thousand bottles for the sultan."

"But why weren't they drunk?" she asked.

"The sultan was deposed," he explained, "and he hid the bottles from his successors. Recently my men found the cache. Of course," he whispered, putting a finger to his lips, "we cannot let the ulema know we are drinking alcohol; the holy men think it is the liquid fire of the devil." His eyes twinkled as he lifted his glass.

"What is it you say?"

"*À votre santé*," she said.

"*À votre santé*," he repeated.

.....

On several occasions the sultan invited her for excursions on his boat. The first day of such an event, I handed Nakshidil her *ferace* and when she had buttoned up the cloak, I gave her a *yasmak* and told her to put it on. "But why?" she asked, and I remembered that only once before had she ventured outside the harem grounds and worn a veil.

"It is your protection," I answered.

"Protection? From what?"

"From dangerous eyes."

"What do you mean by that?"

"You must not be seen by any men," I explained. "This

will keep you from their intrusions. All Muslim women must wear the veil outdoors. But it is even more important for women of the sultan's harem. If you were caught without it, you would be killed."

"I will not hide my face," she said, tossing the white chiffon onto the floor.

I picked it up silently and handed it to her again. "You are a Muslim," I said firmly.

"Do you mean to say that if I were not, if I were still a Christian, I would not have to wear the veil?"

I nodded. "But you would not be a favorite in the sultan's harem," I reminded her.

She flashed her ice-blue eyes at me.

"Nakshidil," I pleaded. "In the past you have put your trust in me. Please do as I say."

She moved her head from side to side to show her doubt, but I continued. "You have a choice. You can refuse to wear the veil and stay indoors, or you can wear the veil and leave the palace grounds with Sultan Selim."

I showed her how to take one of the gauzy cloths and slip it over her head so that it covered her hair and forehead. I tied it in the back. The second piece was to cover her face from below her eyes, and as I knotted it too, I mentioned that the Turkish veil was far better than the ones worn by Arab women. "They can hardly see out," I said.

"I don't care. I feel like a prisoner," she muttered.

"Think of it as freedom," I said. "Freedom from undesirable men."

. . . . .

Never had she seen such a boat! she exclaimed. The long, slender, floating palace was as sleek as a swan, with its brilliant white hull, gilded moldings, and bright green border; the gilt of a palm branch glittered in the sun, and behind it the great gilt falcon, symbol of the House of Osman, rose upwards on the prow. With the help of three of us, she stepped into the caïque and sat beneath the great wooden canopy at the feet of the padishah. Two more black eunuchs shaded them with a parasol of white goose feathers as fourteen pairs of oarsmen—their white caftans gleaming, the blue tassels dangling from their red caps—pulled the boat swiftly away from Seraglio Point and across the sparkling water.

"Please tell me, my wise sultan," she begged from beneath her veil, "where is it you are taking me?"

His eyes twinkled as he answered, "Do not be too curious, my sweet. You shall see soon enough."

We glided swiftly through the Golden Horn, passing, on the left shore, the New Mosque with its two minarets, built by Valide Sultan Safiye in the 1600s, and on the right, Galata Tower, soaring above the hills. We reached a point along the Galata side where high stone walls sheltered verdant gardens.

"Come, my flower," the sultan said, gently taking Nakshidil's hand and helping her up. "I am going to show you my secret hideaway."

It was spring, and the sun shone on a riot of red and yellow tulips, splashing a path to a stone pavilion. "This is Ayralikavak Kiosk," he declared. "You have heard me speak of it, and now you are the only woman, aside from my mother, to see it."

His yellow slippers awaited him at the door, and as soon as a eunuch removed the sultan's boots and helped him into the soft leather shoes, they entered the jewel-like building. We followed, and I saw the rooms, some with brilliant floral designs in the reds, greens, and blues of rare Iznik tiles, others lined with Venetian mirrors, and in a small salon I spied musical instruments resting on the shelves.

"This is where I compose my music," Selim explained to Nakshidil, as he patted a seat slightly lower than his. "I want you here beside me. You are my muse, my inspiration."

Pulling off the white gauze that hid her face from the world, she smiled and took her place.

Flute in hand, he worked on his latest composition; after a while, he signaled one of the eunuchs. "This was a gift to me from the Italian ambassador," he said, as the black slave brought in a violin. "It is a Guarneri. Have you heard the name?" he asked Nakshidil, handing her the instrument.

"Shah of my heart," she answered, "this is the finest

violin in the world, given to me by the finest man in the world."

Stroking the honey-colored wood, she nestled the instrument between her shoulder and her chin and played a few strains from Mozart's Turkish Concerto. When she heard the exquisite timbre of the instrument, she put the bow to her lips and blew a kiss to Selim. The sultan picked up his flute and together they played duets from Bach and Telemann.

"There are others in the harem who would love to learn this," she said plaintively. "Perestu has asked me many times. But I am a poor teacher and the palace tutors do not understand European music."

"Then we must have someone else to instruct them." With that, he raised his glass of sparkling wine and clicked it to hers.

Only a few months later Sadullah Agha, a well-known composer and musician, was hired to teach some of the girls the violin and the harp. Perestu was one of the first to attend his classes.

. . . . .

On fine evenings the eunuchs would call out "*halvet*," the command for privacy, and after everyone retreated from the grounds, Nakshidil and Selim would stroll through the palace gardens.

"If I may be so presumptuous as to ask, what do you and

the sultan talk about?" I said one day as we sat in her rooms nibbling pistachios.

"Of course, you may ask, chéri," she answered. "You know that the sultan is eager to learn what the Europeans are saying and doing, and that, for the first time, he has sent several envoys to establish embassies in Europe. When he heard there was going to be a big reception at the French Embassy here, he asked his sister Hadice Sultan to attend. There was much she admired, but when she saw the gardens, she was so taken with them, she asked to have similar ones for Topkapi. Yesterday we discussed the ideas proposed by the Austrian landscaper, Ensle. His brother was the imperial gardener at the Schönbrunn Palace, and Ensle has done work here in Pera. He has offered to design formal gardens for Topkapi."

"Was that all you talked about?"

"No. Princess Hadice is so enamored of Western style she has commissioned the architect Antoine Melling to design a palace for her. The sultan showed me the plans."

"So landscaping and architecture are your topics of conversation," I said, cracking a nut open with my teeth. "Have you no more interesting gossip than that?"

"Ah, a few days ago he told me about his sister, Beyhan Sultan. Selim complained that she is the bane of his existence."

"But she has just celebrated her marriage. After four days of feasts and gifts, she should be content in her new life. Why is she bothering the sultan?"

"It seems that after the wedding ceremony, the pasha, all dressed in his sable robe, waited for hours for the call from his new wife. Finally, he was brought to his bride's chamber by the chief black eunuch, and proclaiming himself a slave, he fell on his knees to kiss her feet."

"That was the right thing to do. A princess's husband is always her slave. She should have been pleased."

"Instead of welcoming her groom to her bed, she kicked him in the face. When he cried out, "Oh my sultana" and "Mercy, my lamb," the princess only slapped him more, until his cheeks were bright red and his nose was bleeding. The princess literally threw her new husband from their marriage bed. The poor fellow was taken away by slave girls. The next morning Beyhan Sultan came complaining to Selim, who told her he would speak to the pasha."

"What did Selim say?"

"He told him that, as the husband of a princess, he must obey her wishes. 'Whatever her whims,' he said, 'you must follow them.' Then, leading him out of the room, he put his arm around the pasha and whispered, 'You are better off far away from her. I will make you the governor of a province so that you can remain married, but for goodness' sake, be glad you will live apart.'"

"That is quite a story."

"Yes, but after he told me, he looked at me and said, 'As much as I love my sister, I fear she has been influenced by Aysha, the mother of Prince Mustafa. That woman knows I am close to Beyhan, and she thinks that by befriending my sister, she will also be in my favor.'"

"She isn't, is she? What did you say?"

" 'My wise sultan,' I said, 'forgive me for such a question, but tell me, why did you allow Aysha to stay here after the death of Abdul Hamid, may he rest in glory?' "

"What was his answer?"

"He threw his head back, rolled his eyes, and said, 'I remembered how sad I was after my father died: I was kept at Topkapi, and my mother was sent away to the Old Palace. I allowed Aysha to stay here because I wanted Mustafa to be near his mother. But Aysha is spoiled and spiteful, and she has influenced my sister to no good end.' "

"How delicious. And what did you say?"

"I smiled and said, 'My sweetest sultan, my good fortune in life is to be able to please you.' He took my arm in his and as we walked back to the harem entrance, I bent down in a bed of hyacinths, plucked a flower, and placed it in his turban."

"Perfect!" I said, "but look at that pile of empty shells. Please take away the rest of these pistachios. I've eaten so many I'm going to have a stomachache."

It was only a few weeks later that Selim led her out to the gardens and begged her to close her eyes for a surprise. At the end of Seraglio Point, she saw his gift: there stood a dainty kiosk, its design inspired by French kings. Mirrored panels lined the rooms; painted vases and flowered pots filled the niches.

"It's the most beautiful pavilion I've ever seen," she told me, "and he's named it Beloved Kiosk, in my honor."

"The eye of good fortune has smiled upon you," I said and pinched my right earlobe to keep away the evil eye.

10

. . . . .

Hocus pocus: it rarely works. Weeks went by without a call
from Selim. No invitations arrived to his private chambers;
no visits were made to her rooms. She ached for his endless
questions, his warm laughter, his sweet poems set to music.
"Oh chéri, he is the thorn in my heart," she told me. The
deadness of empty hours weighed on her. To stave away despair, she sometimes asked me to keep her company during
the day. We played dominoes and card games, and once,
when she was holding a pair of queens, she said they reminded her of the time when she and her cousin were told
they would both be made royalty.

"Who is this cousin?" I asked. "And who made this pre-
diction?"

"My cousin was called Rose, and, like me, she lived in
Martinique," Nakshidil said. "She was much older than me,

and we went together to a famous fortune-teller in Fort-de-France. When we sat down at her table, the big African woman spread her tea leaves, looked at Rose, and said in a deep, trembling voice, 'You will become more than a queen, but you will not die a queen.'"

"And what did she predict for you?"

"Oh, I was very young, about five years old at the time, and she said something vague—about how I, too, would be touched by royalty. But we thought the news about Rose was more exciting, and when we returned home, we told our mothers."

"What did they say?"

"They lashed out at us for visiting the seer."

"And what *did* become of Rose?" I asked.

"She was sent to France to marry a fellow named de Beauharnais."

"And did you see her when you were in France?"

"No, never," Nakshidil said. "I wrote to her once in Paris, and she wrote back just before I left, but that was the last time we corresponded."

"So, she didn't become a queen," I said, laughing.

"No, I guess not," she answered with a smile, and I was glad to see her sadness disappear, if only briefly.

. . . . .

I suggested to Nakshidil that she join the girls in the music room while they learned to play the violin and the harp. But when she returned one afternoon, she said the lesson left her dizzy with confusion. Was it her imagination, or had she seen Perestu flirting with the teacher?

"With Sadullah Agha?" I asked. "It cannot be. They would be risking their lives. Forgive me, my gentle lady, but I believe you are too eager to see romance, even where it does not exist."

"I saw how she gazed at him," Nakshidil insisted. "And I saw how he looked at her. Believe me, Tulip, I am no fool."

On the following day she asked me to come along. I watched Perestu delicately pick up a violin, show her dimpled smile, flutter her lashes over her big eyes, and beseech the teacher for help. Sadullah Agha seemed more than eager to show her how to hold the bow; perhaps, I thought, that was the enthusiasm of a good tutor. But did I not notice an extra glance in her direction as he turned away?

"Why don't you say something?" I asked Nakshidil, who was obviously upset, but when she called her old friend aside, the girl shrugged her shoulders and shook her braided head.

"You have known the love of a sultan," Perestu said. "Can you not allow me the pleasure of a small flirtation?"

Poor Nakshidil. It was difficult to deny her friend a bit of happiness, but the romance between Perestu and the music teacher made her sulk even more. There was still no word from Selim, yet she had no idea what had put her out of favor.

She begged me to find out from the chief black eunuch

if she had done anything to upset the sultan, but when I questioned Bilal Agha, he shook his long, narrow head and blamed it on the padishah's political concerns.

"The constant threat of Russia hangs like thunder over the Ottoman Emperor," he said. "The cost of the war has been so high that the sultan himself has had to make a personal contribution."

Only recently the harem women had been asked to donate some of their precious belongings to the treasury. Each one had turned in a special piece: Nakshidil contributed a jeweled mirror; others gave baskets and bowls woven in gold; cups and plates trimmed with gilt; candlesticks inlaid with mother-of-pearl; silver coffee trays, ink stands, incense holders, water vessels, vases, ladles, and jeweled pipes; all were donated so that weapons could be purchased in exchange.

"There's more than the Russian threat," the chief black eunuch continued; "yesterday, when we met in the divan, the French ambassador Choiseul arrived with worsening reports from France. A full-scale revolution is in progress."

"How does that affect us?" I asked.

"The French moves towards a constitutional monarchy give the sultan reason to worry: as the news rumbles eastward, the ruling class could turn against him. A few days ago the padishah made a secret foray into town: last time he dressed as a merchant and met with Choiseul in a coffeehouse; this time he disguised himself as a sailor, stopped at several stalls in the Grand Bazaar, and listened to the gossip.

The rich are not at all pleased that he's confiscated some of their land and increased their taxes. And what makes matters worse, the peasants could join them and rise up in revolt."

To counter any possible reactions from his subjects, Selim was considering more ways to reform his government and regain control. He had installed a new set of sumptuary laws, enforcing the strict codes of dress that delineate class; he outlawed the import of foreign fabrics like alpaca that hurt the Ottoman farmers; and he instituted economic changes that benefited the masses.

Most importantly, he wanted to modernize the Janissaries. Once the pride of the empire, the elite force was started in the early days when young Christian boys from captured lands were brought to the palace to be trained as soldiers and taught Islamic tradition. With only a dim memory of their past and a future that outlawed marriage, their only hope lay in their loyalty to the sultan. They became faithful followers of the padishah.

But in the years since, pure custom had given way to corruption: now the boys were often Muslims who bought their positions; allowed to wed and have children, they also lost their fervor, caring more about their families and their farms than about fighting for the padishah; in addition they frequently sold their hereditary right to others, solicited bribes in exchange for protection, and sometimes threatened the populace by setting fires.

The Janissaries' ability to defend the empire was vital, yet as soldiers they had become ineffectual. Just as crucial was their loyalty to the sultan. They served as the backbone of the throne; without their support and protection, the padishah was spineless. Every Ottoman ruler knew that if the Janissaries turned against him, his throne would shatter into splinters. It is with good reason that the adage goes, "The sultan trembles at the Janissaries' frown."

The chief black eunuch told me that while Selim's father, Mustafa III, was still alive, he introduced his son to his military adviser, the French expert Baron de Tott. "For the last three years before he became sultan, Selim was corresponding with the French king, imploring him to aid in rebuilding the weakened Ottoman army. Now after consulting with him once again, Louis XVI has promised to send a group of officers and experts to Istanbul to help make improvements in the military."

"So that's why he calls the new infantry Nizami Cedit, like the French, 'The New Order.'"

"That's correct," the chief black eunuch said. "Selim had studied other European methods as well, and has used a combination of techniques for drills, exercises, and exams. The Janissaries saw this as a threat, and egged on by the reactionary religious leaders, they resented the very idea of being taught by the infidels. The Janissaries' complaints have reached the palace."

If affairs of state diverted the sultan's attentions, that was understandable. But truth to tell, there was more. Gossip filled the harem corridors like swirls of dust, and Nakshidil choked each time she heard of another odalisque called to the sultan's bed. When she asked me what she should do, I told her there was little she could do, except pray that Selim would not forget her.

One morning as we were having such a conversation, we heard a knock at the door. Narcissus, Aysha's favorite eunuch, was standing outside with a package.

"Please, come in," I said.

He threw back his strange head to say no, then thrust the offering at me. "This is from the good lady Aysha," he said, his tongue stumbling on his harelip. "She has heard of Nakshidil's sadness and wishes to send a message of understanding. Please accept it as an offering of friendship."

As soon as he left I slipped off the embroidered cloth and found a selection of sweets. I was always suspicious of Aysha, so I smelled them first and then took a bite. Nakshidil watched me carefully.

"They're delicious," I said with surprise. "Perhaps she really has changed."

Nakshidil took one and bit it slowly. "Not bad," she said, "but I'm not in the mood for sweets. You enjoy them, Tulip. Have another."

I did. And another. Later that night my stomach ached; I hoped it was only from eating too many sweets.

11
· · · · ·

We were strolling in the garden, the summer sun brilliant on the flowers, when Nakshidil plucked a chrysanthemum and wondered aloud if she would see the sultan anytime soon. Besme, her favorite slave, asked if she would like her fortune told.

Nakshidil smiled. "I wonder what happened to Rose," she said almost dreamily.

"Rose? He was taken to the hospital, but now he's better," I said.

"No, not the black eunuch. My cousin, the one who was supposed to become a queen."

"Oh, I'm sorry. It's confusing when we all have the names of flowers."

"I wonder if she is still in France. Or if she was caught in the throes of the revolution. I guess I'll never know." She paused, and a twinkle appeared in her eye. "Do you suppose?"

"Suppose what?" I asked.

"Do you suppose I could send a letter?"

"And how would you get it out?"

"I don't know. You're always clever with ideas, Tulip."

I thought for a few minutes. "There is a Jewess," I said finally, "*a kira,* a woman who comes to sell her goods at the palace. Last week she brought me a sample of her beautiful silks, made in her family's factories. She told me she has family connections all across Europe."

"Perhaps she could send a letter to my family in Martinique."

"It's very dangerous," I warned. "Eunuchs have been beheaded and slave girls have been sewn in sacks and drowned for less than that."

"It's worth the risk," she pleaded. "I know you think I'm wrong, but now that I am no longer a part of Selim's life, I dream again of seeing my family. And wouldn't it be wonderful if they could see Mahmud!"

I looked at her as if she had lost her mind. But all she did was pick another flower and pluck its petals.

"Would you like me to read your future?" Besme asked again.

"Yes, of course, you may read my future." Nakshidil smiled. "But please," she begged the girl, "do not tell me if it is too unpleasant."

As in Africa or Martinique, some slaves in the palace

told fortunes, some practiced black magic, and some even believed in Cabbalah. With their inexplicable lives, who could blame them for seeking answers through such illusionary means? Straw pulled from other places and spun like silk to suit a potentate's fancy, the girls had no roots to reach back to, no future they could rely on. Life in the harem is precarious at best, deceptive in its promises, predictably unpredictable. Palm readings, number patterns, magic potions, tarot cards, tea leaves, evil eyes, and other superstitions serve as veiled answers to the unanswerable. Like most of us, Nakshidil accepted these mystical practices with a touch of suspicion, but also with the wariness of one who knows they may turn out to be true.

Besme had won a reputation for her readings, and now she reached towards Nakshidil. "Hold out your hand, please," she said, and slowly traced the lines on the slender palm. A smile appeared on Besme's lips. "You will have a sea of happiness," she exclaimed. But then her face fell.

"What is it? What is it?" Nakshidil asked.

"You told me not to tell you unpleasant things."

Nakshidil brushed aside her words. "Please, continue," she said.

"I see your sea of happiness disturbed by waves, violent waves . . ."

"And then?"

The girl struggled to follow the lines.

"Do not stop," Nakshidil begged.

"I cannot see; no, I cannot tell what comes next," the

reader said. "I see the tide changing, but I am not sure if that is good or bad. We will simply have to wait."

Nakshidil pulled her hand away. "Do not offer your readings to me anymore, Besme. I do not like to hear such silliness. Go back to work. The girls may need you in the baths."

.....

The hamam provided a congenial respite for the girls, but to Nakshidil the baths seemed more like a golden basin filled with scorpions. She understood the sultan's need for numerous wives and concubines—the horrid rate of infant deaths, the necessity of many offspring to assure an heir— nonetheless, it pained her that Selim had taken two kadins and ten times as many concubines. She found no comfort in the other favorites—though many of them saw each other as sisters—nor in the rumors that Selim sometimes hid behind a secret lattice to watch the naked girls playing in the pools. Nor did her encounter with Aysha one day in early autumn offer any solace.

Awash in loneliness, Nakshidil sat on a marble ledge in the baths, ready for depilation. I noticed Aysha standing nearby, and I wanted to warn my friend to be a little wary, but as I was on my way to help someone else, Aysha reached her first. When I returned, Nakshidil was distraught and told me she had nearly been burnt. I tried to calm her down and asked what had happened. It seemed a slave girl had spread the arsenic paste on her arms and legs and her private parts, and then left her side.

"It sometimes happens," I said.

"The paste was on me for an awfully long time," she went on. "I could feel it searing through my skin."

"What did you do?"

"I was searching around for someone to help me, when Aysha came over. She must have noticed my look of distress and asked what was the matter. When I told her, she went at once and found a slave to remove the paste. Thank goodness, because it was just in time. I realize now, another minute and I could have been scarred for life."

"And where was the first girl?"

"She had been called away by Aysha."

I made a face, and Nakshidil looked at me. "You don't think Aysha distracted her on purpose?"

"We'll never know," I said. "But one thing is certain; it is better to keep one's distance from her."

"I suppose you are right, Tulip. This time I thought she was trying to help. I always realize too late that she cannot be trusted."

Seeing how upset she was, another girl approached Nakshidil. I noticed that as she moved, her towel flicked open, showing the henna design painted on the smooth skin above her opening. I moved away, but knowing of Zeynab's reputation, I kept myself within earshot.

"My dear, tell me what concerns you so," Zeynab said, running her fingers through Nakshidil's long, blond hair.

"Nothing would please me more than to be your loving friend."

Nakshidil smiled. "Your friendship would be welcomed. But it is the gift of a man's love that I long for."

With that, the dark-haired woman slipped her arm around her. "I can give you greater love than any man," she cooed. No sooner had Nakshidil heaved a sigh and closed her eyes, than Zeynab fondled her breast. Nakshidil jumped and quickly moved away.

"Are you afraid, *hemshirem*?" the woman asked with a nasty laugh. Disgusted, Nakshidil refused to answer, saying only, "Do not flatter yourself by calling me your sister."

"There are many others who want me," Zeynab sniffed, tossing her hair back as she sauntered off.

Indeed, there were; the halls echoed with the empty lives of the girls; some sought to fill them with whatever friendship they found. But for Nakshidil, a woman's love could not replace Selim, and she grew only sadder and more disconsolate.

A few days later in the music room again, she and I watched the romance blossoming between Perestu and the teacher. Once again, she called her friend aside.

"What is happening between you and the music tutor?" Nakshidil asked.

"Oh Nakshidil, Sadullah Agha has told me I am the love of his life. I am so happy, I cannot begin to tell you. Please be happy for me," Perestu begged. She smiled and the dimples in her cheeks seemed bigger than ever.

But I realized the depth of Nakshidil's sorrow when I saw her fighting back her tears.

A moment later that devil Aysha walked in, Nascissus shadowing behind her. "It is disgusting to hear that European noise," she said in a loud voice. Her eyes roamed the room, as though she were memorizing the faces of the heretics; suddenly she saw Perestu and her gaze rested upon the girl.

"Something must be done," Aysha snapped at me.

"I find the music quite beautiful," I said.

"It is not the music I am speaking of. That is bad enough. But I have heard about this Perestu and her romance with the music teacher."

"Oh, I'm sure it is only rumors," I answered, worried now about the girl.

"These stories do not come out of thin air. There is always some truth. The chief black eunuch must be informed."

"But she'll be . . . she'll be killed," I stammered, "and so will he."

"They know that is the risk they're taking."

"But only if someone finds out. After all," I protested, "they aren't hurting anyone."

"They are hurting me," she declared. With that she marched up to Perestu, pointed a finger at her, and said, "You slimy creature, sneaking around with a man. Who do you think you are?" And then, she reached over and pulled Perestu's hair.

The next thing we knew, Perestu was pulling Aysha's hair. Narcissus tried to join them, but Sadullah Agha held him back, while the two women were on the floor, kicking and screaming and yanking each other's hair. Nakshidil begged me to try and stop them, but interfering would have been like stepping into a lions' den with raw meat. I had never seen anything like this in the harem. And the worst was yet to come.

Perestu tried to stand up, but as soon as she did, Aysha pulled her down and bit her on the face. If I didn't care for Perestu, I would have said it was better than the wrestling matches with the oiled Janissaries. But truth to tell, it was frightening to see all that jealousy explode. I knew that Perestu was in trouble for assaulting Aysha, even if it was in self-defense. As she lay there moaning in pain, blood streaming down her cheek, Nakshidil rushed to her side, while Aysha walked away and ordered me once again to go to Bilal Agha. I had no choice; not only was she capable of attacking me, the woman was, after all, the mother of Prince Mustafa, heir to the throne. I pleaded with the chief black eunuch to have mercy on Perestu and the music teacher.

"He will be imprisoned at once," the master said.

"And she?" I asked.

He rolled his eyes in reply. The next morning I heard that the sultan had called for Sadullah Agha's death. That was the last I knew until two days later when Selim, still burdened by affairs of state, announced an evening of entertainment preceding Ramadan. At least a puppet show and a concert would offer the sultan some relief.

As always on those festive occasions in the Entertainment Hall, the women were gorgeously adorned in silks, their arms and legs covered with jewels, their heavy perfume mixing with the incense burning in the air. We marched in, the Valide Sultan Mirishah leading the princesses, the kadins, the concubines, and the rest of the slave girls and black eunuchs, and after Mirishah took her seat on the raised platform, the others arranged themselves at her feet. As I stood behind Nakshidil, who sat on the opposite side from Aysha, I remembered the first time Nakshidil had paraded into the room and performed her dancing for Abdul Hamid. How far we've come, I thought to myself as we eagerly awaited the arrival of the sultan.

The mistress chamberlain banged her silver cane, we all rose, and a phalanx of eunuchs escorted in the sultan and the two princes. Once Selim had taken his place on the throne, and Mahmud and Mustafa were cushioned beside him, the Karagoz began.

The sultan's efforts at reform were beginning to take hold, and it was said in the palace that his popularity was on the rise. But the cutout puppets we watched dancing on strings told a slightly different tale. They portrayed a king who tried to change the old ways, only to find himself under attack by an angry populace: a mob was shouting; Janissaries were banging their overturned kettles; and the ulema were haranguing against Christian influence. Observing the show, I wondered how close to the truth they came. While the puppets danced, Selim sat absolutely still, his face blank of emotion.

Did the shadow figures foreshadow the future? I saw Aysha snicker as she watched the mob of puppets attack the cutout sultan, and I recalled rumors that she had been involved in a strange plot: years ago Aysha had tried to blame Selim for an assassination attempt on Sultan Abdul Hamid. She was absolved of any guilt, but it was known that she would do anything to put her own son closer to the throne.

When the shadow puppets finished, and refreshments had been served, the musicians were called in. The evening was hot, the windows were open, and in the quiet pause between the end of the puppets and the start of the music, we heard cries from outside. I edged towards the latticed window and looked below. Palace guards were rowing in a caïque and behind them a eunuch rowed a smaller boat; just as I turned, I saw the guards lift a heavy sack and drop it into the sea. I knew, then, where the cries were coming from, but the girl's screams faded as her body disappeared in the Bosphorus. "Poor Perestu. May God be merciful," I murmured with a shiver. I saw tears in Nakshidil's eyes, and I turned to look at Aysha, but she pretended not to hear the cries.

As if on cue, the musicians picked up their instruments, the cymbals crashed, and the audience sat up to listen. After a few sets of traditional Turkish music, the orchestra surprised us with a new composition. A startled hush came over the room and then a rush of whispers as people asked who had written the brilliant piece. Heads turned towards the sultan, but once again he sat stonelike on his mother-of-pearl throne.

Finally, Selim turned to the chief black eunuch and asked who had created such a wonderful composition. "Sadullah Agha, Your Majesty," he said. "He composed it only the other day."

Tears came to the sultan's eyes and it was clear that he was overcome with sorrow for the man he had ordered killed. "Praise Allah," Selim cried out. "God forgive me for his death. He was a brilliant musician. I had no right to take his life away."

With that the chief black eunuch lifted his head and said, "Your Majesty, Sadullah Agha is alive!"

I wondered if now the sultan would order the death of the chief black eunuch. How could Bilal Agha defy the sultan? Then he explained: "Sadullah Agha, the musician, is to be executed tonight, immediately after the concert," he said.

Surprising us all, the sultan exclaimed, "Bring him here at once!"

Suddenly the room was abuzz as the poor fellow was brought from his prison cell to the Entertainment Hall. Shaking in his slippers, not knowing what to expect, he stepped before the sultan, and the moment he did, Selim threw his arms around him, congratulated him on his composition, and told him that he could have whatever he wanted.

"Oh Majesty, may Allah bless you. It is Perestu I want. I miss her more than anything."

The sultan turned to Bilal Agha. But the chief black eunuch rolled his eyes and said sadly, "You may have as many women as you wish, Sadullah Agha. But Perestu is gone. Tonight her body was dropped into the sea."

"May the heavens forgive our deeds and smile upon Your Majesty," Sadullah Agha said, tears welling in his eyes, and I knew he had lost the only woman he truly loved.

. . . . .

The next day Nakshidil received word the sultan wished to see her. She rubbed herself and her clothes with Selim's favorite fragrance, and as we left the baths, she skipped down the hall in a waft of ambergris. "I'm so happy, Tulip," she said. "And yet, I feel so sad for poor Perestu. If only all of us could feel joy at the same time."

I shook my head and sighed. "I'm afraid that will not happen as long as Aysha is around."

Later when we reached the chambers of the sultan, I wished her well and stayed outside, handing some gold coins to the eunuchs. I did not want to watch for long, only to make sure the reunion was complete. Peeking in, I could see Selim in his bed, a warm smile on his face. Nakshidil glided towards him, stepped slowly out of her silky clothes, and kneeled to kiss his feet. I heard a loud cry of passion, but I could not bear to see any more, so I turned, thanked the eunuchs, and left.

. . . . .

Selim's attentions were as brief as the sunlight in winter. "I miss him so," Nakshidil told Mirishah a few weeks later on the fifteenth day of Ramadan. The valide had spent the morning with her son and the highest officials at the special ceremony in the Pavilion of the Sacred Mantle, where sacred relics from the Prophet were kept and celebrated; now everyone in the harem was gathered for the late-night feast. Mirishah offered her consolation; nonetheless, she was more concerned about a princely offspring.

"You must understand, it is for the sake of the Ottoman Empire," Mirishah said. "Not a single girl has yet to produce an heir; what if something were to happen to Mustafa or Mahmud? My son must concentrate on the women who can guarantee the continuation of the Ottoman state. A woman can be responsible for only one prince. Be pleased he sees you at all."

"It is not just that I miss him so," Nakshidil confided; "it is that I feel so much like a prisoner. It has been so long since I have been outside the palace grounds."

"Perhaps we should have a picnic," Mirishah suggested.

On the day of the outing four kadins and Nakshidil, dressed in pink feraces and dripping with rubies and pearls, followed behind the noble valide sultan like chicks behind the mother hen. At the edge of Seraglio Point a small area of the dock had been curtained off, and as the women stepped behind it, we eunuchs helped them onto the caïque.

"Why do we have this curtain?" Nakshidil asked with a frown.

I explained it was so the boatmen would not see the harem women. "How tiresome," she muttered from behind her chiffon veil as she stepped carefully into the satin-lined caïque.

The oarsmen rowed us to those gentle inlets of the Bosphorus we call the Sweet Waters of Europe. As we passed a place along the shore, Mirishah pointed and said that was the site of one of the fountains she had recently bestowed. Without fountains, she reminded us, the public has no source for drinking water. She looked at each of the girls.

"If you are ever valide sultan, you must give generously to the people," she advised. "It is our duty as good Muslims to contribute to the welfare of others." I remembered hearing that Mirishah had come under the influence of the Sufis and was fervent about her religious responsibilities. In the past year her pious deeds included a new soup kitchen to feed the poor and a mosque for the army to assure her son's support. Pray that the Janissaries continue their backing, I thought.

When we had traveled further up the shore and landed at a closed-off park, some of the black eunuchs stood on guard while the ladies pulled off their veils and relaxed: for several hours they romped around the pleasure garden like a whirl of pink dust, playing tag, swaying on the swings, dipping their toes in the waterfall; and then, in an area where we spread some patterned rugs, they indulged in a feast of stuffed eggplant, roasted lamb, yogurt, kebabs, corn on the cob, creamed almond pudding, and all sorts of sweetmeats. It was the first time in a while I had seen Nakshidil smile. She was lying under a leafy linden tree, stretched out on a cashmere blanket on top of a Persian carpet, her head resting on silk cushions.

"You know, Tulip," she said, "You are the only person in whom I can truly confide."

"But you have your slaves," I reminded her.

"They are sweet and well-intentioned, but they do not understand me, chéri. You and I come from privileged backgrounds. We are kindred souls in a way."

It is a rare privilege to be the confidant of a concubine, and I held her secrets close to my chest. This was not the first time we had talked, of course. Usually we gossiped about people in the palace, but, sometimes, in the quiet of her rooms we spoke surreptitiously about her past. Now, recumbent under the summer sun, she chewed pensively on a fig and told me she had awoken in a pool of sweat the night before. When I asked her why, she said that once in a while she still had nightmares about the pirates. "Tell me more," I said. "It is better to expunge these things from the soul."

12

. . . . .

Nakshidil put down the fig and dipped her fingers in a bowl of rose water. Wiping her hands on a linen cloth, she began: "I left the convent and set sail for Martinique in a cabin far smaller than the one we had occupied three years earlier. Zinah, my nanny, and I had to squeeze ourselves and our extra belongings—all the gifts we were bringing home—into the crowded bunk.

"For two days we sailed in misery, shoehorned into the cabin, suffering *mal de mer* as the winds churned up the seas. The captain shifted the sails to fight the storm, but he did not tell us that the ill winds carried more than just the dangerous elements; they bore the curse of Barbary pirates.

"I lay on my narrow bed, nauseous from the tossing waves, and then I felt the boat's tossing change to a gentle rock. It rocked me to sleep."

"Thank goodness," I said.

"The sound of men's voices awakened me, shouts and strange noises in a language I did not understand. Later I found out that the captain had spied the oars of a pirates' galley."

"Why didn't he pull away?"

"The becalmed waters had made it all but impossible for our sailboat to escape. The corsairs encircled us and climbed on board."

"What did you do?"

"The door of my cabin burst open and two foul-smelling men pulled me out of bed. Before I could say a word, they slipped heavy chains around my feet and locked my wrists with iron cuffs.

"I watched helplessly as one of the pirates, shirtless, with tufts of hair coiled like worms across his chest, rampaged the room, yanking open drawers, boxes, suitcases, searching for booty. Suddenly, he spun around and strode towards me, his eyes gleaming. I wrapped my arms around myself, but it was too late: the pirate had spied the gold locket dangling from my neck. I touched my throat, and, as I did, I felt his hairy paw push away my hand and tear the chain from my neck, and my skin began to burn."

"I remember, Nakshidil, when you told me about that locket," I said.

"I still miss it," she murmured, touching her throat. "I thought of Cervantes, and his tales of imprisonment at the hands of the Moors. His poem floated back to me: I wanted my soul 'to fly aloft to abodes of bliss in heavenly lands,' rather than face whatever cruel fate lay before me."

"How long were you on the boat?" I asked.

"The days and nights melded into one. After a time, one of the pirates shoved a bayonet at my back and forced me to trip my way up to the deck. I hadn't seen the light in days, and to my surprise I felt the warmth of the early morning sun, and watched it embrace the whitewashed buildings on the shoreline of Algiers. Slowly the rays grew brighter and more buildings came into view, white stone houses with terraced roofs rising like rows of choirboys up the hillside. The sight filled me with hope."

"And what happened when you landed?"

"They took us onto the dock and I stood behind the ships' crew and the male passengers who were still in chains. My blue dress was torn, and my arms and legs were scored with bruises, but I felt that I could breathe again. I searched for Zinah, but the woman was nowhere in sight."

"What happened to her?"

"I dread to think. For months afterwards I dreamed of her, her warm round face and bright eyes, but I never saw her again."

"And what did they do to you?"

"They marched us in forced procession, until one of the corsairs pulled me away. He put a sharp weapon at my back and a muscled hand on my arm, and dragged me up five hundred steep steps. My body felt as tossed as a capsized boat as I stumbled through the labyrinth of narrow alleys that crisscrossed the Old City. I moved limply along, but when his hand brushed against my chest, I lunged angrily and tried to bite it . . ."

"Good for you!"

"But the best I could do was some spittle. The ruffian slapped me and I nearly fell down on the cobblestones. At last, I reached the top of the hill and saw the walls of the huge, brick Casbah, and the palace."

"Was it like this one?" I asked.

"He pushed me inside so swiftly that I did not see much. Inside the palace, I was thrown at the feet of the bey."

"He's called the one-eyed monster," I said.

"I was determined not to show my fear before that ugly face, so I raised myself up and held my head high in defiance. If this was their gruesome leader, I thought, I refuse to cower before him. Instead I showed him my blue eyes and smiled as brightly as I could."

Nakshidil paused for a moment and took a sip of sherbet.

I told her that the bey bin Osman was under the thumb of the Turks, and at that time he still provided generous gifts to his patron, Sultan Abdul Hamid. "Bin Osman knew you were a gift the old Turk would love. What did he say when he saw you?" I asked.

"He looked me over with his one good eye and pointed a long bony finger at me. 'This one is too good to waste,' he growled at his leering men. They chained me and took me back to the dock."

"Back on the boat?"

"This time Christian slaves pulled the oars of our ship, and with the corsairs' whips at their backs, they rowed hard against the sea. Days went by, and then, once again, the pirates dragged me on deck. I saw Constantinople rise into view, with spiraling minarets and domed mosques glistening in the sun. 'Istanbul,' 'the City of Seven Hills,' they shouted, cheering as dozens of caïques swept by and wild ducks fled out of the way. Our ship slid through the narrow waters dividing Europe and Asia, and when finally it came to a halt and docked at the foot of the palace, four halberdiers grabbed me by the arm. I recalled the words of Dante: 'Then we came along to the desert shore that had never seen anyone sail upon its waters who had known a return after.' "

"Your Dante was right."

"No, I told myself, he can't be right. I *must* return. When I cried, 'Where are you taking me?' the soldiers' only answer was a strong pull on my arm. And then I saw a strange group approach and I felt doomed."

"A strange group?" I asked.

"It was the eunuchs," she said, lowering her eyes.

"We've all had our rough journeys," I said.

"Like mine?" she asked.

"No," I said and turned away.

. . . . .

I often found myself at the Grand Bazaar doing errands for Nakshidil. Wandering through the narrow, crowded lanes I reached the cosmetic stalls to buy ointments, or the book-sellers' stands near the entrance at Beyazit Square, where I bargained with the Armenian dealers over French books sold off by some returning diplomat. A flood of advisers from France had caused a growing interest in French culture—French clothes, French food, even French books were in de-mand—and competition from Ottoman merchants and members of the ruling class had driven up the prices.

Nonetheless, even under Selim, it was not easy to smug-gle books into the harem, the religious teachers being wary of any Western ideas, and once in a while I had to bribe the guards at the gate. But in general, Nakshidil and I developed a scheme: I would wrap the small volumes inside a bocha and carry them in the embroidered cover as nonchalantly as I would a bundle of heavy silk. The difficult part for Nakshidil was to hide them. Despite the fact that she now had her own apartment and her own coterie of slaves, her privacy was not secure. The head chamberlain held the keys to every cham-ber and every cupboard, and at any time the woman might steal in and see them; we never knew whom she might tell.

Nakshidil used the books to teach Mahmud, and by the age of nine, he had learned to read poetry and history. In the comfort of her rooms, he nestled close to her and lis-tened as she cushioned the tales of her harrowing days cross-ing the seas. He was eager to study maps, and liked to trace his fingers along the mountains or through the waters con-necting Turkey and France. He would travel by hand across the Mediterranean, skimming the shores of Tunis and

Tripoli, moving north towards the Aegean and the islands of Greece, turning into the Sea of Marmara and through the straits of the Bosphorus. "It is an easy journey," he would say, and she would smile, not telling him how painful it had been. Sometimes they played chess or backgammon, and nothing delighted her more than seeing him win.

In the afternoons her "lion" went off with a tutor for Islamic instruction: he was learning to read in Arabic, memorizing important phrases from the Koran, and studying the history of Islam. He had even begun to learn calligraphy, copying letters from his illuminated alphabet, although to Nakshidil's displeasure, the calligraphy teacher, Muhammad Rakim, was an imam firmly opposed to influences from the West. Once, when the beady-eyed prayer leader arrived, they were reading Voltaire, and Rakim growled. "I have heard of Voltaire," he said. "That man is worse than an infidel; he is an atheist." Each time after that, the imam viewed Nakshidil with suspicion.

Indeed, Mahmud was off with his teacher, Rakim, when Narcissus, the eunuch, knocked on Nakshidil's door. She was startled at the sight of him, with his misshapen nose, broken once too often, and his twisted mouth. To me they were symbols of his twisted mind.

"It would be my mistress Aysha's greatest honor to have you as her guest at her apartment this afternoon at four o'clock," he said thickly, his tongue stumbling at the roof of his mouth. "She looks forward to the pleasure of seeing you then."

"How kind," Nakshidil replied, surprised at the invitation.

I shivered at the name, remembering some encounters over the years: her threat to Nakshidil of aborting a future child; the henna spilled on Nakshidil in the baths; the depilatory cream that nearly scorched her. The death of Perestu. What did Aysha want now?

"Is she trying to make up for the past or is this a ruse? Is she scheming something new?" I asked.

"It is hard to say," she answered. "After all, this invitation was extremely polite. It's been nearly a year since the burning paste incident; and I don't think she blamed me for Perestu's flirtations. Perhaps now she truly wants to be friends. You know," she said wistfully, "I was fortunate to be called to the sultan's bed, but it's been six months since I've seen him. If Aysha is still close to Selim's sister Beyhan, perhaps she'll have some news."

"I suppose at the very least, you'll have an interesting afternoon."

Readying herself for the visit, she buttoned the pearls down her caftan and wound a silk scarf round her neck, a touch I had seen no one else do. "You look divine," I said, watching as she chose some baubles for her fingers and ears. She tucked a lace-edged handkerchief into the folds of her soft belt, and then reached to take a second one for Aysha. She hesitated, reluctant to part with the cloth she had so carefully embroidered. Then, remembering her loneliness, she folded it again and turned to me. "I'm looking forward to the meeting," she announced.

Aysha's two rooms and private bath faced onto the courtyard of the valide sultan and, like Nakshidil's, were warmed not only by a brazier but by a fireplace, a mark of the woman's status. But, despite the cashmere-covered divans and the finely woven carpets, I thought the apartment seemed dark and ominous.

Surrounded by her staff of slaves and Narcissus, Aysha reclined against a pile of pillows, wrapped in the tubes of a narghile. She was dressed and jeweled to the hilt, and her lips issued words of welcome. But I felt the swords of the slaves' glances and suspicion cut right through me.

Nakshidil smiled and kissed the hem of Aysha's silk dress to show her respect. "It is so kind of you to invite me, hemshirem," she said.

"You are most welcome, my sister. It is so good of you to come." Aysha offered her a seat at the tandour, while I stood behind them, next to Narcissus. "Slip your feet under; this will keep you warm on such a cold day. Perhaps our friendship will grow warmer too," she said, taking a puff of the fruity tobacco. I looked at Narcissus, but he returned my glimpse with an icy glare.

"I thought it would be a good idea to get to know each other better," Aysha went on. "Until now we have not spoken with any intimacy. Sometimes, I even feel you try to avoid me." She raised her hand and curled her fingers, signaling her servants to offer coffee, tea, sherbets, and some rather ordinary pastries.

"I am honored by your hospitality," Nakshidil answered, waving away the offer of tobacco. "It warms me like the tandour. And please, do not take offense if I have been reticent; it is just that I am rather reserved."

They chatted politely about this and that, gossiped about the new kadins and the concubines, noted that none of the girls had borne an heir, and agreed how embarrassing it had been when one of the kadins announced she was with child and the story turned out to be false. Nakshidil did not let slip how vacant she felt, or how much she would have liked to carry the sultan's child. And then, Aysha commanded a slave to bring them her domed casket, and like two good friends, she and Nakshidil happily fingered the ropes of pearls and colored stones.

But the redhead soon became more sober and ordered the treasure chest be taken away. "It seems the sultan is having many problems," she said.

Nakshidil sighed. "I suppose it is true. It is not easy to do away with corruption in the empire."

"Indeed. I know that sometimes reforms must be made, but Selim has gone too far. What does he know of the military when he spends his time writing poems and playing the ney? The Koran says: 'Not equal are those believers who sit at home and those who strive and fight in the Cause of Allah.'"

It was hard to deny that Selim's passions lay more in music than in the martial arts; to Nakshidil, it made him even more appealing. "He is a wise sultan," she replied. "I am certain he knows better than we what is good for the people."

Aysha raised her eyebrows and threw back her head, her big emerald flashing against her neck. "Do not be so sure. Power sometimes interferes with clear thinking." Circles of smoke curled through her lips.

"What is it you are trying to say?" asked Nakshidil.

"I have heard that the ruling class is ready to rise up against him. Revolution is in the air. The ulema are fed up with his interest in the European infidels, and you know they are a powerful force. As the religious leaders, they are part of every mosque: they are the muezzins, the imams, and the sheikhs who give the sermons. And their law, their sharia, is the law of the land."

"But the ulema do not have physical force," Nakshidil argued.

"You forget that then there are the Janissaries. They are furious about the New Order army. They resent the money that is being spent, and they feel it is a threat to their own system. With the ulema behind them, they can dethrone Selim. My son Mustafa is the eldest prince and therefore next in line. And then comes Mahmud. There is no one else, my sister. Selim has no heirs himself. He has spent too much time with the pages."

Nakshidil listened quietly. She felt dizzy hearing about the Janissaries and the ulema. And the talk about the pages was like salt in an open wound. She too had heard the rumors that the sultan enjoyed the young boys as much as he did the girls in his harem. It was strange that Selim had taken so many women to his bed, yet not a single one had given birth to his child.

Aysha continued. "You must choose, Nakshidil. The day will come. Mahmud will be destroyed along with Selim, or he can be an ally of the next in line. Mustafa wants him on his side."

The words were harsh, but Nakshidil had to face the truth: though she loved Selim, he had taken others and tossed her aside like last night's meal. Yet what about Mahmud? If Selim really were overthrown, and Mustafa came to power, he could order his brother killed. No doubt, Mustafa would be more popular if he had Mahmud's allegiance. If Nakshidil declared her loyalty to Mustafa now, her son might enjoy great power in the future. But that would mean aligning herself against Selim.

Aysha had finished speaking, but Nakshidil remained still. I could have sliced the air with a sword, the tension was so thick. Finally, she put down her cup of mint tea. "This has been such an enlightening afternoon," she declared.

With that she rose, and, not bothering to kiss the woman's hem, she turned and left. I followed, still carrying the handkerchief she had planned to give as a gift. As soon as we were safely away, she turned to me. "I'm certain Bilal Agha will want to hear of this, don't you think, Tulip?"

I smiled and said nothing, only twisting around my finger the ruby ring she had given me recently as a gift. But I knew the chief black eunuch would have more than a passing interest.

13
. . . . .

The week of the circumcision the whole harem was in a tizzy:
two princes at the same time—nine-year-old Mahmud and
fourteen-year-old Mustafa—and thousands of boys across
the empire would be circumcised as well. What festivities
were planned! Feasts for a thousand guests at the palace,
flowers spread like carpets across the city, gold coins distributed like candy, concerts and marching bands, performers
everywhere: Topkapi had not seen anything like it since
Ahmed III had four of his sons circumcised nearly fifty years
before.

A throne was brought to At Meydani, the outdoor square
between the Blue Mosque and the Mosque of Haghia Sophia,
where the ancient Romans held their chariot races. Guests
arrived from around the world, and for two mornings they
came to pay homage to the sultan. Wrapped in a stiff caftan,

long sleeves hanging to the ground, Selim sat on his ceremonial throne, while the queen mother, along with Selim's
sisters, Beyhan and Hadice, and the princes' guardians,
Nakshidil and Aysha, watched from a nearby pavilion.

Poor Mirishah had plenty of work to do, keeping the two
women from scratching each other's eyes out. Aysha had
done everything she could to prevent Mahmud from being
circumcised at the same time as her son Mustafa: she had
sent special gifts to the valide sultan, offered to donate
money for a fountain, and attempted to bribe the chief black
eunuch with her jewels. Nakshidil tried to be civilized, and
even offered to put off Mahmud's circumcision.

But Selim was determined to make this a major celebration, and he wanted both his heirs included. Now the
women were forced to sit together politely, as one after
another, the wives of officials came to pay their respects,
while the provincial governors, the foreign ambassadors, the
holy men, and the vezirs threw themselves to the ground,
kissed the hem of the sultan's robe or the tip of his sleeve,
and made obeisance to the padishah on his gold-plated
throne.

On the third afternoon of the celebration, the palace
women, wearing gossamer and glitter, were gathered in
Mirishah's reception room. Seated cross-legged on the
floor at the feet of the valide sultan, they smoked jeweled
pipes while slave girls passed trays of sesame sweets and small
gold cups frothed with coffee. The valide had insisted that
Nakshidil and Aysha sit side by side in the center, but some-

how Aysha had sidled up to Beyhan and drew her to her left, hoping, no doubt, that her honeyed platitudes would glue the princess's friendship.

The head chamberlain entered the rococo room and announced, "You must see the gorgeous gifts we have received in honor of the circumcisions." Slaves followed behind her carrying trays piled so high with presents we could scarcely see their faces. We watched with delicious anticipation as they carefully unwrapped glorious blue-and-white porcelain vases from China, brilliant crystal goblets from Austria, endless yards of the finest cotton from Egypt, soft damask from Syria, and rubies the size of walnuts from India. "Those are mine, of course," Aysha murmured to Nakshidil, as the blood-red stones flashed in the light.

The latter looked at her with dismay. "They belong to both of us," she said. "Both our boys are being circumcised."

"Don't be ridiculous," Aysha said, blowing a puff of smoke in Nakshidil's direction. "This is my son Mustafa's celebration. He is fourteen. Mahmud is still young, and not even your real son. If not for your conniving, Mahmud would not have had his ceremony for at least two more years. You are here because you pushed your way in, and you don't deserve these presents. Besides," she added, "I hear you are not interested in jewels, but only in Western books."

Nakshidil was aghast. "How does Aysha know about my books?" she whispered to me. "Muhammad Rakim," I murmured, reminding her that the calligraphy teacher and Aysha were friends.

And then, I watched with disbelief as Aysha nodded at her eunuch. Narcissus slid his fingers through the pile of rubies, pouring them into the knot of his sash. As he made his way towards the door, I marched up, glared into his ugly face, and stuck my foot in his path. Splat! He tripped and fell to the ground, and the rubies went flying across the room. There were more than a few gasps as everyone saw the jewels he had secretly stashed. Mirishah ordered him to pick the stones up from the floor and bring them to her; then she sent him away for a beating with the bastinado.

That night fireworks lit the sky, and the following day the festivities continued: a military review; fencing duels; a Janissaries' wrestling match, with the soldiers' bare chests and leather-clad legs oiled like snakes; and a circus, complete with lions, a leopard, fighting cocks, and dancing dogs. But the highlight of the celebration was a game of cirit with Mustafa and Mahmud on opposing sides. To Nakshidil's chagrin, Mahmud's team lost by seven points.

"Too bad, Nakshidil. I know how much you wanted Mahmud to win," Aysha said, pretending to offer sympathy. Then, in a warning tone, she added, "You really must be more careful. It seems like Mahmud has a tendency to choose the wrong side."

"I don't know what to do, Tulip," Nakshidil said to me later. "I can't imagine allying myself with that woman. But if

I don't, she'll make it her business to destroy both me and Mahmud."

"Stay as far away from her as possible," I advised, "but if circumstances force you to be with her, pretend to be her friend. And for goodness' sake, don't let her goad you." We were sitting in the garden, and I could see that not even the jugglers, or the clowns, or the pyramid of nine men balanced on each other's shoulders, could make her smile. Finally, an idea bounced into my head.

Word had arrived that the sultan wanted the women to entertain him. The first game the girls played was "Beautiful or Ugly." We tied a blindfold around the sultan's sister Hadice, and after she chose two people, she called out, "Beautiful," and the girls posed. Then Hadice Sultan tore off the blindfold, looked at the girls and decided which one had the better pose. The winner was then blindfolded. This went on several times until it was Aysha's turn. I was surprised when the redhead chose the sultan's sister Beyhan as one of the players and Nakshidil as the other. But as soon as she called out "Ugly," I understood.

Nakshidil and Beyhan Sultan made up their poses, and when they were ready and told her to take off the blindfold, she looked at Nakshidil and laughed loudly. "That's not a pose," she said so Sultan Selim could hear her, "that's just your normal, ugly face." I saw Nakshidil wince, and I wanted to put my arms around her, but of course I couldn't. Instead, when Selim turned his head, I gave her an understanding wink.

When Beyhan Sultan announced they would play that silly game "Istanbul Gardens," I decided to put my plan into action. Out came the princess, wearing a man's fur coat turned inside out, with a mustache painted on her face. She mounted a donkey backwards, balanced a melon on her head, and holding the donkey's tail in one hand and a clove of garlic in the other, she laughed and cried out, "Catch me!" The girls all ran after her as she rode the donkey across the lawn. After a few minutes, Aysha caught her, and then it was her turn.

Beyhan gave her the coat and the melon, while one of the slaves painted a mustache on Aysha's face. Then, just as Aysha called out, "Catch me," I rushed up to her. "You've forgotten the garlic," I said, and as I handed her the cloves, the donkey tripped over my foot. I guess I'd gotten rather good at that, because the donkey fell, and Aysha went flying and landed flat out on the ground. Poor dear; she was lucky she didn't have a broken leg. I apologized profusely and hoped the sultan would not blame me and order the bastinado. But Selim seemed to slough off the matter. And for the rest of the week of festivities, Aysha was laid up in bed, too bruised to move.

The next day was the big event. Wearing their finest embroidered caftans—Mahmud in yellow brocade, Mustafa in blue—the two princes appeared before the sultan in the Circumcision Room. From there they were brought to a special chamber where the procedure took place. I was with Nakshidil, alone in her apartment, waiting nervously for news, when an imam arrived, trailed by a eunuch carrying a gold tray.

"My good lady," he said, "as you are the closest to Mahmud, you must see that the occasion has been successful. It is my highest honor to show you." With that he lifted the velvet cover; my knees buckled and I fell to the floor. The next thing I remember, Nakshidil was fanning me with a linen cloth.

"Tulip," she cried, "are you all right?"

I looked around and saw that I was laid out on her divan. "Yes, I think so."

"You fainted," she said. "Do you know why you passed out?"

At that, I recalled the moment when the imam pulled back the velvet cloth, and I saw the knife and the slice of foreskin on the gold tray.

"It reminded me of something," I said, my voice still faint. "Something that happened long ago."

"But you must tell me, chéri. Remember what you once said to me: You must exorcise it from your soul."

"It is not a story you would like to hear."

"I have told you my own unhappy tale," she reminded me.

"It was the tray," I whispered.

"The tray?"

"Yes, the tray with the knife, and the foreskin."

"Go on."

"Remember I told you that my father sold me in exchange for gold? When the transaction took place, I was sit-

194

ting outside our mud hut, whittling a tool; some strange men walked over to me, and just as I was about to say hello, they grabbed my hands and chained them. Then they chained my ankles and dragged me on foot, and before I knew what had happened, we had left our village and were heading north. I walked for days, maybe weeks, like that, until somewhere in the desert of Egypt, they stopped at a Christian outpost. I still remember the huge cross and the two brown-robed monks coming towards me with such an odd look in their eyes. They took me from the others, brought me into a bare tent, strapped me to a table, and bound my arms and legs."

Nakshidil cringed, and I could see it was difficult for her to listen. But it was too late. I had to continue my story.

"They did not cover my eyes, but made me watch, so I could see the knife and the blade coming down. I screamed, first with fear and then with pain; I was bleeding like a fresh-cut pig. I must have passed out, because the next thing I knew I was buried up to my chest in the sand. I stayed that way for days. They told me the sand would stop the bleeding, but the pain was so great I was not sure I wanted to live to find out. I asked myself, was it better to be among the few who endured such barbaric acts, better to survive this horrid castration, or was it better just to die? Oh God, how comforting death must sometimes be!"

Nakshidil could not hide her revulsion, but she knew I needed to talk. Her face scrunched in a grimace, she asked weakly, "Were you alone?"

"There were many boys in the desert, all lined up like cactus. I heard their moans and watched them slowly dying. Finally, after seven days and nights, one of the white men told me I was healed and took me away. As we left, I saw more corpses buried in the sands.

"They took me to Cairo and put me on a boat with dozens of others: we were held in irons and packed together like spoons, so close you could breathe in the next man's sweat. We were like that for days, and I was still red and sore and in agony: every time I urinated I wanted to die. I remember when we reached Istanbul, and the chief black eunuch came to meet us. I saw his misshapen face and bloated figure, and I knew my fate was sealed."

The flood of memories was too much. I started sobbing and I could hear Nakshidil weeping as well. "I'm sorry, Tulip," she said through her tears. "I'm sorry."

"It isn't your fault," I said. "Besides, you would never treat people so badly."

She looked at me and said nothing.

. . . . .

Six months after the circumcision, in the winter of 1794, the valide sultan announced she was leaving the palace. As a Sufi mystic, she explained, she needed more time for prayers and reflection; her devotion required a tranquil retreat on the Bosphorus. Time passed at Topkapi much as it had, like an

empty vase waiting to be filled, made more hollow by the absence of Mirishah.

Silence prevailed as always, but the tinkle of laughter that
sometimes broke the quiet was gone. The days were marked
by the rituals of meals and prayer and the change of costume
that accompanied them. The seasons came and went, reminders that nature had its own agenda: the plane trees covered themselves in leafy green cloaks and then suddenly
bared their limbs; tulips, hyacinths, carnations, and roses
danced in the warm gardens and then disappeared in the
cold hard ground; hot breezes blew across the Bosphorus
until icy winds chased them away. And while spring turned
into summer and fall succumbed to winter, the concubines
lay in waiting for the sultan, lolling themselves into a stupor
with their hashish-laced tobacco or their little opium pills,
but Nakshidil's small pleasures came from reading a book or
completing a piece of stitching or playing a brief sonata. Or
gossiping with me.

"What do you hear in the harem?" she asked me as I arrived one afternoon. It had been a while since I had seen
her, and she was eager for any news.

"I'm delighted you asked," I said.

"Oh?"

"The chief black eunuch told me last night that Selim
had called him in and told him he was fed up with Aysha."

"Oh, Tulip," she said, "that's the best news. Why didn't
you tell me right away?"

"I just sat down," I reminded her.

"What made the sultan feel this way? Did Bilal Agha say?"

"I suspect it was some message from Mirishah. Even though she's removed from the palace, she hears what's going on. You know, the valide sultan has her own network inside Topkapi."

"What do you suppose she heard?"

"There have been rumors that the Janissaries are plotting a rebellion. The ulema are part of it; the imams, the sheikhs, and the muezzins have been egging on the army, calling Selim a traitor for allying himself with the unbelievers. Every time there is a new innovation, like the new army engineering school with European teachers, or the printing press the French just started in Pera, they denounce it and call it the work of the devil infidels. And Aysha is considered one of the instigators. You know how close she is to Muhammad Rakim. Well, the two of them have been gaining support among the ulema for her and her son."

"That's serious. She could be drowned in a sack for far less than that."

"You are right. But Selim is so kind, he has ordered that she be sent to the Old Palace."

"Maybe we should give her a farewell party," Nakshidil said with a laugh.

"With poisoned sweets," I added.

There wasn't even time. The next morning we watched Aysha and her eunuch, Narcissus, climb into the oxcart and rumble away to the Eski Saray.

14
. . . . .

Three kira were permitted to come to the palace to sell their goods. Two of them, a Greek woman who dealt in jewels and an Armenian who offered furs, had been hardened by the years. But the third, a Jewess, was the most intriguing. Esther Kamona was young, a mere slip of a girl, with thick wavy hair, a high forehead, and dark eyes that seemed to know of things beyond the world of Istanbul.

When I went to greet her on a summer morning, in the room near the eunuchs' quarters reserved for meeting the kira, her eyes twinkled as she pointed to a velvet bocha. "I have something for you," she teased. "Shall I open it?"

"Please," I answered, eager to see what she had brought.

She nodded to her slave and the black woman unwrapped the cover. Esther drew out the fragile tissues, uncoiling a snake of brilliant pinks, turquoises, and tangerines more gorgeous than I could have imagined. Anemone, the palace eunuch who had escorted them in, stepped nearer, his eyes glittering as he caught the smooth silk between his gold-ringed fingers; he held it up to his chest, hips thrust out as though it were a dress for him to wear.

"I think she'll like it," I said and took the cloth.

"Keep it in the bocha," Esther insisted, and I knew that inside the soft pouch there was something more.

I hurried to Nakshidil's rooms, and when she saw the fabrics, she gushed. "That woman is a genius. How did she come up with fabrics even more exquisite than I had dreamed of? Oh, what glorious dresses they will make." As she unraveled the silks, a letter dropped out from the folds. Nakshidil broke the seal of the envelope and we read it together.

June 25, 1795

My dearest Cousin Aimée,
 What an extraordinary piece of good fortune to find your letter when I returned from Martinique. But how dreadful that I could not answer you until this time. The wretched circumstances of revolution would not allow me the luxury of writing letters. Any evil informer could have had me killed for an indiscreet word here or there!
 Oh my poor cousin. What fates have brought us to such places. Where to begin? My marriage to Alexandre de Beauharnais was, to put

it bluntly, a disaster. I am obliged to admit that, even as he took me on
my marriage bed, he was in love with another woman.

Of course I can understand a flirtation here and there, maybe even
a discreet romance or two—after all, what man can hold up his head if
he lacks a mistress—but it was our relationship that I found so abhor-
rent. Instead of caring for me as his adoring Creole wife, he treated me
callously, as though I were no more than a household slave.

I had little choice but to escape to a convent. I am pleased to say
that at Penthemont I not only came across the most divine ladies
(do pardon the pun but I mean the guests as well as the nuns), but the
convent also served as my finishing school. I realized I could create a
life for myself worthy of my dreams.

And yet, after my stay, I found myself at the age of twenty-five and
alone. My husband was gone and my darling young son Eugène gone
with him. Longing to see my parents, I gave in to an impulse and set sail
for Martinique. Would you believe it? The ship I left on was called the
Sultan, and we sailed at almost the very moment in 1788 when you
were setting off from Nantes. To think our ships might have crossed on
the high seas!

I am sad to say I found my parents in poorer straits than mine.
Nonetheless my visit went quite well until the following summer when
word came of the upheaval in Paris.

It wasn't long before the slaves of Martinique were up in arms,
proclaiming their rights to freedom. By August, when the National
Assembly in Paris announced the Declaration of Rights of Man and
Citizen, and our own people followed suit with a Colonial Assembly, I
suspected it was time to leave the island, and I returned to France.

I assume you have heard, by now, of how the crowds stormed the Bastille. I still cannot get over the sight of human heads and hearts impaled on spikes and carried through the streets! What base levels civilized men can sink to! I found little to eat and less to heat my house. Rats scurried in the streets and men and women rushed about, almost as ugly as the rodents, in their dirty peasant clothes. My wonderful Paris had disappeared. I did enjoy the salons at Germaine de Staël's, but I sat quietly and listened to the gossip. You know, I am too indolent to take sides.

Of course, I have always liked to help people, and with my debts piling up, some of those I helped repaid me with generous gifts; one or two even became my lovers.

After all, who is to say that a woman should have only one man in her life? Are we not just as entitled as our husbands to be free? What is this fight for independence all about? And, I might add, who knows better how to please a man than a woman who has had experience?

But all of this was of no importance when that vile man Robespierre came to power. The masses flocked like moths around a candle to watch the deaths at the guillotine. My poor dear Alexandre was killed by the executioner's hand. I too was condemned to the putrid Carmelite prison. Only by the grace of God and the help of my friends did I survive.

Thank the Lord, Robespierre himself was put to the guillotine, and now the country breathes more easily. As I told my friends at dinner the other evening, recalling the fortune-teller's words in Fort-de-France, "that horrid Robespierre nearly upset the prophecy." Well, the New Year soon approaches, and who knows what it will bring?

I have met a most interesting man. Too short, and too stocky, but

with a smile that lights up my heart and blue eyes that penetrate my soul.
He is even good at reading palms! Everyone says he is the most brilliant
soldier to come along in years. He will be a force to be reckoned with.
I'm sure you'll hear of him someday, even in far-off Constantinople.
His name is Napoleon Bonaparte. What is most strange is that he will
not use my name, but insists on calling me Josephine.

I pray that you will have the happiness I have found with him. I
feel certain we will be married within the year!

My dearest Aimée, be assured that I have tried my best to inform
your family of your whereabouts. But due to the British blockade, com-
munications have been cut off between France and Martinique.

Please know that you are always in my thoughts, and that I remain,

Your most loyal and true cousin,

Rose

Rose's letter was like a favorite perfume, wafting with memories of other times and other places. Nakshidil read and
reread the pages until she knew every word by heart. She
asked me to make a copy and hide it in my room; if anyone
found the original, at least she would have another. She had
to admit, she said, that despite the independent attitude of
the women, life in France did not sound so much better
than life in the seraglio.

From the inlaid writing box she had asked me to buy in
the bazaar, Nakshidil selected a clean pink sheet, dipped her
reed pen in ink, and scrawled a note to Rose. Filling her in
with the latest news, she ended her letter with a reminder: "*I*

long to hear from my family. Please do what you can to help." With that she sealed the folded paper with perfumed wax and handed it to me. "Please give it to the kira," she said, "along with this shawl I have embroidered. I want Rose to have it as a gift."

"Wouldn't it be wonderful if she were to succeed in reaching your family?" I said.

Nakshidil put her palms together. "At least I know I have tried."

. . . . .

For more than a year Nakshidil continued to move about like a spiritless ghost, a shadow haunted by her memories. And then circumstances changed. Towards the end of 1796 reports reached Topkapi that Catherine of Russia was dead. The new Russian czar wanted to keep his country out of war with Turkey, even extending offers of peace to the sultan. Good news was also coming from the West. The new French ambassador in Istanbul had arrived with gifts of heavy weapons, telling the Ottoman officials that the revolutionary regime wished to maintain friendly relations with the Sublime Porte. Reassured by the reports, Selim and his vezirs felt confidant that the new French commanding general looked favorably upon the Turkish throne. It was as if in one breath Allah had blown away the black cloud that hung over the Ottoman Empire. And Nakshidil came back to life. Once again she experienced the kind of happiness with a man that her cousin Rose had enjoyed.

With his mind at ease, Selim had more time for poetry and music, and more time for Nakshidil. "My sultan, light of the world, you cannot know how I have missed you, how your absence has pained me," she told him, when, finally, they were together.

"What did he say?" I asked, when I saw her the following day.

"He told me, 'Only he who feels real love knows the joy and sorrow of life.' "

"Ah," I said. "For in love there is sweetness and bitterness."

"How did you know he said that, Tulip?"

"Selim was speaking the words of an eighth-century poet," I replied.

For twelve months life was so sweet that the sultan called for a tulip fete. The last one had been held by Sultan Ahmed III, who, sad to say, was dethroned for his excesses. But Selim had much to celebrate, and under the light of a full April moon, he sat on his throne in a garden kiosk, while his guests gathered in viewing pavilions. After much cajoling, Mirishah had agreed to leave her palace on the Bosphorus and join us, and in a latticed kiosk beside the sultan, she and the sultan's sisters and the women at her feet sipped coffee from diamond-studded cups and nibbled sweets while nature put on a spectacular show.

Tulips of every size and color burst from vases placed on shelves of varying heights in the gardens; torches filled with colored water lit the sky; canaries and nightingales emitted sweet songs; crawling turtles carried flaming torches on their backs; and thousands of tulips bloomed everywhere. Guests feasted and slaves danced. "Let us all laugh and play, let us enjoy the world's delights," the poet Nedim had written, and we did. "How different it is without Aysha," Nakshidil whispered, and I nodded my head happily in agreement.

On other occasions, with Nakshidil at his side, Selim played the ney to her violin and read aloud his poems. Once again he brought her on his boat for excursions along the Bosphorus. Alone together, with only us eunuchs to serve them, he revealed his relief over the new Russian czar and confided that more French military men were on their way to help him modernize the army. His only disappointment was that a brilliant officer, who had offered to come, was now unavailable. Nonetheless, the man, General Bonaparte, was behaving well towards the Turks.

"Did you say he is called Bonaparte?" Nakshidil asked, stunned at hearing the name.

"Yes," he replied. "But why do you ask? Does the name mean anything to you?"

She was tempted to tell him that her cousin Rose was going to marry this man, but she held back, and later, when she asked my advice, I told her not to say a word.

"Imagine if he found out you were sneaking letters out of the palace! Too many girls in the past thought they were in the sultan's favor, only to discover that one misstep and they were on their way to banishment or death. Leave well enough alone," I warned. "He adores the fact that you are French. And with this Bonaparte in command, things can only improve."

How wrong I was.

15
· · · · ·

The first indication that matters were not going well occurred in March 1798, when the council learned that
Bonaparte had been made admiral of the Orient. Why the
Orient, the ministers wondered, when his troops had been
fighting in Europe? Soon after came the reports his army
was sailing east. The sultan demanded a meeting with the
French ambassador. The conference was set for the following week, on the Janissaries' payday, an august occasion
meant to impress the foreign envoys with the size and power
of the sultan's special forces; it was, as always, a visual feast.
The chief black eunuch asked me to accompany him to the
meeting of the divan.

Prayers were performed at Haghia Sophia, after which
we rode in a grand procession. Passing through the First
Courtyard and the Executioner's Fountain, we reached the

Second Courtyard and the Divanhe, the yellow council building where scores of young pages stood outside and thousands of yellow-turbaned Janissaries flanked the twenty-two marble columns. The chief white eunuch, the chief black eunuch, the chief of the admiralty, and the head of the treasury—all wearing various heights of turbans to indicate their rank, and dressed in green satin robes lined in sable—entered the richly painted Council Hall and took their seats on the silk sofa that stretched along the back wall. Then, escorted by hundreds of soldiers, the grand vezir Ibrahim Pasha arrived, the head minister's tall white turban banded in gold, his white satin robe lined in sable, his neck and chest adorned with yards of diamonds, pearls, and precious stones. He marched up the marble stairs, and at the door of the divan, the chief water carrier bowed and murmured, "Oh, Your Excellency, deign to come in."

Everyone rose to greet the grand vezir. Parting from the soldiers who remained outside, Ibrahim Pasha turned to his ministers. "May your morning be auspicious," he said, and took his seat in the center of the sofa. The sheikh-ul-Islam, our highest religious authority, led the green-turbaned vezirs in prayer, while the rest of us stood on the side of the room; the sultan stayed upstairs, seated directly above the grand vezir and hidden from view by the filigreed cage.

The French ambassador, M. Dubayet, small and thin and monocled, arrived with much pomp and circumstance and a score of aides. Much to his chagrin (I could see by the frown on his face), he was given a seat on a backless stool.

Such are the indignities that often befall the infidel at Topkapi.

While he looked on, white eunuchs brought a sample of the Janissaries' food, to be tasted by the vezirs: a tureen of soup, pilav, and a saffron rice sweetened with honey. When the ministers finished their tasting, they shook their purple-turbaned heads to signify the food was untainted, and the Janissaries stationed outside rushed into the courtyard. Imagine the shock of the broken silence as they raced across the open square, and then the noise as their long metal spoons clanged against the huge cauldrons of soup and rice. The sight and sound of the ten thousand tall-turbaned men was enough to frighten anyone.

After they had eaten and quieted down, mountains of leather purses filled with coins were piled along the floor, stretching from the feet of the grand vezir all the way to the door. Ibrahim Pasha was handed an imperial decree, and after he kissed the sultan's seal, he read out loud the authorization to distribute the coins. Immediately, several Janissaries were invited to take the heavy bags and hand out the pay to the sultan's special army. Thanks be to Allah, they were pleased. Otherwise they might have overturned their soup kettles, rushed into the hall, and attacked us!

By now we were all quite hungry and silently cheered as our meal was carried in. I cannot remember how many dozen courses we were served, but I can tell you that the French ambassador seemed overwhelmed as platter after platter of roasted lamb; kebabs of beef; broiled chicken;

grilled quail; pastries with chopped spinach, beef, and veal; poached fish; stuffed aubergines; stewed zucchinis; chopped tomatoes; pickled cucumbers; yogurt with garlic; mashed beans; steamed grains; baked pilav; and lentil balls were placed before him. And for dessert came ripe melons, huge berries, juicy oranges, jellied apricots, fresh peaches, plump dates, and piles of honeyed sweetmeats. He seemed a bit awkward, eating his food with his fingers and rinsing them afterwards with rose water, but I must admit he managed to get enough of it into his stomach.

At last, it was the ambassador's turn to make his case. While the sultan took leave for his throne, M. Dubayet was wrapped in an ermine robe, and his aides were cloaked in camels' hair. When all were ready, the head doorkeepers grasped the envoy under the arms, lifted him up, and swept him off to the Throne Room.

I followed behind and entered the room where the sultan was enthroned on a velvet sofa. Pearls adorned the crimson covers, emeralds studded the cushions, and gold thread was woven into the carpets that covered his feet. A canopy hung above his head, and over it, three globes symbolized his worldly power.

The ambassador of France crossed the silk carpets on the marble floor, bowed three times before the sultan, kissed the skirt of his gold-embroidered caftan, and stepped backwards towards the wall. The grand vezir officially greeted the foreign envoy, and the Frenchman began to speak; I served as interpreter. Ahmed Bey, the sultan's secretary, was taking notes. Only recently Ahmed Bey had told the divan he blamed the tumultuous events in France on atheists like Rousseau and Voltaire: their antireligious writings were, he said, responsible for the heresy and wickedness spreading through their country.

"It is well known that the basis of order and cohesion of every state is a firm grasp of the roots and branches of holy law, religion, and doctrine," Ahmed Bey declared, echoing the ulema in the divan. He told the chief black eunuch that he wished the French uprising "would spread like syphilis to the enemies of the empire" and hurl not only France but all of Turkey's opponents into conflict. But the chief black eunuch told me that others in the divan differed, and felt sympathy for the French.

"The infidels' rejection of Christianity is an indication they understand that Islam is the true religion," one of the vezirs had said in way of explanation.

Standing so near the sultan, I could see the concern in his eyes: which of his own factions were to be heeded; was the ambassador to be trusted or not. Still, he said nothing and listened closely to the diplomat's words.

"Exalted sultan, majestic padishah, God's glorious shadow on earth," proclaimed M. Dubayet in a rush of politesse. First, he wanted the sultan to know he carried with him the sincerest regards of the Directory, the new government of France, and he wished to express its highest desire for the continued good health of the great sultan. "May the caliph live a long and fruitful life," he said. He hoped that the Shah of

Shahs was pleased by the numerous gifts he had brought, enu-
merating the enameled porcelains, the fine perfumes, the silver warming trays, the gold-rimmed coffee cups, the gold
candlesticks, the gold watches, and the ormolued desk. And he
hoped that the valide sultan, the grand vezir, and the chief
black eunuch would find his gifts to their fancy. He thanked
His Majesty profusely for the generous way in which he had
been treated. Then he put on his monocle and got down to
business.

It was true, he confirmed, that the French army was
moving east, but they were headed for India, he said, where
they were determined to destroy the British trade routes.
Surely, he said, the great and wise sultan would understand;
after all, England had long been an enemy of the Turks as
well. Please be assured, he begged, that France was out to
help, not hinder, the great Ottoman Empire. France wishes
to be your friend, he said, and to aid in any way possible
against the enemy Britain.

With that, he made the appropriate obeisances and
backed out of the room. I hoped the ambassador was telling
the truth; otherwise he might find himself, like other men-
dacious envoys before him, a prisoner in the Seven Towers.

. . . . .

In June of that same year, all hell broke loose.

The ambassador's promises were nothing but a bunch of
lies. Bonaparte's troops had landed in Egypt, one of our

most important provinces, and it was now clear that the general was out to destroy the Ottoman Empire and then take on the English in India. Soon after his soldiers arrived at Alexandria, in the Aboukir Bay, they headed south towards Cairo and struck a serious blow at the Turkish troops. The battle at the Pyramids was a disaster; by August 1798 Cairo was in French hands.

Generally, Turkey has been able to balance the scales. Whenever we have felt overwhelmed by one European country or another, we called on our opponent's enemy to come to our side. I suppose that is why they say "the enemy of my enemy is my friend." Sometimes the scales seemed more like a seesaw as we changed back and forth between the British and the French, the Russians and the Austrians. Wasn't it just yesterday that the French were our closest friends? This time, it was the British who rushed to our defense. Admittedly, Admiral Nelson was more concerned about protecting India against the French than about maintaining the Ottomans' hold on Egypt, but *malesh*, to our advantage, the British admiral destroyed Bonaparte's fleet.

With most of his ships gone, the French general mapped out a land route, and in January 1799 he marched his troops east across the Sinai Desert to Palestine; there, in Jaffa, our soldiers were overwhelmed and surrendered, but the barbarous French murdered them anyway: three thousand men, along with women and children, were drowned in the sea. But by the will of God, three months later, when the French moved up the coast towards Syria, our New Order army rose to the task: at Acre, two thousand of Bonaparte's troops were destroyed, their heads slit by our swords; the rest turned on their heels in retreat.

The French returned to Aboukir. Ottoman forces were waiting for them once again, but sad to say, they were not equal to the enemy. In a tragic turnaround, the French soldiers forced our troops towards the sea: thousands of our men drowned in the bay, while Bonaparte installed his rule over Egypt.

.....

At home, the people were in an uproar as word of defeat reached our shores. The humiliating loss of such an important province was made worse by the deaths of so many Ottoman soldiers. The sultan took his revenge on the French at once. Anything linked to France was condemned. Not only were the French ambassador and his aides imprisoned; all French advisers to the Porte were ordered to leave the country; all French commercial property was seized; all French citizens living in the Ottoman Empire were ordered to register with the Muslim courts; all pro-French vezirs were put in jail; and all references to France in the palace were eliminated. I need not tell you what this meant for Nakshidil.

Of course, there was no more Western music, no more

Western dance, no more wine sipped even secretly. But worse, there was not a word, not an invitation, not even a whisper of her name. Her mere presence was a cause célèbre.

For a while Nakshidil shed such tears I thought we would run out of handkerchiefs. "What am I going to do?" she cried. "How am I going to live? I'm being humiliated beyond belief. I cannot show my face to anyone."

"You must not worry about what people think," I said, knowing, however, that word had already spread, and the whole harem was gossiping about her predicament.

Afraid to be seen, she avoided the concubines' baths as much as she could, using the hamam when others were not around. She ceased her visits to the music room, and only once in a while, removed her violin from her cupboard shelf, turned the pegs, and, not daring to play her favorite pieces, stroked a melancholy Turkish tune. She buried her French books even deeper in her cupboards, and read them only when I stood on guard. In the gardens, she walked alone, dropping petals as though they were tears. And when she sewed, her needle pierced the cloth like pricks at her heart.

You cannot imagine how difficult it was for me when, again and again, I had to inform her that, upon the orders of the sultan to the chief black eunuch, her privileges were being removed. First, her rations were all reduced: her bread, butter, sugar, honey, coffee, tea, flour, meat, vegetable, and fruit allotments were cut by more than half. A few weeks later came word that her allowance was dropped by

two-thirds. And the following month, most of her jewels—
diamond and ruby necklaces, ruby earrings, sapphire rings,
pearl and diamond sashes—had to be returned to the treasury. And most of her slaves would have to go. Only two
girls, Besme and Hurrem, remained.

What's more, in August 1798, Prince Mahmud had
reached the age of thirteen, and as was the rule at Topkapi,
only a few months later he was scooped up from the nursery
and delivered to the palace *medrese,* the school run by the
ulema. Living in the Princes' Cage, along with his brother
Mustafa, he was officially being groomed, under the tutelage
of the sheikh-ul-Islam and the religious hierarchy, to become a sultan of the Ottoman Empire and caliph of the
Muslim world.

In past times, Mahmud's big, shining eyes and little-
boy's thirst for life had enlivened Nakshidil's spirits. But
now he was being drenched in the teachings of Islam. In the
Princes' Cage, the ulema saw to it that the Muslim tradition
reverberated from the blue and white hexagonal tiles with
geometric patterns, to the densely knotted prayer rugs, to
the detailed map of Mecca, to the wooden ceilings gilded
with inscriptions from the Koran; and the imams' rigorous
lessons included everything from calligraphy to music to religion and law, all based strictly on Islam.

"How could they take Mahmud away!" Nakshidil complained. "They are deliberately keeping him from me."

"We all live at the sultan's whim," I said. "It is a great
honor to enter the Cage. At least, thanks to the interven-

tions of Selim, it is no longer an island of cruel isolation as in the past, but, rather, a comfortable lair. Just think! Someday, Mahmud will be sultan."

"As long as Aysha is around, his life is tenuous," she said. "And if the day comes when Mustafa is made sultan, Mahmud and I will both be finished."

"I doubt it. Even if Mustafa becomes sultan, and God forgive me, may Selim live and rule until his grandsons have white hair, the boy is so thickheaded he will not survive on the throne."

Nothing I said seemed to calm her. "What about my slaves?" she asked. "How will I do without them?"

"I will still be here, and I will do my utmost to see to it that you are comfortable. You will feel as though you had a hundred slaves. In any case," I added, "it is better to be here than in the Palace of Tears."

"Perhaps that is true. But doesn't the sultan know I have only his best interests at heart?"

"Indeed he does," I replied. "According to the chief black eunuch, anything that reminds him of what the French are doing in Egypt enrages him. Yet he has taken a risk and allowed you to remain at Topkapi. I'm certain that after a while his anger will pass. He will calm down and return to his senses. This will be over quickly, I am sure."

But how could I have known that Muhammad Ali, the provincial governor in Egypt, would use the situation to claim his independence from the sultan? And once again there were problems with Russia. Selim had signed a new alliance with the czar, but almost before the ink was dry, the Russians were interfering in Greece, in Anatolia, and in Bulgaria, spurring on the provincial governors to proclaim their independence. And with every incident the ulema blamed Selim and his ties to the infidels.

16

. . . . .

The sight of Mahmud standing in her doorway brought tears of joy to Nakshidil. "Ah, mon chéri," she cried, forgetting for a moment the ban on everything French. Hugging the boy and smothering his face with kisses, she led him inside.

"Nadil, please," he begged, putting a finger to his lips. "Do not speak to me in French or we will both be in terrible trouble."

"But no one will hear us, my lion. Only Tulip is here."

"You never know," he said, nodding hello to me. "If, by chance, someone does, we will suffer harshly."

"Forgive me. I'm so delighted you're here," Nakshidil said. "But how is it that you were able to come?"

"It's been six months since I left here for the Cage. I told the imams you were sick and that I had to see you."

Seraglio

"And how are they treating you?" She was scurrying around, bringing out plates of fruit and sweetmeats.

"I have been well. But I know it has been a difficult time for you, and it has been the same for me. The imams have used the sultan's rage against France to strengthen their own position."

Nakshidil nodded and pushed another plate of food towards him.

"And you know," Mahmud continued, swallowing a piece of halvah, "that Selim has replaced the sheikh-ul-Islam with someone far more conservative. He hopes that if the highest religious figure is a reactionary, it will placate the Janissaries' anger over the New Order army and encourage them to fight." The boy's voice cracked as he spoke, and I realized it was not emotion but adolescence that was the cause.

"Even before these current problems, the holy men were against the West," Nakshidil said. "I always tried to ignore them."

"Yes, but now they are wild. It's impossible to ignore them. They speak with venom, and recite to me every day how the West is evil, the West is corrupt, the West is satanic. Forgive me, but they say the infidel women prostitute themselves and show their bodies and their faces to all men; they say the infidel men drink alcohol, gamble with their money, and pray to false gods. They mock Westerners who rely on philosophy instead of faith, and call them unbelievers ignorant in the ways of Allah. When I arrived they grabbed my French books and ripped them apart."

"But the more you know of both the East and the West, the wiser you will be."

"They do not understand, dear Nadil. They say that all of Islam speaks in one tongue, Arabic, which is holy, while Europeans speak in so many different tongues: they say it is proof that Christianity is discordant and inconsistent. They speak with disgust of the foods of Christians, especially pig, and say that anyone who eats this filthy animal is swine himself. They tell me Europeans are dirty and do not bathe with soap and water, but soak themselves with perfume."

"But my child, you know that all this is not true."

"It does not matter. They are using it against me."

"What can I do to help you, my lion?"

"Nothing. I just wanted to see you and tell you I love you."

"I am so grateful to you for coming here. I have worried about you every hour of every day. Please, do not be intimidated by Mustafa or the ulema. You must know that their ways are rigid. You must be flexible and walk forward towards the light." She hugged him again, then drew him back to look at him.

"You have grown taller, and I see that you are changing. Do not think about how things were, or how they will be," she said. "Remember the words of the mystic Bedreddin,

'There is no past, there is no hereafter; everything is in the process of becoming.'"

But truth to tell, everything was becoming worse.

.....

Two months after Mahmud's visit, word arrived that Valide Sultan Mirishah had taken ill. The palace physicians could do little to help. Even the English doctor, Neale, summoned from Pera, found nothing but frustration when he came to see her at her retreat. The chief black eunuch greeted him, offered him coffee, sherbets, and sweets, and introduced him to the Greek physician who had tended the valide. Apparently Mirishah had suffered a high fever on and off for many weeks, over which time the good Greek had bathed her in ice water and watched the fever decrease, only to see it rise again.

Finally the chief black eunuch led the Englishman to the patient. The frail woman lay hidden behind a curtain, and unbeknownst to Neale, the sultan was hiding behind a heavy grille. The only parts of the valide's body the physician was allowed to see were her hands and wrists from which he could take her pulse. The doctor tried to do his best, but with little for him to examine and her illness so far along, his efforts were to no avail. Eight days after he saw her, we heard the muezzins around the city announce her death. The following day there was a procession to bury her in her turbe, and the people came out to pay their respects. Mirishah had given generously to the Ottomans, with soup kitchens, fountains, a hospital, and a mosque, and in her honor Selim declared that food and money be distributed to the poor.

Her passing brought more sadness. "She gave me Mahmud and for that I will always be thankful," Nakshidil said. "She was a kind woman, and I felt she was sympathetic to me. Of course, I was disappointed, sometimes, that she did not do more to help me with Selim. But I suppose it is natural; her first loyalty was to her son."

"God knows," I said, "a sultan must be able to count on his mother. The others around him are as fickle as the wind."

"She was the one who saw to it that I was educated for Selim," Nakshidil went on. "I am grateful to her for that too. I will miss her."

And she did, languishing as days crawled into weeks, weeks slugged into months. The kira Esther came to the palace with cloths for the sultan's five kadins, and though Nakshidil was not privileged to purchase goods, I had been able to smuggle a letter out with her, and now she carried one back. The sight of the French seal lifted Nakshidil's spirits, but not for long.

October 1799

News arrived this year that saddened me, my dearest Cousin, and, I am afraid, it will sadden you as well. First, I learned that my poor mother had taken a turn for the worse and before I could adjust to that news, I received confirmation that she had died. Now comes word from a traveler that your mother and father have both passed on too. It is a terrible thing not to say goodbye to one's parents in their old age, but such has been our fate.

I am sorry that I have to be the bearer of bad news, but I hope this brief letter finds you in good health.

Your most loving cousin, Rose

Nakshidil handed the letter to me. "I'm so sorry," I said, "is there anything I can do?"

She shook her head. "There is nothing you can do, Tulip. There is an emptiness in the pit of my stomach that makes me feel sad and alone," she answered. "My family is gone, along with the possibility of ever seeing them. The ulema have been so cruel, they not have allowed me to see Mahmud since his visit six months ago. I feel like a tiny cork bobbing up and down in the vast sea."

We did not see Mahmud for another two months, and when he returned I was taken aback: he was taller by at least three inches, his chest was broad, he voice was deep, and his face was covered with stubble. Though he had changed a great deal, he said that little had changed in the Princes' Cage. If anything, the atmosphere had grown worse. The extremists held tight control, and they insisted on the strictest adherence to Islam. Anything that hinted of European was forbidden, *harem*.

"Even my brother Mustafa is using it against me. He reminds me constantly that you are French, and that you have taught me French things."

"And what about Mustafa's mother?" I asked. "Does he see her?"

"All the time," Mahmud replied. "She has even come to the Cage. She has encouraged Mustafa to be close to Muhammad Rakim, the calligraphy teacher, and he is close to the sheikh-ul-Islam. They are doing everything they can to poison my name. It is foolish, I know, since my brother is older than I am, but still, nothing I say will reassure him that I wish him well when he takes the throne. In any case, as I keep telling him, Selim is young, and praise be to Allah, he will rule for many years."

The ulema, he said, questioned why Nakshidil was allowed to remain at Topkapi, and it was only Mahmud's pleas to Selim and Selim's intervention with the religious men that kept her in the palace.

"Thank you, my child," she said, "for taking such a risk and looking after me. But what can I do for you?"

"I am nearly fifteen," Mahmud said. "It is time for me to have a woman. I know Mustafa has his slave girls, and I must have my own."

"I'll send you one of my slaves," Nakshidil said, smiling at the thought of the little boy becoming a man. "I have only two, but tell me which one pleases you, and she shall be yours."

Mahmud eyed the girls as they came in and out of the room. Before he left, he indicated the one he liked.

"Hurrem shall be yours, Mahmud. But please be careful. You know the palace rules. She cannot carry a child. If she does, her life and the life of the child will be ended. And yours will be endangered."

As soon as Mahmud had gone, I asked her if the voluptuous Hurrem was safe. "She's awfully young," I said. "Why not send him Besme; she is older and past the childbearing years."

"This is the girl he wants," she replied. "I will speak to her and she must promise to take precautions."

That was as close as Nakshidil came to a sultan's pleasures. With little prospect for her return as Selim's favorite, or even the chance to amuse him, or entertain him, or just converse with him, time passed for her at a tortoise's pace.

I, however, was kept busy. With the empire engaged in war with France, and envoys constantly shuttling to and from the divan, the chief interpreter called on me to translate for foreign dignitaries, almost all of whom spoke French. And the chief black eunuch sent me to the Avret Bazaar to inspect the girls at the Friday sales and to see if any were up to the standards of the palace.

Each time I came to the slave market I felt a wave of nausea. A herd of black girls, newly arrived, was displayed outdoors on a platform, and old men with soiled turbans and dirty fingernails squeezed their breasts or examined their orifices, all the while jiggling the gold in their own pockets. I learned to push away my disgust at the degradation and take a deep breath, reminding myself how fortunate I was to be representing the sultan.

Indeed, the best girls were saved for me. I entered one of the private salons, settled onto a comfortable sofa, and took a cup of coffee passed on a tray. The usual pleasantries were exchanged, and when I was relaxed and ready, the white girls were brought in, one by one. Mostly they were young peasants with rough hands and bad teeth, and I did not even bother to inspect them. But once in a while I looked them over, checked their mouths and their bodies, and smiled. Knowing I had found a dark-eyed beauty with smooth skin, I bargained, and bought her at a good price.

In addition, I was attending to Nakshidil, and to the kadins as well. There were six of them now, and they were always ordering me here and there: to buy fabrics from the kira when she came to Topkapi; or to buy trinkets at the Grand Bazaar, or ointments at the spice market. The one thing they all sought was the secret potion that would help make them pregnant. "Ask if this will work," one would whisper, adding the name of something new she had heard about. "Find out what they have," another would say, "there must be something that the infidels use."

I worked my way down the narrow lanes of the Grand Bazaar, through the throngs of eager buyers, knowing that though there were thousands of stalls selling everything from armor and books to carpets, silks, turbans, and jewelry, only a few were worthy of the palace. Over the years I had made friends with some of the merchants of the Old Bedestan, and the moment I entered the vaulted halls where the finest merchandise was housed, I was welcomed with scrapes and bows. It is no small thing to be shopping for the sultan's harem. At this place or that I stopped, took a cup of coffee, heard the day's gossip, and bargained for something on my list.

Then I would head to the *misir carsisi* and wander past thousands of brilliantly colored sacks brimming over with spices, herbs, and pharmacopoeia: hashish, henna, hyacinth, caraway, sandalwood, cinnamon, linseed, peppermint, white poppies, opium, ambergris, ginger, nutmeg, and yarrow. Again, at my favorite shops, I would take a coffee, chew over the news, and, with the girls' pleas in my ears, purchase the latest elixir. But to no avail: there were still no new heirs for the sultan.

Even Nakshidil sent me to the bazaar, but her requests were different. "I have hidden my books well, but I am too afraid that Muhammad Rakim will find them and have me punished," she said. "I am sad to let them go, but see what you can get for them. At least it would be helpful to have the money."

The market for French books had shriveled up like an old lady; anything having to do with France was frowned upon. Nonetheless, I did my best, flattering the dealers as though they were young virgins, and little by little I sold off her books until there were only one or two left.

One wintry afternoon when I came back from the bazaar, I brushed the snow off my caftan and stopped by to

see her. "There is great excitement across the river in Pera,"
I reported.

"Why is that?" Nakshidil asked.

"Well, for us it is the year 1214. But for the infidels, it is
the end of the old century and the start of the new one."

"My God," she said. "Is it really 1800? That means I've
been here twelve years, Tulip."

"And I've been here twenty-five."

.....

It was in December of that year, twelve months after
Nakshidil sent Hurrem to Mahmud, that the girl came scurrying back to the apartment. She arrived late in the afternoon, carrying a thick bocha under her arm. "Please,
please," she whispered, as soon as I had closed the door.

"What is it?" Nakshidil asked impatiently.

The plump Hurrem placed the bundle on a divan and
carefully unwrapped the contents. Layers of cashmere swad-
dled a brand new baby. A piece of cloth stuffed in the child's
mouth kept it from making noise.

"My God, Hurrem, are you crazy?" Nakshidil asked.

"Oh, my lady, I am so thrilled," Hurrem squealed.
"When I discovered what had happened to me, I was so excited, I wanted to tell everyone."

"I hope you kept it a secret," I said.

"Did anyone notice your belly?" Nakshidil asked.

I looked at her full-fleshed figure and knew the answer.

"It was not difficult," she replied honestly. "I am not so thin, and the layers of clothes helped me hide my stomach."

"And when did you give birth?" Nakshidil asked.

"Early this morning."

"Does anyone know?" I asked.

"I don't think so. I have tried my best to keep it quiet. It did . . . it did cry once or twice before I gave it my breast."

"If anyone sees the child, it will be strangled," I said. "You will have to give it up."

The girl was too emotional to listen. "Imagine, a daughter of the sultan!" she said.

"He is not a sultan yet, and he never will be, if this is discovered," said Nakshidil. "Mahmud can be killed for this. And so can you."

Hurrem tried to protest, but Nakshidil would hear none of it. She was right. The risk was far too great. She motioned for me to come into her sleeping room. Her whole body was tense, and she stood with her shoulders hunched, her arms crossed tightly against her chest. "What are we going to do, Tulip?" she groaned. "We can't keep this baby here."

"I've been thinking," I said, "and I believe I have a solution. The kira Esther is coming tomorrow. Hurrem will stay here tonight and feed the baby. Tomorrow we'll wrap it in the bocha, and, please God, it will stay quiet. I'll give the infant to Esther. She'll find a family for it."

"Oh, Tulip, you always come up with the best answers," Nakshidil said and kissed my hand. "But what about the girl? If she tells anyone, we're all finished. It's just the kind of excuse that Mustafa needs to destroy Mahmud. He'll tell the imams and they'll call in the executioner."

"And you will face a similar fate because Hurrem was your slave," I added.

"We can't allow the girl . . ." Nakshidil said.

I nodded and raised my hand to stop her from saying any more. I knew what I had to do.

The next morning I awoke, eager to wrap the infant and take it to the kira. I walked into the room where Hurrem had slept; the girl was crouched on the floor, in tears. "You'll forget this after a while," I said. I looked down, but all I could see was the folded blanket.

"I gave it milk, I did everything I could," Hurrem said between sobs. "She's gone," the girl wailed. "Gone."

I bent down and unwrapped the cashmere cover. The baby was still, its tiny body rigid, its breathing stopped. It had not made it through it the night. My head swirled with emotions. For an instant, my heart went out to the slave girl; she had brought this being to life. And now, twenty-four hours later, it was dead. Yet I had to confess, I was relieved. The gods had done their work.

"My baby, my baby," Hurrem wailed, rocking the stilled child back and forth in her arms. "How could this happen?"

"It happens often. Life is fragile," I said and shrugged. "Only the strong survive." I pulled Hurrem up from the floor and shook her. "Do not ever, ever tell anyone about this child," I warned. "Do you swear?"

She hesitated for a few moments, then nodded her head.

"I swear," she whispered weakly, "I swear," but her words were unconvincing.

I scooped the dead infant in my arms, wrapped it again in the cashmere bocha, and carried it to the gardeners. They were also the palace executioners; they would know what to do with it.

Later, when I returned, I found Nakshidil sitting alone in her room. "I heard her crying," she said, "but I thought it was because we were giving the baby away. I had no idea . . ."

"It's easier this way," I said. "Where is she now?"

"She's in the other room," she answered, pointing to the small space where the girl had slept. "I know she has to be punished, but maybe she's learned her lesson."

"It's too late for that," I said. I turned and left, knowing the gardeners would be coming soon.

17
· · · · ·

Like the colors of a prayer rug that fade with time, Hurrem
and the baby faded from memory, and once again Nakshidil
adjusted to the monotonous routine of the harem: rising
at dawn, she said her prayers, breakfasted, and dressed;
sometimes she read the small volumes she had hidden in a
bocha in the cupboard, and after the midday meal she
sewed; she had stopped playing the violin, but from afternoon until dusk she gossiped with me or Besme, the only
slave she had left. Once in a while Besme offered to read
her palm or spread a handful of cards, but Nakshidil refused, insisting she had heard her best fortune back in
Martinique. "I have been touched by royalty, just as the
soothsayer told me," she said, "and now I know how difficult
that can be."

.....

Perhaps it was the new century that turned our luck. It took another year, but, finally, things began to improve. Joining forces once again with England, the Ottomans were able to rout the French from Alexandria. Bonaparte was defeated in the East, and in March 1802, Turkey signed the Treaty of Amiens, affirming peace with France and reestablishing our sovereignty over Egypt.

Not long after that, the French ambassador was let out of prison and returned to his embassy, French merchants were given permission to engage in active trade, and Nakshidil was no longer persona non grata. Not that she was suddenly called to the sultan's bed. That remained for others, when the sultan had time. But at least she was able to take pleasure in her books and her music and enjoy the company of the other women.

I was kept busy, not only with my regular duties, but serving as an interpreter for visiting envoys; every week another foreign diplomat paid a call on the palace. As Chief Black Eunuch Bilal Agha said one day on his way to a meeting of the divan, no one ever claimed it is easy to rule an empire. As he explained, the sultan had to balance the powers of the French, the British, the Austrians, and the Russians, all of whom were hungry for a piece of Ottoman turf. Recently, the czar had snatched some influence in Moldavia, and only with the help of one of our best military commanders, Alemdar, were we able to stop them from seizing our territory.

"Selim has to play one country against the other, like a juggler tossing balls in the air," said Bilal Agha. "Any time one of them tries to throw the sultan off step, he has to use the others to equalize the weight."

So, when Bonaparte was crowned the ruler of France on May 18, 1804, Selim, thinking it best to appease both the British and the Russians, refused to recognize him as the new emperor. That turned out to be a mistake. A year later the French army destroyed the Russians at Austerlitz in Moravia, and the sultan watched his balls drop to the ground. Bonaparte was on the march again; this time, the sultan acknowledged it was better to be on his side, and in February 1806 he declared his recognition.

.....

Not long after our renewed alliance with France, a letter arrived from Rose.

"My dearest Cousin," she wrote in March 1806:

> *It pleases me no end that your Sultan has reestablished his friendship with France. Though I must tell you that my own relations with Bonaparte are not what they once were.*
>
> *Since we last corresponded, so much has happened. You know, of*

course, of my marriage, and my coronation as Empress in December
1804—you see, the fortune-teller was right!

But I can confide in you, my own flesh and blood, that my hus-
band's petty flirtations with the ladies of my court are a strain. God
knows, I try to keep Bonaparte happy. Nonetheless, rumors abound that
he will demand a divorce, and I am resigned to whatever happens.
Misery treads on the heels of joy.

"How well I know," Nakshidil said, when we both had
read the letter.

"Look at it the other way around," I answered. "You have
had your years of sorrow. Now comes the joy." But I have
never been good at predicting the future.

. . . . .

Besides balancing the foreign powers, Selim had to keep a
watchful eye on his own possessions. At any given time, the
local notables, spurred on by Russia, Britain, or France,
might try an insurrection against the Turks.

"The Ottoman Empire may not be as great as it once
was," the chief black eunuch said one afternoon as we waited
for yet another ambassador, "but it still stretches to Serbia,
Romania, and Greece in the west, and Syria, Arabia, and
Egypt in the east. The sultan is constantly shuffling provincial governors and shifting army troops from one place to
another to quash rebellions."

In the east, there had been problems in Damascus. The Mamluks, the military class that once ruled Egypt and Syria, attempted to wrest control, but the provincial governor had managed to put things back in order. In Arabia, however, the Wahabis were a serious threat. The conservative sect, bent on purging Islam of any deviation from their strict decrees, refused to recognize the sultan as caliph and guardian of the holy sites. Those reactionaries, who called themselves "true believers," had beaten our men and taken over Mecca and Medina.

"It is an insult to all of us that the Wahabis have seized the holy cities," Bilal Agha said. "Do not forget it is my job as chief black eunuch to manage Mecca and Medina. It is no secret that the taxes we collect from the thousands who make the pilgrimage to the Prophet's birthplace help to fill our treasury vaults. Now the Wahabis are pocketing the tariffs from the Haj, and we will not have sufficient funds to pay the Janissaries. The Janissaries have already accused the sultan of favoring the New Order army. This will give them an added grievance. Mark my words, Tulip, trouble is brewing. I am worried the Janissaries might turn over their cauldrons and rebel."

After all, the chief black eunuch added, in Serbia, the Janissaries had allied themselves with a group of corrupt Muslims, and, with covert help from the Russians, had actually established their own autocratic rule. The only way the sultan was able to regain control was to support the local Christian peasants who were willing to fight against his own troops. Thanks to them, and help from a few loyal Ottoman officers, the Janissaries were defeated. "We were fortunate to have Alemdar as one of the Ottoman commanders," Bilal Agha said. "He has become a true reformer. But the Janissaries won't forget this, and I am afraid we will pay the price."

But that was for the future. In the meantime, in the strange way of politics, the balance shifted, or you might say, the bedfellows changed: Russia declared herself our enemy, the sultan broke off relations with Britain, and Bonaparte was once again our friend. And in the divan, as he had done before, the sultan changed his vezirs, demoting the pro-Russian and pro-British advisers and promoting those who were pro-French.

.....

"For all the adversity the sultan faced outside the empire, first with Russia, then France, then Britain, who would have guessed that his greatest threat was at home?" I was folding Nakshidil's clothes, preparing them for her journey.

"On the other hand," I continued, "you could say that, having disguised himself more than once as a sailor or a merchant and gone to town to hear the gossip, Selim should have known what would happen when he ordered the Janissaries to put on the uniforms of the New Order."

"Then again, they should have been proud to be part of such a modern army," Nakshidil said.

"In any case, the Janissaries used the order to justify their actions, and the volcano erupted."

"Frankly, I think the ulema had a lot to do with it. They had been preaching anti-Western ideas for so long."

"And the economy was in such a bad state," I noted. "The high taxes, food shortages, staggering inflation—people blamed their troubles on Selim's European ways. Especially the Janissaries: they hadn't been paid enough or received their salaries on time for two years, and they were seething."

"I suppose that's why being told to wear the uniforms of a European-trained army was the last straw," said Nakshidil.

"Yes, but never forget Aysha. She had been plotting this for a long time. Remember her warning when you were in her apartment years ago. And her friendship with Muhammad Rakim and the ulema. She wanted only one thing and that was to seat Mustafa on the throne. She would do anything to put him there as sultan."

The revolt began in February 1807 when a British fleet sailed into the harbor of Istanbul. It seemed the British were so concerned about our renewed alliance with the French, they sent seven battleships to anchor in our port; they thought this would deter our friendship with the Franks. With the ships threatening Topkapi, the sultan ordered his men to fortify the seawall. In the face of our three hundred cannons, the British withdrew, and the city heaved a sigh. But only for a moment. Russian control of Romania had stopped the shipment of wheat and other grains to the capital. And Russian ships blockading the Dardanelles prevented our boats from bringing in other foodstuffs. The sultan needed the Janissaries to help him fight the czar's army, and he needed them equipped in the latest ways.

In May 1807, an order went out to the Janissaries: they would be trained in the methods of the New Order army. A team of New Order officers, led by the sultan's emissary, arrived at a fort on the Black Sea and demanded that the soldiers garrisoned there put on the Western-style uniforms. Furious, the Janissaries rebelled. They attacked the sultan's emissary, slaughtered the New Order officers who had come to train them, and even killed some of their own officers. Knowing that more teams were sent to train other Janissary garrisons, they sent out word to murder the New Order men.

To pacify the Janissaries, the sultan agreed to send the New Order army back to their barracks and keep them there. But that only made it easier for the insurgents. Hundreds of Janissaries left from their various forts and headed towards Istanbul. Within two days thousands were gathered in the city, joined by religious students from the medreses. While the populace hid in fear, the Janissaries made a list of demands, calling for the removal of Selim's pro-reform advisers.

But the next morning, prodded by Aysha, the sheikh-ul-Islam went even further. The highest religious authority issued a fatwa to remove Selim from the throne. The Janissaries marched towards Topkapi, like tigers growling for prey. We heard their shouts becoming louder and louder as they reached the outer gates: "Sultan Mustafa, Sultan Mustafa," they bellowed, celebrating their victory as they clamored for Selim's defeat. Their roars grew even louder as the rebels came through the courts. The girls were so frightened that many of them hid under their beds. Word swept through the palace that the sultan's secretary, Ahmed Bey, had been killed, and the next thing I knew the chief black eunuch came running into my room, saying that Ahmed Bey's head had been delivered to Selim, and that Nakshidil had better hide.

"Where is Mahmud?" she cried, when I told her what had happened. She was thirty-one, and the years had taken their toll. Her face was drawn with deep lines, her eyes were dim, and her blond hair was turning silver.

"He is still in the Cage."

"They'll come after him. Tell them they can take me. They can do anything they want with me. But do not let them have Mahmud."

"Bilal Agha swore he'll be all right."

"And what about Selim? Will he be executed?" Tears were streaming down her face.

"The Janissaries, the sheikh-ul-Islam, and three of the deputy vezirs presented him with the fatwa. They accused him of acting against Islamic law. And they say he has failed as a sultan because he has not produced any heirs. When Selim saw the fatwa he realized he hadn't any choice. It is sharia, the word of law."

"How can we save him? What can we do?" she asked, wrapping her arms around herself.

"They are wise enough to know that he is still popular with many people. He is a good man. When he was told that he would be removed and Mustafa would succeed him, he said only, 'May God increase the days of his life.' Selim will be allowed to live in the Cage with Mahmud."

"Thank God. If Mahmud and Selim are safe, I can breathe easier now."

I looked down at the floor.

"What is it?"

"I did not want to tell you this, Nakshidil. But you know that with Mustafa on the throne, Aysha will become the valide sultan. She is returning from the Old Palace tomorrow, and she has already given the order. I am sorry. But you are being sent to the Palace of Tears."

There wasn't much for me to do as I helped Nakshidil pack for her banishment. She had been allowed only a few new outfits over the past years and the old ones were ragged with age. She still had a handful of jewels, and I wrapped them carefully in cloths, not wanting to damage the precious stones. Nakshidil watched me as I fondled a string of emeralds.

"They are yours, Tulip," she said.

"What do you mean?"

"I want you to have them. I don't need them in the Old Palace."

"But they are worth a fortune."

"They are my gift. You have been so kind to me over the years."

"You've given me gifts already," I protested, "the pearl sash, the ruby ring."

"You've given me more than that," she said. "You can't know how much it means to me—all that you've done."

I smiled. "And I am grateful for your friendship," I answered.

"Ah," she sighed, "I have learned that real friendship in the palace is as rare as a butterfly in December. I knew I could always trust you, Tulip, even if I did not want to hear what you said. Now that I am going off, I want you to have this to remember me by."

I bit my lip to stop my tears. No one had ever given me such presents. "I am sure you will be back in Topkapi very soon," I said. "When you return, these emeralds will be waiting for you."

Nakshidil put her hand on mine. "The old saying is true: 'What you give away, you keep.' I have given you those emeralds but I will keep much more. Yes, we will see each other soon, *inshallah*." We hugged, and I could feel her whole body shaking. But we would see each other sooner than I thought. The following day I was told that I, too, was being sent to the Eski Saray.

18

· · · · ·

Nakshidil and I were ordered to leave together for the Palace
of Tears, and we stepped into our carriage at Topkapi just as
the procession for the new valide sultan reached the palace
grounds. It pained me to wave goodbye, and then see Aysha,
swathed in satin and jewels, arrive in the imperial coach. "To
think that that woman is now the valide sultan!" exclaimed
Nakshidil. "How dreadful to think of her in such a position!"

"And to see Narcissus as the chief black eunuch," I
moaned as that detestable figure marched by, dressed in the
turban and cape of the kislar aghasi.

"Poor Mahmud. Poor Selim," Nakshidil said. "Who
knows what will happen to them? I pray for them both. God
help us all."

We rode through the gates of Topkapi, said farewell to

the Mosque of Haghia Sophia and rumbled along the cobblestones, past the Blue Mosque and the bazaar. At the square where Selim had held court for the circumcision festivities, Nakshidil remembered the time of Mahmud's celebration.

"It's been thirteen years. So much has happened since then," she said, "it seems like a lifetime."

It took more than an hour to reach the Third Hill and the Eski Saray. As we approached the high walls, I felt a rush of sadness for all we were leaving behind, and a sense of misgiving over what was to come.

"I shall always be indebted to you," I said to Nakshidil.

"Oh, Tulip, you are exaggerating. It is only a necklace."

"I don't mean the necklace. You saved me from being banished to this place twenty years ago. If you hadn't pleaded with the chief black eunuch to let me stay at Topkapi, I would have been living in the Old Palace all this time."

"I dread to think what it would have been like all those years without you," she said.

On orders from the head chamberlain of the Eski Saray, Nakshidil was given a small room and I an even smaller space in the old wooden palace. Instead of the fine carpets and cushioned sofas of Topkapi, we found bare walls peeling with paint, wood floors splintered from age, and thin, lumpy mattresses strewn over broken divans. And if the walls and floors and furnishings were badly in need of repair, the sullen tenants were badly in need of love. Sad-faced virgins, who had never been given the chance to know a man, wives and concubines of dead sultans, wizened black women, and embittered eunuchs haunted the hallways like ghosts of unfulfilled dreams.

Dozens suffered from tremulous diseases of the nerves; their eyes twitched, their lips trembled, their hands shook, their stomachs groaned, their backs ached, their limbs were sore, their necks were pinched, their bowels were inflamed. What's more, when winter came, cold and dampness pervaded the rooms, and with not enough braziers to go around, at night you could hear the desperate coughs of those ill with tuberculosis or pneumonia. In the harsh light of day we watched their frail figures carried off on litters, little more than skeletons of their once beautiful selves.

Our allotment of food was reduced to yogurt, pilav, and bread, and I remember many afternoons with Nakshidil, shivering under the tandour, chewing slowly on our meager rations, whispering about the new sultan Mustafa and recalling that fateful day when Selim was overthrown.

"To think that almost all of his good advisers were killed," Nakshidil said not longer after we arrived, "and Mahmud and Selim were allowed to survive. Praise be to God. It's almost a miracle."

"It's true," I added. "The only reformer who lived was Alemdar, and that's because he was far away from the capital."

Mustafa had hardly been put on the throne when rumors spread that he had undone all the reforms Selim had put in place. The New Order army was destroyed, the new taxation system repealed, land seized from the rich was returned, and the Janissaries were allowed to go back to their old corrupt ways of bribery and nepotism.

The only satisfying stories were the ones that showed the public's distaste for the new sultan. Mustafa had done nothing about the Russians' grasp on our grain in the Balkans, and the city was suffering from severe shortages. On a Friday afternoon when the sultan rode to the mosque, with the Valide Sultan Aysha behind him, he found himself face to face with defiant crowds of women protesting the price of bread.

And there were endless stories that claimed Mustafa was too weak to control the very people who had put him on the throne. Infighting was rampant, the military had split into factions, and the ulema were arguing with each other. Muhammad Rakim, who was appointed as sheikh-ul-Islam, and the deputy grand vezir had conspired together to assassinate the grand vezir. Shortly after that, the two were conspiring against each other. A power vacuum had allowed the Janissaries to grab control, and marauding soldiers rampaged the shops and abused the citizens in the city, while others hunted out and killed New Order soldiers hiding in the countryside.

.....

We had endured Gehenna for more than a year when a messenger from Topkapi arrived with news. It was the middle of

July 1808, the Old Palace was stifling, and we were sitting in Nakshidil's room, the windows too warped to open, the air thick with flies that had flown in some open door in the Eski Saray. At first, I thought it was the heat that made the sweating messenger stumble over his words. Then I realized he was so shaken he could hardly speak.

"Mahmud . . . Selim . . . Mahmud . . . Selim," he stammered over and over, as Nakshidil wrung her hands. "What is it? What are you trying to say?" I snapped. That's when he told us what had happened:

"A secret committee was formed to oust Mustafa and return Selim to the throne," he said. "The man in charge of the plot was Alemdar. At the beginning of July he marched his forces—fifteen thousand strong—from Edirne to Istanbul on the pretext of helping Mustafa. But his true aim was to save Selim."

"How would he do that?" I asked, brushing away the flies.

"Soon after Alemdar reached the capital, he ordered his men to surround the city walls while he tried to see the sultan. He wanted to tell Mustafa the only way to restore order was to step down."

"And did he?"

"The sultan refused to see him. Alemdar organized a small corps and sent them to the nearby guardhouse to assassinate the chief of the Janissaries; another group was sent to capture the new grand vezir at his home. Alemdar led the rest of his soldiers onto the palace grounds and marched them past the gates to the Second Court, where he found the sheikh-ul-Islam, Muhammad Rakim, in the Council Hall. He ordered Rakim to tell the sultan to step down, but even though the order was carried out, the sultan refused to abdicate.

"What audacity! Imagine refusing to obey an order of the sheikh-ul-Islam," I said.

"Yes, but even worse, the sultan ordered his Chief Black Eunuch Narcissus to find Selim and Mahmud and have them strangled."

"I'm not surprised," I said, swatting another fly. "If there were no one else to succeed him. Mustafa knew he could keep his throne."

"But where are they now?" Nakshidil asked frantically. "Where is Mahmud? Where is Selim? What happened to them?"

"Selim was in the harem in the music room when Chief Black Eunuch Narcissus and his henchmen broke in. Some of the girls who were there told us Selim was dressed in a green turban and caftan, calmly playing the ney and singing his composition:

" 'O Ilhami, do not be indolent and do not trust in the things of this world.

" 'The world stops for no one and its wheel turns without ceasing.' "

What irony, I thought; of all the poems Selim wrote, that was his favorite!

"But what did he do when the men came in?" Nakshidil asked.

"He begged them not to hurt anyone and promised that he would surrender peacefully. But they attacked him nevertheless. He fought as hard as he could, but with only his wooden flute as a weapon, he did not stand a chance. The harem girls stood by. Some of the women screamed in horror while the men sliced him with their swords, and two fainted at the pool of blood on the floor. The men threw his severed body, limb by limb, into the Second Court to show Alemdar, and shouted, 'Behold the sultan ye seek!'"

"My God," Nakshidil moaned, covering her face with her hands. "Poor Selim. He was a kind, sweet man. A man who tried to help his people. He didn't deserve this." A fly buzzed and she slammed it. "And what about Mahmud?"

"Alemdar and his men rushed to the seraglio and found the sultan cowering behind his eunuchs. They seized Mustafa, and put him in chains. At the same time Alemdar ordered some of his men to find Mahmud and save him.

"And did they?"

"Little did they know," said the messenger, "Mahmud was in his apartment when the chief black eunuch and his men crashed down the door. Thanks be to Allah, when one of Mahmud's slaves heard them coming, she took a bucket of hot ashes from the brazier and threw them into the villains' eyes. As soon as she did, two more slaves grabbed Mahmud and pulled him through a chimney and up to the roof for safety."

"Thanks be to Allah," I said.

"No, wait," the man stopped me. "It was only a few minutes before Mahmud and the slaves heard the sounds of footsteps again; they knotted their sashes into a ladder and Mahmud slid down the cloth, landing near an empty room. He ran in and hid under a pile of rolled carpets. Once more, he heard the sounds of men rushing in and tried to bury himself deeper under the rugs. But the men were determined to find him, and after searching the room carefully, they did."

"My poor Mahmud," Nakshidil wailed.

"It took a long time before the men could convince Mahmud they were not on the side of Mustafa, but had been sent to save his life. Finally he understood; he crawled out from his hiding place and followed the men to their chief, Alemdar.

"'It is our lord Sultan Mahmud,' they told Alemdar; they were so excited they had already given him his new title. Alemdar dropped to the ground and kissed Mahmud's feet.

"'But where is my brother, Sultan Mustafa?' Mahmud asked.

"'He has been taken prisoner,' they told him.

"'What about my cousin Selim?' Mahmud wanted to know.

"Alemdar gave him the sad news: Selim was dead. 'Majesty,' Alemdar said, 'you are now our new sultan.'"

"Thank God, Mahmud is safe," said Nakshidil. "May he live a long and fruitful life."

"The Ottomans are fortunate to have him as their sultan," I added. "What happens now?"

"Sultan Mahmud's first act was to appoint Alemdar as the new grand vezir," the messenger said. "Tomorrow we will bury Selim, may he rest in glory, and celebrate Mahmud's ascendance to the throne. People will throng the streets and the First Court. The band will play the 'Sultan's March,' the crowds will sing, 'May he live a thousand years, and may he see his grandson's hairs as white as the driven snow.' The next day the sultan will receive his last haircut. Then he will visit the Pavilion of the Sacred Mantle and kiss the Prophet's mantle."

What happens to us, I wondered, but I kept my thoughts to myself. We would find out soon enough. The following morning the same messenger returned.

"Last night, before the celebrations began," he said, "the new and glorious Sultan Mahmud issued a decree."

"What does it say?" I asked.

The messenger pulled himself up to his full height, and spoke as if he were reading an official edict: "'Let it be known to all the Ottoman people that Nakshidil is my mother, and that she will be the valide sultan.'"

"Praise be to God," Nakshidil said, clasping her mouth. "I cannot believe it. Tell me I am dreaming, Tulip."

"No, no," the fellow said. "It is true. In two more days you will officially become the valide sultan."

"Inshallah," I whispered.

"God willing," she repeated.

The fellow rose and started to go, but halfway through the doorway he turned and said, "I almost forgot. You must prepare for the Valide Alay."

Mashallah! It had been little more than twelve months since we had been sent to the Old Palace. We had dreamed every day of returning to Topkapi, but never did we believe we would go back in an imperial procession.

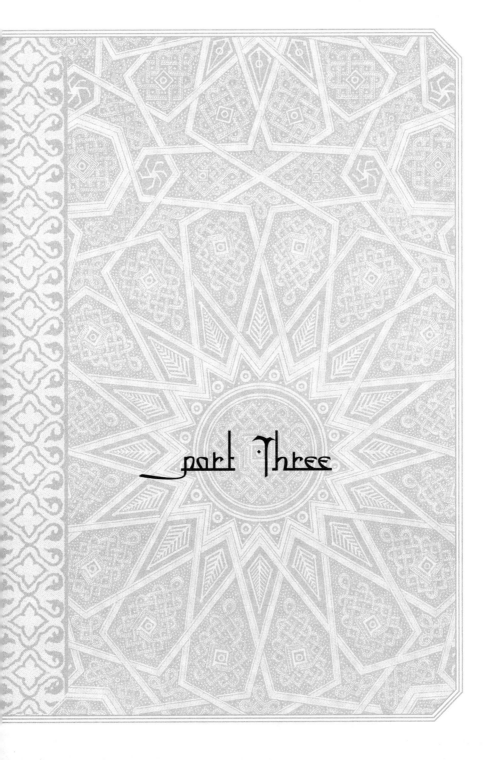

part Three

19
·····

A gentle knock on the door was all that was needed to awaken Nakshidil. I stood in front of her, beaming, knowing this was to be a day like none before.

"I've been lying here for several hours, turning from side to side," she said, running her fingers through her silvery hair. "I tried to picture myself at my ordinary morning tasks, but all I could see were gilded coaches sweeping along the road like swans gliding across a pond."

Slowly, Nakshidil lifted herself from the veil of half-sleep, stretched her arms and smoothed the layers of her sleeping clothes. The bright rays of sunrise had not yet burst upon Istanbul, but even in the shadowy light of early dawn, as she sat, childlike, on the edge of the bed, it reminded me of her early days in the harem, an angry child, alone and scared, refusing to obey the rules of the palace. Now she was mistress of all the slaves and the most important woman in the empire.

. . . . .

We knelt together, the soon-to-be valide sultan and I, on the frayed rug, and performed the prayers to Allah. When we had finished, she kept her eyes shut, and I saw her bring her fingers to her forehead, then to her chest, to her left breast and her right. As she crossed herself, I heard her pray in another tongue and for the first time, I wondered if she merely masqueraded as a Muslim.

I myself have never taken to heart the words I mumbled in prayer; they impart no meaning on my life. Who is this Allah in whose name young boys are castrated, young girls are raped, and tens of thousands of all ages are enslaved? What god does he represent that brings out such evil in man?

Not that Allah is alone: the Christians have done their fair share of slaughter; the Jews have filled their bible with tales of war; and neither Africans nor Asians have perfected a god of peace. No, religion offers no solace to me; only the truth that those who pray with the greatest fervor are the greatest peril to all.

I looked at Nakshidil and wondered how much she pretended and what she really believed. I remembered the story of Mehmed the Conqueror and how he had proclaimed his love for his Christian wife and shown her off in the palace courtyard; and then, because she was an infidel, he ordered his men to slice off her head. Would others look at Nakshidil as an infidel? Would Nakshidil always feel herself a Christian, even though she had taken the Muslim vows? I dared not ask for fear of putting her in danger.

"Please, Tulip," she implored, when she opened her eyes and saw me staring. "Do not tell anyone about my Latin prayers. I have done my best to be a Muslim, and I will continue to try. But deep inside I feel I deserted God, and I have paid a price."

"Perhaps it was He who deserted you."

"I cannot think such thoughts. Besides, I believe He has given me one last chance."

"What did you pray for?" I asked. My question was not so much one of theology but curiosity.

"I prayed that God gives wisdom to my son and protects us all from evil forces. I prayed that my son be the sultan who saves the empire, and that I be the queen mother who helps breathe life into it. I asked that my son be safe from angry Janissaries, safe from rivaling vezirs, safe from vicious ulema. I prayed that the city be safe from fires and safe from earthquakes, that the palace be safe from resentful mothers, and all of us be safe from illness. I asked that you, Tulip, be safe from jealousies, and that all my slaves be loyal."

"Amen," I answered.

.....

She did not rush through the day, but caressed it, drinking in her breakfast tea as though it were the warm chocolate of her youth. "I want to linger over everything," she said, running her finger along the rim of the cup. "I want to be aware of all that crosses my path, to notice the chip on this cup, and the crack across that plate. For the past year I have tried to blot out the ugliness from this place that has been my prison, that has marked my doom. I have tangled with Destiny more than once, and now it smiles on me. I wish to savor every moment, so that I can enjoy, even more, what is to come."

In the baths she made note of the marble and how it had yellowed from age and cracked from abuse, and the towels worn through with the years. But if the objects had decayed, the atmosphere was alive with excitement, the odalisques fluttering like new birds learning to fly. She watched closely as the slaves pasted her arms and legs with arsenic cream, doused her with warm water, scrubbed her with loofahs, and soaked her in her favorite new scents of cinnamon and vanilla. Sighing, she inhaled the essence and let the strong sweet smell intoxicate her like wild spirits inhabiting her soul.

Wrapped only in a threadbare linen sheet, she strode on pattens to the dressing room where other slaves lined her eyes with kohl, drew her brows together with india ink, and tipped her fingers with henna. She watched carefully as they combed and plaited her long hair. "Here, not there," she said more than once, as they sprinkled the jewels on her tresses and then covered her head with a paisley patterned turban. A huge white plume reared from the back, and in the center of the cloth, above her forehead, they pinned a jeweled aigrette cascading with pearls; three times they pinned it and three times she had them take it off; her sharp eye could see that the large, rectangular ruby was a hair's width off center. When she finally pronounced the word "perfect," the headdress resembled a brilliant spray of fireworks bursting into the night sky.

An array of clothing and jewels had been brought from Topkapi the day before, and she ran her hand along the silks, inspecting them for any flaws or creases. She chose a brilliant pink satin caftan embroidered with gold to wear over a jade silk vest, and a striped magenta skirt to cover her thin, wide pantaloons; and when all the diamond buttons had been carefully looped, she curled a broad cashmere sash, encrusted with gems, around her hips. She selected her jewels carefully, inspecting each one for texture, holding it up to the light for color, trying it on for shape, until her ears dangled with diamonds and rubies, and her neck and fingers were smothered in diamonds, rubies, sapphires, emeralds, and pearls.

She had to admit, she said, laughing as she glanced at herself in the mirror, baubled bracelets tinkling on her arms and ankles, yards of glitter around her neck, she was at least as dazzling as any valide sultan preceding her. She knew the whole world would see her, or at least imagine it did, as she rode from this Palace of Tears to her new home in Topkapi, for if her son the sultan was deliberately kept remote, she was to be visible to the empire.

"I am ready," she announced, her face exposed to the world, and nodding to her veiled slaves, she wished them well on the journey they were all about to take. At the front door of the Old Palace, in the bright July sun, we lifted her under her arms, holding her like a bird from beneath its wings, skimmed her down the crumbling steps and across the front lawns, and eased her down gently at the imperial carriage. Once more, she waved to the others, climbed into the gilded coach, and settled herself on the jeweled cushions spread out on the purple satin floor. For just a moment, she opened the latticed windows and looked back. "On to Topkapi!" she ordered.

At the front of the procession several hundred of the Imperial Cavalry rode, dressed in armor and short taffeta robes, mounted on gaudily caparisoned horses. Three hundred heralds, their heads topped in brightly pleated turbans with arching feathers, marched behind them. Directly after them came scores of Imperial Gardeners—the Royal Executioners—in pleated turbans; and dozens of mufti, wearing the green turbans of holy men.

The valide's palace adviser came next. Holding a gold scepter in his hand, he wore a thickly wadded turban, and a cloak trimmed with sable and wide sleeves—the twin symbols of his high status. A double rank of harem bodyguards followed, each armed with an ax and a long pole. I took my place behind them. Wearing my tall pointed turban and sable-trimmed cape, and holding my scepter with three tails, I walked proudly as the new chief black eunuch.

Glancing back, I nearly cried at the sight of the gorgeous

horses covered in brilliant silks, pearls, and gold, leading the coach of the new valide sultan. Alongside Nakshidil's carriage, halberdiers carried tall spears topped with six red horsetails—only one less than the sultan—to symbolize her power. After them came palace officials throwing coins to the onlookers; boys and girls raced into the streets, grinning from ear to ear as they caught the money.

Four score of coaches rode in the wake of the imperial chariot, a retinue of servants attending the Princesses Hadice and Beyhan, and other daughters of the late sultans Mustafa III and Abdul Hamid, may they rest in glory; six carriages held ice and refreshments to sustain the sultanas during the three-hour journey; one carriage held Cevri, the new mistress chamberlain. If she had not thrown ashes in the eyes of the enemy, Mahmud would not have lived to be sultan. All around were loyal Janissaries, some on foot, some on horseback, intimidating the crowds with their looming headdresses and long mustaches that drooped like horses' tails around their mouths.

The procession moved sluggishly in the summer heat, crawling through the city streets past turbaned throngs, their colors proscribed by law—Greeks in black, Jews in blue, Armenians in violet, and Muslims in green—stopping at the guardhouse in Beyazit, where the chief Janissary came forward. Bowing deeply, he kissed the ground of the sultan's mother, and, as he did, the broad sweep of feathers atop his turban brushed the dirt. In return for the agha's obeisance, and hoped-for loyalty, the valide cloaked him with a robe of honor and handed out gifts for him and his staff of soldiers.

At each of the Janissary guardhouses along the route, the entourage stopped, and the act of gift-giving was repeated. Each time beads of perspiration glistened on Nakshidil's forehead and along her upper lip, and I hastened to her side and handed her a freshly perfumed handkerchief to dab them.

When we reached the huge walls of Topkapi Palace, I looked up and pinched myself: it was all too good to be true. And then in the First Court in front of the bakeries, we saw Mahmud, mounted on his horse. I smiled at the sight of him and looked at Nakshidil, who beamed with pride. Just twenty-three years old and he was the sultan! Resplendent in his stiff red satin caftan, he bore the aura of Ottoman power and the gravitas of imperial woes.

As Nakshidil's carriage approached, the new sultan dismounted and stood before her, the gold embroidered stars and silver crescents of his ceremonial robe gleaming in the noonday sun, his turban spraying the sky with its diamond aigrette, his dark eyes sparkling against his pale skin. Making obeisance to his mother, he salaamed three times, bringing the finger of his right hand downward from his broad forehead to his upturned nose to his thick chest. Then he took his mother's hand and kissed it. With great reverence, he lowered his body and knelt before her on the ground.

"*Arslanum*, my lion," she whispered proudly, and he led her through the palace courtyards, past the curtains of cypress trees and the gray buildings where they minted and stored Ottoman money; past the ten imperial kitchens, where one hundred and fifty cooks prepared the food for the thousands of people who live and work in the palace. Sweet smells wafted from the cooking halls, and as I had not eaten since dawn, my mouth watered at the thought of the halvah and the honeyed sesame sweets.

We passed the Imperial Divan and I tried to picture the new sultan holding audiences with foreign envoys or concealing himself behind the lattice during meetings of his Council of State. I was so excited by the events of the day, I barely noticed the flowering gardens, the pavilions overlooking the sea, the gazelles dancing on the lawn, the peacocks strutting, or the birds splashing in the fountains. But at the iron gates to the seraglio, I stopped dead still: the spectacle made me sick. Thirty-three heads, still steaming and dripping blood, were impaled on spikes, while balanced on a silver platter glared the hideous head of Narcissus, the former chief black eunuch.

Later we learned that Grand Vezir Alemdar had ordered dozens of Mustafa's officers strangled with silken cords, and I confess, I sighed with relief at the news that Sheikh-ul-Islam Muhammad Rakim had met the same fate. As for the women in the former sultan's harem, they were stuffed in weighted sacks and thrown into the sea. "There will be no offspring from these evil females who stood by while Selim was murdered," Alemdar, the man who had saved Mahmud, declared. Despite the gory revenge, however, Mahmud retained kindly feelings for his family: the new sultan insisted that his brother Mustafa be allowed to live in the Cage and that Mustafa's mother remain unscathed. Somehow, it seemed, Aysha always survived.

20

· · · · ·

The formal celebration had ended, the festive meal con-
sumed, when Nakshidil and I proceeded to the private quarters of the valide sultan. As she surveyed the reception room,
she looked even more dazzled than she had two decades before, when Mirishah had informed her she was in the eye of
Sultan Selim.

"Do you remember the first time we came to the valide's
apartment together?" I asked.

"Of course, and how strange it all is. Wonderful things
have happened since then. And terrible things too. Even before that, there was the horrid night with Abdul Hamid! And
then the delicious times with Selim! And becoming the
guardian of Mahmud!" She was suddenly quiet, and when
she spoke again her voice had become more sober. "I shall

never forget Perestu's death: how awful it was. And all those confrontations with Aysha."

"And now you are officially Mahmud's mother and valide sultan," I reminded her, not wanting the memories to end on a sour note.

She ordered sherbets and coffee as we relaxed on a divan, and it pleased me to watch the girls in the coffee service, each doing her special dance: one carried the velvet-covered tray, another the silver pot, another brought in the tiny cups encased in gold. I liked to see how the pourer kneeled, holding the pot high, tipping it so the coffee flowed like rapids into the cup, frothing as it reached the rim. Then, when the girls had served us, they rose like graceful tulips and took their leave.

I took a sip from the jeweled cup and thought for a moment about the changes in my own life. "When I arrived here as an innocent boy, castrated and scared, I lived in fear of the chief black eunuch, and now I am the one in that powerful position. And someone else who's just arrived, young and terrified, will follow me someday." I took another sip and stared into the dark liquid. "A Persian poet wrote that life is a passing wind, but I believe it is a continuing cycle," I said. "The wheel goes around and around: sometimes we are at the top, sometimes at the bottom, but the wheel keeps moving and our lives go with it."

Nakshidil stirred her coffee with a gold spoon. "Yes, I understand what you mean. No matter what happens, the cycle continues. First this was Mirishah's, and I was a slave;

now I am here, and I will choose other slaves to be favorites and kadins." Her eyes swept the rococo room. "What a privilege to live here. It really is magnificent: the gilded boiserie, the painted landscapes."

She rose and walked across the flowered carpet to the tiled fountain. "It took me a long time to appreciate the ceramics," she said, running her hand along the smooth wall. "When I arrived as a young girl at Topkapi, I could not distinguish Iznik tiles from Italian or Delft. It was only after a few years that I learned to treasure the vividness of the colors and the intricacy of the patterns." She pointed her finger to the staircase. "Seeing the bedroom just now, I was overwhelmed by the tiles: the peacock patterns and the floral sprays; imagine the delicate brushwork that went into painting them, and then glazing them to such brilliance."

I saw her eyes searching above the doorway and along the walls.

"What are you looking for?"

"Do you remember the inscription to Mirishah that was on the wall? 'A sea of benevolence, a mine of constancy.' It was written by Selim, and I've always remembered those words. You pointed it out the first time we were here. But I don't see it now."

"Most likely it was removed," I replied. "Probably on Aysha's orders." Later, my suspicions were confirmed.

. . . . .

Over the course of the first few months, events moved at a furious pace. In the harem, the black eunuchs were ranked by the amount of time they had served; and a new female staff was put in place. A number of girls had arrived as gifts from pashas and provincial governors, but additional ones had to be bought at the slave market, and more than a dozen mistresses had to be assigned, from head of the wardrobe to head of the sick, each with an array of females to assist her.

In the divan, advisers were called in from all corners of the empire to review the affairs of state. The sultan, sitting face to face, not concealing himself from his council, agreed to tax the people fairly and justly throughout the empire; the provincial governors promised that taxes to the sultan would be paid in full in a timely manner. At Alemdar's urging, steps were put in place to reform the Janissaries: promotions were to be earned; soldiers were to be disciplined; training was to be done in the Western style. The New Order army was restored, and renamed so as not to anger the regular troops; and instead of considering them as a separate force, the new Segbans were called an auxiliary to the Janissaries. Word went out that further changes were under way.

. . . . .

Early one morning, I was summoned to see the sultan. He was in the baths, having the hair removed from his body, when I arrived.

"Ah, Tulip," he said with a smile. "There are some things a eunuch can feel fortunate about."

I looked at him, a bit surprised. "Your Majesty?" I said, not knowing what he could have in mind.

"I do not mean to make light of your situation. But at least you do not have to go through this process, do you?" He pointed to the foul-smelling cream smeared across his body. "Your lack of body hair makes it that much easier to be a good Muslim."

I nodded slightly, certain there were more serious things he wanted to discuss. He motioned for me to sit. As soon as the paste had been scraped off and his body thoroughly washed, he signaled the bath slaves to leave; only a mute black eunuch was allowed to stay and serve him.

When the sultan began to speak, I noted a weariness in his eyes; his shoulders were hunched, as though the weight of the world was upon them. "Tomorrow is Tuesday, Tulip, and it is the next meeting of the divan. I am pleased to have you there as Chief Black Eunuch."

"My sublime sultan, I am most grateful and supremely honored to be kislar aghasi," I said, and looking up from my marble seat I saw Nakshidil enter the room; the baths connected the valide's suite to the sultan's, allowing them the opportunity to speak with no one else around.

As she joined us, the sultan welcomed her and said, "It is good that both of you are here. There is much on my mind, but my primary concern is the Janissaries. The ulema are stirring them up, telling them the new Segbans are usurping their power."

I nodded my head in agreement. "Majesty, I have heard similar reports. The sheikhs have been giving sermons in the mosques that the Segbans are dangerous and take their orders from the infidels."

"It is an outrageous lie," said Mahmud.

"It is the same problem as Selim had when the tried to modernize the military," noted Nakshidil.

"I wouldn't doubt if Aysha is behind it," I added, but my remark was ignored.

The valide sultan turned to her son. "My lion, Grand Vezir Alemdar must be more clever. It is he who installed the Segbans. He must make the Janissaries proud to have the Segbans attached to them. He must make them feel as if they deserve the credit for the Segbans' success."

"I believe you are right," the sultan answered.

"Forgive me for such boldness, Majesty," I said, "but an idea has entered my mind."

"Boldness is what we need. Tell me."

"Perhaps we should make some gesture to assure the Janissaries of His Majesty's support." I looked around the room. "A fountain, perhaps."

"I will offer something even better," said Nakshidil. "My stipend is exceedingly generous. I will use some of it to build a mosque for the Janissaries. That will show support not only for them but for the ulema as well."

"A magnanimous idea," I said, "in the true spirit of Muslim charity." With that I rose, thinking that Nakshidil had come to talk to Mahmud in private. The sultan told me to stay.

"You are the chief black eunuch now," he reminded me, "and you have always been loyal to my mother. I value your advice." We moved to the cooling room, and Mahmud signaled the mute eunuch to bring him a narghile. We watched the black slave fill the amber cup with apple tobacco and then light it with pieces of heated charcoal. The sweet smell of the tobacco and the gurgling of the water in the pipe calmed us, and for a while we were each lost in our own thoughts. Slowly, Nakshidil came out of her reverie and turned to Mahmud.

"I have seen the worry in your eyes, my son," she said. "I know that you are uneasy, and that you bear the burdens of the empire."

"There is much to worry about," the sultan said. "It will take a great leader to steer the right course."

"You must remember that great leaders are not born; they become," Nakshidil said. "They grow in strength, and as they do, they give strength to their people."

Mahmud puffed on his pipe. "I have thought of little but this since I became padishah. But who knows what history will hand me?"

"History is made by human beings. God gave us this world, but real leaders shape it. I know there are those who think that events occur, like storms in the sky, but events are made by people. And it is people who respond."

"It's true," I said. "Think of Istanbul. Constantine the

Great founded this city, the only one that stretches across two continents, and for a thousand years Constantinople was the capital of Byzantium. It took Mehmet the Conqueror to make it ours in 1453."

"Look at Russia today," said Nakshidil. "Catherine defied the world, and we trembled at her name. Since she died, our fears have disappeared. Now it is Napoleon who captures our attention and turns our heads towards France. Some rulers lead the stampede. Others let events trample them. You come from a line of warrior horsemen, my son, and you must show the way."

"But what are you suggesting?" Mahmud asked, frowning. "Surely, not to conquer foreign states?"

"Chéri, the Ottomans are no longer what they were. They are not a conquering nation as in the time of Süleyman the Magnificent; he expanded the empire from Belgrade to Baghdad. But sadly, some of what was conquered by him in the sixteenth century has already been lost to Russia, Austria, and France. We must preserve what we have. It is up to you to make this nation great again."

The sultan nodded for her to continue.

Nakshidil reached over and put her hand on top of his. "Turkey is like an ancient tree rooted deeply in the ground: its trunk is broad and strong, and its long limbs reach out. The Oriental soil nurtures the roots; but the European sun nourishes the buds. Let the tree's limbs bend towards the sunlight, so they can blossom with new ideas."

The mute eunuch came around, passing a tray of sweets,

and the sultan took a piece of halvah. He bit the sesame paste and said, "Continue."

"You must gaze beyond the horizon," the valide sultan went on. "Remember that now the French are pointing in the right direction. The revolution did terrible things, as we know, but it also brought us new ideas of liberty. And then there is Bonaparte, a brilliant military man. His armies are fierce; yet his people flourish. I tell you, my son, if the Ottoman Empire is to survive, then we must look to the French."

"But as Selim learned, reforming the military is not enough," I said.

"You are right, Tulip. Mahmud must change the way people think." She turned again to her son. "As sultan, you must educate them, give them the opportunity to learn and think freely."

"And how would the padishah do that?" I asked. "Not in the medreses. The ulema are not interested in giving that kind of education."

Mahmud swallowed the last bit of the sweetmeat, and wiped his hands. "We should begin with the military," he said. "There is no doubt they need new training and new schools. The valide sultan is right. We must build a modern army to defend ourselves, but we must also build people's minds. We all know how important education is. Look at you, Tulip. You have taught yourself to speak several languages and it has opened your eyes to the world. Without educating the public, we will be walking blindly in the dark." With that, the sultan rose and kissed his mother's hand. "Let us hope we can make these changes soon."

21
· · · · ·

For the first two weeks of Ramadan, which the moon had ordered for early May, we followed the laws of the Prophet, fasting from sunrise to sunset, and then, at the sound of the cannon blast, feasting from sundown to dawn; fasting and feasting every day for fourteen days, sleeping for much of the day, stuffing ourselves at the sundown meal, then supping again at three A.M. and breakfasting before sunlight.

"We are desperately in need of an heir," Nakshidil blurted out one afternoon. We were in the midst of a game of backgammon, trying to divert our thoughts from food.

"I would not be concerned," I said. "We have been here less than a year, and, I am sorry to say, the combination of the two coups, first against Selim, then against Mustafa, and then the death of Selim, have been deeply troubling for the sultan. Added to that is the current situation with the

Janissaries: keeping the army content while at the same time installing reforms is a challenge to any leader. Mahmud's worries have made him depressed, and he has not given the concubines the proper attention."

"Perhaps he has not found the right girl for inspiration."

"There are plenty of pretty girls," I remarked; "three hundred women, all wanting the affection of your son." I paused, kissed the dice in my hand, and rolled. "It's odd, isn't it; here you are ruling them, and I remember how much you hated having to vie with others for Selim's affections."

"But you know, Tulip, in those early days I did not understand the purpose of the harem. It took a while before I realized that this is not a prison, but a refuge; not a pleasure palace for lustful men, but a sacred womb to bear the offspring of Ottoman sultans." She studied the board and bore off a checker. "Remember, Selim had no offspring; there are no more heirs to the Ottoman throne, and after Mahmud, the line dies out; yet the bellies of the concubines are empty. My most important task is to assure the continuation of the empire."

"I predict, even without the help of tea leaves, as soon as everything is calm, you will have a grandchild."

"Inshallah," she said, and forcing my checker onto the bar, she rolled a three and bore off her last piece.

It was my responsibility to see to it that the entire harem was entertained during the month-long holiday. At the valide sultan's request, the wives of important men were invited to the evening feasts in her reception room, and in the second week Nakshidil invited Selim's sisters, Hadice Sultan and Beyhan Sultan, to join us. After a repast that included everything from soup and caviar and kebabs to sweet Ramadan cake, the women lounged on soft cushions while slaves danced, storytellers spun their words, fortune-tellers read tarot cards, and musicians stirred us with the haunting strains of Turkish melodies. Some of the ladies smiled when Nakshidil played a violin piece by Mozart, but I noticed frowns on the prune-faces of the conservatives.

Nothing, however, scandalized them as much as seeing Beyhan Sultan. The daughters of the sultans live a life of privilege, from the generous stipends they receive, to the grand palaces in which they reside, to the slavish husbands they rule. But no matter how powerful they may be, even princesses cannot control all mortal things, and recently Beyhan's husband had passed away. Since the death of the pasha, she had come to be called the *delhi* sultana for her crazy ways.

The princess had taken to riding in her ox-drawn carriage from her home in Ortakoy to the European quarter; sitting in her araba, lumbering along the cobbled streets of Pera, she lured attractive males like a charmer lures its snakes. The men fell under her spell and followed her to her palace, where some were shaved and painted and made to dance in female costumes, while others were favored with her cup of pleasure.

Word of her activities had reached the valide sultan, and now Nakshidil was trying to tame the lecherous woman. "To think she was once a friend of Aysha's!" the valide whispered to me. "I don't know which is worse, to have Beyhan Sultan behave like this or to have her aligned with that woman."

"I think I know the answer," I muttered.

Princess Hadice, too, was enamored of the West. Fond of the architect Antoine Melling, she was constantly coming up with projects for him to do, from the rendering of her palace on the Bosphorus to the design of her knives and plates. On this particular evening, she had brought along plans for the latest additions to her residence overlooking the sea: one, a garden labyrinth, amused us all with its twisting paths and puzzling dead ends. But if the European maze was interesting, the second idea was even more intriguing: the princess had proposed a secret panel on the ground floor of the palace.

"Look," Hadice said, her eyes wide with delight as she showed us the drawings. "There will be a section of the wooden floor that has a panel with a spring. All I have to do is push this panel down and it will open, so we can swim out in the Bosphorus."

Beyhan looked carefully at the architect's pictures. "That's wonderful," she exclaimed, "and maybe some of our male friends can push it from below and swim in to us."

With that, the music began and the dancing girls appeared. "Take a good look," I whispered to Nakshidil, who nodded knowingly. As each of the slave girls stepped from the circle, I felt pleased with our recent additions. The first girl showed off her full breasts; the second one flirted with her almond-shaped eyes; another had legs as long as a cypress tree. But it wasn't until Fatma came forward that I really paid attention. Her wide-set eyes and cupid's lips gave her an air of sweet innocence, yet her swiveling hips left no doubt she could give a man great pleasure. I looked at Nakshidil and noticed that she, too, was taken with the girl. When the evening was over she told me to prepare Fatma for the sultan. "I think we've found the inspiration," she whispered with a smile.

.....

On the fifteenth day of Ramadan I rose early for one of the holiest rituals, the ceremony of the Sacred Mantle.

This was my first official holy day, and my first visit to the pavilion where the sacred relics were kept; only the highest members of the palace hierarchy were ever allowed in. As I retrieved my dagger from the hidden closet between my bedroom and my prayer room, I thought about the privileges of being the chief black eunuch: my richly furnished apartment; my staff of slaves; my large income; my influence with the sultan; my right to preside over ceremonies such as the one taking place in a few hours. I had paid a great price, yet today it seemed almost worth it. While my slave girl held the mirror, I buttoned my fur-trimmed robe and straightened my cone-shaped turban. I took a deep breath and headed for the passageway that connected the chief black eunuch's apartment with that of the valide sultan.

"I wonder what the Prophet's mantle will look like," I said to Nakshidil.

The weather was cool and she was wearing a pale blue caftan lined with sable. "I should think the Prophet's robe would be beautiful," she said, running her hand along the dark fur. "Of course, I've never seen the Holy Mantle either, but I'm sure it will make my own coat look poor by contrast."

I straightened my turban again, adjusted the dagger at my side, and escorted her outside. The princesses and the dignitaries' wives had gathered in the valide's courtyard, and with Nakshidil at my side, and the others behind me, I led the twenty women in a procession. We marched out through the gardens to the front of the Fourth Court, filed through a narrow passageway to the Third Court, and proceeded to the Pavilion of the Sacred Mantle. At the small building, just opposite the treasury, we were met by hundreds of Janissaries standing on guard.

Nakshidil touched my arm. "Look at their new European uniforms. How smart they are!" she said excitedly as we marched forward, up the steps of the veranda.

I wondered if the Janissaries would agree. Or did they resent having to wear the Western style? We could never forget that Selim was overthrown when he ordered the army to put on European uniforms. I was glad that Grand Vezir Alemdar was pushing reforms, but I still worried he might overdo it. On my last foray into the bazaar, I had heard mumblings of criticism from many people.

Inside the four-room pavilion, I led Nakshidil to the Room of the Armchair where she took her seat. Once she was comfortable under the canopy, I left the room, knowing that the women would each come forward, kiss her hand, and seat themselves below her in order of rank. They would wait until the men had made their visit to the Room of the Mantle, and then the guardian of the mantle would call them in.

I hurried past the reception room and the waiting male dignitaries to the special room where the Holy Relics were kept. Here were the Prophet Muhammad's personal possessions: two gold swords studded with jewels; a letter written by him on leather; his personal seal; his broken tooth; his black banner; sixty hairs of his beard encased in jeweled boxes; his footprint embedded in stone; and most important of all, the mantle he had given to one of his followers.

I entered, smelled the burning incense, and looked around: it was the first time I had seen the famed tiled walls, peacocks glazed a blue as dazzling as the Sea of Marmara. Above the tiles, gilded oil lamps and jeweled pendants hung from the domed ceiling of the hall, and on the far side of the chamber, I saw the new fountain that Mahmud had just installed. In front of it stood Sultan Mahmud and Grand Vezir Alemdar.

From behind a curtain came the sounds of the Koran being chanted as we three took our places in front of the silver canopy that protected the Holy Mantle. The sultan, robed in fur-lined red satin and turbaned with a brilliant aigrette, stood in the center; the high-turbaned grand vezir stood on his right; I, the chief black eunuch, on his left.

With his dark eyes burning brightly and his broad chest thrust out, Sultan Mahmud proclaimed in his powerful voice, "In the name of God, the Merciful, the Compassionate," and took the key, which he alone possessed, to open the gold box containing the mantle. Once he unlocked the box, he took out an embroidered satin square and unwrapped it. Inside was another embroidered bocha, and inside that, another. We watched as he slowly unfolded the squares until he reached the fortieth one, the bocha that held the precious mantle.

There we were, each in our gorgeous robes, waiting to see the cloak that the Prophet had worn. I held my breath as the sultan pulled it out and showed us the fragile cloth. What a disappointment! Frankly, I thought it would be woven of gold or silver, but instead it was small and black, a worn, wool cloak lined in tattered beige, with nothing to distinguish it but its wide sleeves. Nonetheless, it was considered the holiest of holies, so I gushed like the others. The agha of the muslin, who was the guardian of the room, touched the mantle with a small piece of embroidered linen and the sultan kissed it. The grand vezir and I did the same.

Then the dignitaries entered—ulema, vezirs, and other high officials—each one making obeisance to the sultan, bowing down and sweeping his right hand to the ground, then lifting his head and touching his heart and his forehead. With that, he was given a piece of embroidered linen that had touched the mantle, and after he put the linen on his head, he stepped backwards to join the others of his rank.

We stood for hours as the visitors threaded through, and though I tried to concentrate, the chanting in the background caused my mind to drift. I thought about that Holy Mantle and the holy men of the ulema, and how they might be in alliance with Aysha and the Janissaries. What was Aysha up to, I wondered. I had heard little about her since she was sent to the Old Palace. Was she really keeping her promise of loyalty to the sultan? Or was she still plotting behind our backs?

The last of the men had finished, and now the women came in, one by one, kissing the sultan's coat and a piece of embroidered linen that had touched the Holy Mantle, putting the linen on their heads, and stepping backwards to assume the stand of obeisance with their arms across their breasts. Then the valide sultan came in, gently kissed the sultan's hand, kissed the symbolic piece of mantle, carefully put it on her head, turned, and led the ladies out. Finally, the sultan wrapped the mantle back in the bochas, placed them in the gold box, and returned it to the silver canopy.

As we began the procession back to the harem, I took a long look at the phalanx of Janissaries guarding the Holy Relics; it struck me that their physical nearness to the Prophet's belongings symbolized their alliance with the ulema. I suddenly remembered Nakshidil's Latin prayer: "May the sultan be safe from angry Janissaries, safe from rivaling vezirs, and safe from vicious ulema." I heaved a sigh, relieved that on my first official holy day, all had gone well.

22

· · · · ·

Boom! Boom! Boom! Three times the cannons of Topkapi
Gate fired the news that a baby was born. Naturally, we all
had wanted seven salvoes, but a male child was yet to be our
good fortune. Boom! Boom! Boom! They repeated the
shots five times that day. You can imagine the joy, since
there had been no child born to a sultan for nineteen years.

The excitement started on Tuesday, nine months to the
day when Fatma was sent to Mahmud. As soon as she announced her first pangs and water trickled down her legs, I
called for the *ebe,* and when the midwife arrived in Fatma's
apartment, she determined the pains were real and that we
should bring in the childbirth chair. Fatma adjusted her
bulging body against the high spindled back and arms, con-
forming her shape to the cutout carved in the front.

The valide sultan came almost at once, accompanied by

some of the harem women; close behind them were the palace dwarf to entertain and the musicians to play their instruments; Nakshidil insisted they play Handel and Bach along with Turkish melodies, so that the newborn infant would learn to appreciate both cultures.

At first Fatma's pains were brief and far apart, and while she sat on the hard seat, the women, cross-legged on the floor and on the divans, tried to soothe her with amusing stories. She laughed as they mimicked the girls in the harem or teased each other, and when a contraction came, she held up her hand so they would pause. After a while the pains sped up, and every time Fatma suffered a spasm, I saw Nakshidil grimace in sympathy. As the contractions grew longer and closer together, one of the women washed Fatma's face with a cloth soaked in rose water, and another massaged her back, while everyone urged her to "push," "push harder."

At last the midwife looked down and announced she could see the baby's head. Fatma screamed and pushed hard. We all said, "Allahu akbar!" God is great! Fatma screamed and pushed hard again. "Allahu akbar!" we said. Then another scream, another push, and miracle of miracles, out came the precious baby and everyone pronounced the Bismallah, the words that begin every prayer: "I bear witness that I will worship no god but Allah and that Muhammad is His slave and His prophet." With that the ebe washed the infant and cut its cord. "May her voice be beautiful!" she declared and sprinkled the girl with fennel seed.

While Nakshidil took Fatma and some of the women to the valide sultan's apartment, the rest of us stayed with the midwife to dress the baby. As quickly as we could, we swathed the little body in gold brocade, tying a silk sash across the infant's middle. With her cries tickling our ears, we lifted her wrinkled head and covered it with a gold cap sewn with gold coins, cloves of garlic, and blue glass beads. We had attached a diamond tassel, and just for good measure, to ward off the evil eye we added a blue cloth stitched with a few lines from the Koran.

When the infant was all wrapped, and her faced veiled in green chiffon, we bundled her up in the arms of the ebe. Off we went with the musicians accompanying us, as I led the little parade to Nakshidil's apartment to present the beautiful baby to Fatma. Dear Fatma lay on her mother-of-pearl couch, stretched out on red satin quilts studded with emeralds and pearls, beaming from ear to ear! But no one glowed more than the valide sultan; "a grandmother," she whispered in my ear, "can you imagine, I'm a grandmother! Look at that beautiful baby." She paused for a moment, and I noticed a change in her expression. "Where is Mahmud?" she asked. "This is his child."

"I'm sure he'll come to the reception tomorrow," I answered.

She shook her head sadly. "If it had been a boy, he would have come today."

"She's fortunate to be a girl," I said. "She'll have all the privileges of a sultan's child—a big stipend for life, beautiful palaces, plenty of slaves—and none of the dangers faced by a prince. No one will try to kill her to get the throne, or threaten her mother's life."

"It's true," Nakshidil agreed. "A sultana has all the freedom and none of the fears. She even chooses her own husband."

On the following day as the cannons boomed, a throng of female guests arrived, eager to congratulate Fatma and the valide sultan. The queue twisted around the corridors, down the stairs, and along the courtyard, as princesses, and the wives of vezirs, ulema, palace officials and other important women, came to pay their respects. You can imagine my shock at the end of the day when I saw Princess Beyhan and the back of the head of one of the guests.

"It can't be," I whispered to Nakshidil.

"It can't be what?" she asked.

"It's impossible."

"What's impossible? Please, Tulip, try to make sense."

"How many dignitaries' wives do we know who are redheads?"

"There aren't any that I can recall."

"That's what I thought."

"Then why did you ask?"

"Because there is a redhead at the top of the line."

"She must be the wife of a foreign envoy."

"Or the wife of a dead sultan."

"Really, Tulip, you're making me mad. What are you trying to say?"

"Who is the redhead we both know?"

She was silent for a moment. "Aysha, of course," she suddenly said, and then as if stunned by her own words, she shrieked, "What is Aysha doing here?"

"I don't know."

"Well," she said, lowering her voice, "you'd better find out."

I signaled Princess Beyhan that I wanted to speak to her alone, and quickly reported back to Nakshidil what I had learned. "Somehow that woman Aysha convinced the head mistress of the Eski Saray that she should be allowed to leave the Old Palace and come to celebrate the baby's birth. Then she convinced her old friend Beyhan Sultan to bring her here."

"What did she say to them that was so convincing?"

"She told them, 'I am the mother of the only Ottoman prince. Certain things are appropriate. If I don't show up, the world will be dismayed. It will be an embarrassment to the empire.' "

There was little either of us could say, except to welcome her graciously and offer her some refreshments; the last thing we wanted was to spoil the party by making a scene. At least, by then, it was late in the afternoon and the crowd of visitors had thinned. "I will give Aysha a few minutes and then escort her out," I told the valide sultan. But my plans were quickly foiled.

As I headed towards Aysha, the head chamberlain entered the room, her silver baton in hand: "Rise for the arrival of His Supreme Majesty, Sultan Mahmud," Cevri announced. The women scrambled to their feet, and we all stood as the sultan made his entrance with his sister Hadice Sultan behind him.

Ordinarily, I would have been there with him, but he wanted to surprise us, and surprise us he did. I could not believe my eyes. I suppose that no one else could either, for as soon as he walked in, despite the strict rule of silence in his presence, a chorus of gasps escaped from everyone's lips. The sultan was almost unrecognizable.

And then, above the hush, I heard Aysha ask in a loud whisper: "Where is his turban? What's on his head? What on earth is he wearing?"

Indeed, it was true; the thing on his head was certainly strange. Instead of his usual turban, Sultan Mahmud, padishah, God's shadow on earth, the caliph, the leader of all Muslims, was wearing a red fez!

The smiling sultan marched across the room to the seated Fatma and kissed the hand of the new mother; then, as she lifted the infant in her arms, he pressed his lips against its forehead, and the tassel of his fez tickled its cheek.

Nakshidil, standing next to Fatma, smiled with delight. "Congratulations, my lion," she purred, kissing his hand and his sleeve.

With that, the sultan thanked them both, turned around, and left, leaving us all in a state of shock.

As soon as he was gone, Aysha rushed up to Nakshidil. "What is this all about?" she demanded. "What kind of infidel is your son? Don't you know what we say: 'The turban is the barrier separating belief and unbelief'?"

The valide sultan smiled and turned away, leaving it to Hadice Sultan to reply. "It is only natural that in our great sultan's move to reform the Ottomans he should change the style of his headgear," she said. "New clothing outside, new thinking inside."

"It's disgraceful to think of the caliph without a turban," Aysha said. "It's blasphemy!"

"It's delightful to see him looking so modern," I retorted, though I wasn't quite sure about the fez. What would the Muslim religious leaders think?

"If he keeps this up, soon he will be praying with the infidels," Aysha taunted.

"If you keep this up, soon you will be praying for your life," said Nakshidil. "How dare you speak about our sultan like that!" With that, she ordered two eunuchs to escort the woman back to the Old Palace. And I signaled the musicians to entertain.

Later, I learned from Nakshidil that she had spoken earlier with the sultan: the fez was a gift from the ambassador of Tunis. "He said that just as Fatma's baby brings new life to the palace, he wanted to bring us a new idea."

"But does it go with Islam?" I asked. "You know what the holy men say: 'Two prostrations with the turban outweigh seventy without the turban.'"

"I'm surprised at you, Tulip," she said. "That is a saying that reflects the past. The ambassador told Mahmud that today the fez is worn by all the Muslims in Tunis. In fact, the flat top is supposed to remind us of the flat prayer rug, and the tassel is the promise of Heaven."

"And when did the envoy give this to the sultan?"

"This morning. Mahmud told me about it in the baths, but I had no idea he would wear it to the reception," Nakshidil said. "What a surprise!"

What a surprise, indeed. And not long after, the Janissaries gave us their own surprise.

23
. . . . .

As I grow older, the years grow shorter. Annual holidays race the calendar, coming around so quickly it is as if time has been compressed. It hardly seemed a year since we celebrated Ramadan and sent Fatma off to the sultan, and yet, since then, Fatma had given birth and Ramadan was upon us once again, arriving like a sudden cloudburst.

This time, however, distracted as we were by Fatma's baby, the days of fasting almost slid by. And in the evenings, as usual, I organized the feasts and the entertainment for visiting guests. After the sun set, and the women came, we indulged in smoked aubergine, sweetmeats, and aniseed cake, while the girls danced, the dwarfs jestered, and the storytellers told their tales.

Midway through the month-long holiday came the time for the visit to the Pavilion of the Holy Mantle. Wrapped in my cone-shaped turban and fur-lined coat, I led the parade of Valide Sultan Nakshidil, Fatma who was now a kadin, the princesses, and the wives of the vezirs and ulema, to the Pavilion of the Sacred Mantle. But even as we left the gardens and emerged from the narrow passageway into the Third Court, I saw the pavilion and sensed that something was amiss. As we neared the small building, my feelings were confirmed. Nakshidil tugged on my sleeve. "Look, it's the Segbans standing on guard," she whispered. "They've replaced the Janissaries."

"I see," I murmured. "Alemdar must have made the change. I hope he knows what he's doing." And without even thinking, I stroked the silver dagger at my side.

As I had done the year before, I led the valide sultan to the Room of the Armchair of the pavilion, left the women to attend her at her canopied chair, and entered the Room of the Holy Mantle. I looked around, noted the Holy Relics on display, and saw the silver canopy. But the sight of the two men standing in front of it left me bewildered: there was the grand vezir dressed in his caftan and high turban, and there was the sultan, wearing his ceremonial robe; but, for the second time, the sultan had replaced his traditional turban with a tasseled fez. Pressing my lips together, so as not to show my surprise, I took my place beside him.

In the now-familiar ritual, the sultan unlocked the special gold box, unwrapped the forty bochas, and held up the Prophet's mantle; we each took a piece of symbolic linen, kissed it, and put it on our heads. The dignitaries were called, and I noted that as each man reached the doorway, saw the sultan, and registered the fez, he could hardly hide his surprise. But no one dared say a word. Instead they each performed the sacred ritual in silence. When they had finished, the women were signaled, and, once again, I saw the startled looks, suppressed, as they carried out the sacred rites.

When the ceremony ended, the sultan folded the mantle inside the bochas and put them back in the gold box. And once again, as our procession left the pavilion, I took a long look at the Segbans standing out front: I thought about the Janissaries, and thanked Allah that all had gone well.

As soon as I delivered the valide sultan to her apartment, I returned to my quarters and put my dagger in its cupboard. It was time for afternoon prayers, and kneeling on my rug, I repeated Nakshidil's words: "May the sultan be safe from angry Janissaries, safe from rivaling vezirs, and safe from vicious ulema." I heaved a sigh. It was then that I heard the noise.

I looked around and told myself it was the sound of people running from a fire, or a pack of animals that had broken free; but I knew that what I heard were not cries of fear but calls of fury. They were the shouts of soldiers, and my worst nightmares were coming true. The Janissaries were storming Topkapi. How many times had we talked with dread of such an act, and now here it was, happening to us!

I knew that the Janissaries regarded the protection of the Pavilion of the Holy Mantle as their right. Later I was told that as soon as they heard that Alemdar had taken away their privilege and given it to the Segbans, the Janissaries became irate. They abandoned their guardhouses around the city, and, gathering supporters along the way, they marched en masse to Topkapi. At the front of the palace they stormed past the halberdiers and rushed to the First Court, but the guards had signaled the Segbans, and the loyal soldiers raced from their posts at the Pavilion of the Sacred Mantle. Thanks be to Allah, the Segbans fought off the rebels.

But early the next morning the insurgents were back. Again from my apartment I heard the noise, and this time three of my eunuchs came rushing in with reports. Once again the Janissaries had pushed their way past the guards of the First Court, but this time they stormed into the Second Court where the council building stood. While some of them raced towards the Divanhe looking for Grand Vezir Alemdar, others sped to the kitchens. There, they found the soup kettles, and true to their tradition, turned over the bronze caldrons and banged them with their spoons to an- nounce their rebellion. My quarters were in the Fourth Court, far removed from the action, but the noise and clamor were terrifying.

"Where is the sultan?" I asked the eunuchs who had come to report, and they quickly assured me that Mahmud was in his imperial offices in the Second Court, protected by his Segbans and commanding his troops from there. "And Nakshidil?"

"She's in her apartment with her slaves," one of them said.

"Then come with me. We've got to make sure she's safe." Reaching into my cupboard, I grabbed my dagger and hid it under my robe.

I headed towards the valide's apartment, but just as I came to her courtyard, I heard the roar of cannons and then a huge explosion. "Look back!" one of my eunuchs shouted.

I turned and saw smoke and fire billowing from the armory in the First Court, where weapons and gunpowder were stored. A dazed-looking Segban was running towards us.

"Get inside and hide," he shouted, "the Janissaries are everywhere. They're racing from building to building, from the Imperial Treasury to the hospital, even the laundry, searching for anyone of high rank."

I indicated he should come along with me. "Who have they found?" I asked.

"Grand Vezir Alemdar," he said, keeping up at my side. "He was in the armory with some of the Segbans. When the Janissaries found him, they dragged him out and attacked the building, and his men fired back. With all the shooting back and forth, the gunpowder in the storeroom exploded, and everyone inside the magazine was killed."

By now I had reached the apartment of the valide sultan.

I banged on the door, shouting that it was me, and when the frightened slave girl opened it, I saw Nakshidil: she was sitting in her reception room, playing cards.

"My God," I shouted, "you can't just sit there like that. You've got to hide."

"I will not hide," the valide said.

"But your life is in danger. The Janissaries are everywhere."

"My life is in danger no matter where I am. I refuse to cower to those ruffians." With that she slammed the cards down. Another black eunuch came running into the room.

"There is no more water in the palace," he said. "We have just received reports from outside that the Janissaries have cut off the water supply to Topkapi. And thousands of ulema and their students are setting fires around the city. If you look outside you can see the flames."

I moved to the window and opened the lattice. Just as the eunuch had said, in the distance thick black smoke was belching from buildings, and flames were leaping like angry gods across the seven hills of the city. I looked down and saw more smoke on the palace grounds and heard the blasts of cannon fire in the Third Court. I turned back towards the room and noticed smoke seeping under the door.

"Get some towels and wet them," I said, ordering the slaves to use the water stored in the baths. In the background gunshots crackled the air, and now, inside the room, the smoke was thickening. My eyes began to burn, and I saw

Nakshidil wipe her watery eyes; we tried to keep our faces covered with the wet cloths, but our mouths were dry and our throats were burning.

One of the girls was coughing badly. "I must have something to drink," she cried, but we hardly had enough water to keep the towels damp. Nakshidil started coughing too, and so did the others; I thought we would all choke to death. Between her coughs, Nakshidil insisted we find Fatma and the baby.

I sent two of the eunuchs on the mission. "They are either in Fatma's apartment or in the nursery. When you find them, wrap the infant and take it to my apartment," I said, explaining how to hide it in my revolving cupboard. "One of you stay in my room, and don't let anyone near it. The other should remain with Fatma in her apartment. She'll want to go with the baby, but it's too dangerous for her in my quarters. They'll never suspect the infant is there, but if they find the kadin, they'll kill them both."

With that I heard a huge noise and moved to a different window. At least a dozen Janissaries were headed towards the courtyard of the valide sultan. I opened the door a crack, wanting to see if anyone was nearby, but I was nearly trampled by another eunuch.

"The sultan sent me," he said; he was out of breath and could hardly speak. "Word has reached us that Aysha is behind the plot. The Janissaries freed her this morning from the Eski Saray, and now she's on the way here."

"That's good," I said, rubbing my hands. "I look forward

to her arrival." The sound of stampeding men disrupted my words, and a few minutes later I thought I heard a woman's voice calling out "Death to Nakshidil." I knew, of course, it was Aysha, and I wanted to run out and strangle her myself, but I had all I could do to protect the valide sultan.

"Go in the prayer room," I pleaded with Nakshidil, "and hide behind the stack of rugs."

"I will not," she said defiantly, removing the damp cloth from her face. "I am staying right here with my girls."

"Please, I beg you, go in there and hide behind the stack of rugs, at least for a little while." I was about to order the eunuchs to carry her into the room, when one of them shouted, "Look out the window. The Navy ships are at the seraglio dock."

I ran to look, but even before I had opened the lattice again, the door of the apartment flew open and five of our troops rushed in.

"What's going on?" I asked worriedly. "Why are you here, and not outside fighting the Janissaries?"

"You need not fear," the lieutenant said. "Everything is under control. The insurgents have been subdued. We made a pincer move, the Segbans at the front of the palace, and the Navy at the rear. The rebellion is over, but the scene outside is horrendous. There are body parts and corpses everywhere."

"And what about Aysha?"

"We have a little present for you," he answered, and with that he signaled two of his men. I confess I felt victorious as they carried Aysha in, her arms and legs in irons, her mouth stuffed with a cloth, her face as mad as a wild woman's.

I pulled out the cloth and looked her straight in the eye. "I think you know what's coming next."

She spat on the floor. "I am the mother of a prince," she growled. "A prince who will soon be the sultan."

"Not anymore," the officer said. Then turning to me, he explained, "Mustafa escaped from the Princes' Cage. Our men found him with the Janissaries."

"Where is he now?" I asked.

"He is in two places: his head is in front of the Council Hall, and the rest of his body is in the sea."

"You're only saying that to torture me. You wouldn't dare," Aysha sneered.

"You can see him if you like," the man answered.

"My son is the real sultan," she said scornfully. "You threw us out once, but the time has come for him to be back on the throne. We know what's best for the people. Mahmud and his fez are a sham. And Nakshidil is the reason: she has turned him into an infidel."

"It is you who are a sham," Nakshidil answered quietly. "You pretend to care for the people, but you are a greedy woman who cares only for her own power. You are right; your time has come, but not to be on the throne."

"You cannot harm me," Aysha said. "I have the Janissaries on my side."

With that, another eunuch rushed in. "The sultan is coming," he said. I looked towards the door and saw a stream of eunuchs and, then, Mahmud. The sultan's eyes were red and his clothes were covered with soot. He looked weary and spent.

"Majesty," I cried, kissing his sleeve. "Thanks be to Allah, you are all right."

"I am fine," he said in a broken voice, "but I have sad news. Alemdar is dead. They brought me his head."

"Ha!" Aysha cried out victoriously. "You bring us great news."

"I bring you the news that your son Mustafa is also dead."

"No, it can't be," she cried. "I will revenge his death for the rest of my life."

"That won't be long," said Nakshidil, rising from her seat. She moved towards Aysha, and, narrowing her eyes, she pointed her finger at the woman. "You have plotted against me and my son from the moment I arrived in the harem. I cannot forget all the cruel things your son did to Mahmud. I cannot forget your vicious threats. Or your attempts to poison me. Or your fight with Perestu and your order that caused her death. No, you cannot pretend to be a decent person. You are not. You are a hateful woman. And you will have the end you deserve."

The room was hushed. The valide sultan had been patient for many years, pretending to ignore Aysha's evil ways in the hope her behavior would change. But now the truth had sunk in. I turned to the naval officer and led him towards the door.

"Here," I said, reaching into my caftan. "Take this dagger and use it for Aysha's head. Then sew the rest of her in a sack and drop it in the sea. Do it tonight, so we can watch."

That night under a sliver of moon, I stood at the window with Nakshidil and saw the eunuchs carry a weighted sack into a small boat. When they had rowed a short while, they lifted the heavy sack and threw it into the sea. Then they turned and sent up a flare, signaling as I had asked. I put my hand to my lips and blew a kiss. "Farewell Aysha," I said, as her body joined the mound of corpses lying at the bottom of the Bosphorus.

Nakshidil took my arm. "It is a cruel fate for anyone," she said. "But the whole empire breathes easier."

The following morning I went outside to see for myself. Bodies were strewn everywhere, their limbs torn apart, their rotting skins covered with flies. I stepped between them on the bloodied ground and walked to the Third Court. There, impaled on the iron gate, was Aysha's head, shorn of most if its hair, but with enough red strands to assure me it was hers. Next to it was the head of Mustafa.

At sunset, when the cannons sounded, the sultan sent a message that he would join us for a quiet celebration. I sighed with relief that the rebellion had been put to rest. But as we readied ourselves for Mahmud, Nakshidil confided that her fears were still not quelled.

"I am more aware than ever that we need an heir," she told me, plumping a pillow with her fist. "Imagine, God forbid, if Mahmud, himself, had been attacked: there is no one to take over; the military would grab control and the Ottoman Empire would cease to exist."

"He has shown us he is a fertile man," I said. "Send him more concubines, and I am sure he will produce an heir."

"I hope you are right," she said, and, putting down the pillow, she looked around and smiled. Mahmud was standing at the door, his broad figure clothed in a dark blue caftan, his handsome head topped with a fez. She rushed to kiss his hand. "Congratulations, my lion. You have shown that you are a true leader."

The sultan shook his head sadly, and when he spoke his voice was filled with emotion. "My good mother, we succeeded at great expense. The courtyards are filled with corpses and the flower beds are rivers of red. There has been too much blood shed, and the stench of death pervades the palace." With that he took his seat on the velvet divan.

"You are right, my son," Nakshidil said, seating herself beside him. "There has been too much tragedy here; too much intrigue, too much hatred, too much blood spilled at Topkapi. Perhaps we should heed the words of the poet Rumi: 'The past has vanished. Everything that was uttered belongs there. Now is the time to speak of new things.' "

"Amen," I murmured.

The sultan put his hand on Nakshidil's. "Let us start now," he said.

24
. . . . .

(W)e sailed in the valide sultan's golden caïque a mile north of Topkapi, close to Pera, to see the new palace. Beshiktash stood on the European shore of the Bosphorus, a splendid combination of Western design and Oriental detail, replete with tiled fountains and marble baths, open courtyards and colonnades.

It had taken three years to build the palace, a sweeping break with the past, and every decision required the sultan's approval. One side of the huge square building faced the sea; the other looked upon lavish gardens composed of formal parks, flowered labyrinths, and ornamental topiaries.

In only a few more weeks the sultan's entire household— white eunuchs, black eunuchs, pages, princesses, head mistresses, concubines, and kadins, along with the valide sultan and the sultan himself—would move from Topkapi to

Beshiktash. But Nakshidil had asked, on this first day of spring, that we take a picnic on the new grounds. I organized the slave girls and eunuchs, ordered the food, and even made sure that the new marching band be there to greet us; it was led by Donizetti Pasha, the Italian musician who had come to Istanbul on a visit and, at the sultan's request, agreed to stay. As our satin-lined boat pulled up to the pier and the valide stepped on the ground, we heard a flourish of trumpets, cymbals, and drums.

It was not often that the valide sultan went on trips anymore; she had been sick for several months, and the illness had made her frail. But in the last few days a bit of her strength had returned, and she suggested a visit with her granddaughter to survey the palace.

"I've made a decision," Nakshidil said. We were standing in the petting zoo, and little Perestu was feeding nuts to the animals.

"Oh?" I asked, not quite sure what to expect.

"I've been thinking about my slave girls. I've decided to do something about their situation."

"What's that?"

"Some of them have served for many years. They've been loyal and hardworking, but it's time they had their freedom."

"That's very generous of you, Majesty, but where would they go? After all, they're rather like the gorgeous animals in this gilded cage."

"What do you mean?"

"These zebras, giraffes, and gazelles have been taken care of for so long—well fed, groomed, exercised—that if they were allowed to be free in the jungle, they'd have a hard time surviving."

"But I'm not sending them out in the jungle to survive. They can go back to their families."

"That's not possible." I rolled my eyes, and one of the monkeys mimicked me. "They could never go back to their families. Those girls have lived a life of privilege, surrounded by the greatest riches in the world The harem has become their home. You can't really believe they could live as peasants anymore."

"I suppose not. But think how happy they'd be to see their families."

"I'm not so sure. For the most part, their families would be ashamed."

"Ashamed," one of the parrots repeated.

"They'd think the girls had been sent back because they were failures in the palace," I said, ignoring the bird.

"They could live here in Istanbul."

"On their own?" I asked. "No, I don't believe so. If you want to give them their freedom, you must marry them off. There are plenty of pashas who'd be eager to have a palace woman as his wife."

"You're right, Tulip. Please begin to make the arrangements as soon as we return to Topkapi. We'll make the announcement tonight. Ten girls will be set free."

"That's wonderful," I said. "Of course, it will make all the others envious."

"They'll have nothing to worry about," she answered sadly, shaking her head. "I'm feeling a little better today, but this illness has caused me to think more about my life, or rather, about the end of it. When I die, Tulip—and I know the time is not far off—I want all my girls to be freed. Please, promise me you'll see to it that those who want to leave the palace will be married to good men."

"I promise," I said and waved at the friendly monkey. He waved back and gave me a wide grin.

I saw that Nakshidil was tired and suggested we move to a place on the grass where we could sit; the eunuchs had spread a carpet and cushions. I called over the little girl and smiled at the sight of her: the child was surprisingly almost a duplicate of Nakshidil, with her father's upturned nose and her mother's cupid's lips. She skipped to her grandmother's blanket and folded herself at her side.

"Ah, Perestu," Nakshidil said, putting her arm around her. "Do you know why you have that name?"

The three-year-old looked puzzled.

"That was the name of my good friend, and I wanted to keep her memory alive through you. Friendship is most important," she said, giving the child a squeeze. "As you grow up, you will find there are few people you can really count on. Remember to cherish them and give them your love." She looked at me and smiled.

The child nodded, not quite understanding, but knowing she should acknowledge her grandmother's words; and in another instant she wrested herself free and ran to play with one of the black eunuchs.

Nakshidil turned again to me. "Whenever I think of Perestu, I realize how important it is that there be peace among the girls. Promise me, Tulip, that you will make sure no Ayshas arise among the concubines and kadins."

I promised her I would do my best. But how could we ever stop the intrigues in the palace? Each time a new girl entered the harem, or a concubine was called to the sultan, or a child was born, the jealousies flared, and the plotting began again.

Soon after our visit to Beshiktash, a second girl was born to Mahmud, but we still hoped for a son. Though Nakshidil remained in poor health, from time to time she took walks in the gardens, or entertained some visiting wives while the palace musicians played Mozart and Bach and compositions by Selim. And she dressed as beautifully as ever, always in her own style, tying her shawls in different ways, wrapping sashes together, using fabrics and colors and jewels as an artist uses his brushes and palette.

Slowly, as her heart gave way, she succumbed and took to her bed. The palace physician tried his usual remedies of herbs but none of them helped; the Venetian physician and the Greek physician from Pera were both called in, but there was little they could do. And so I watched her, frail and weak, wanting so badly to converse and engage in life; I would sit by her bed in the palace at Beshiktash while she listened eagerly to my gossip, trying herself to settle matters in the harem. At times we talked about the past, about the days with Selim, and her cousin Rose, and about the Janissaries and the ulema.

"Whatever you do, Tulip, please make sure that no one is allowed to use religion as an excuse to control others," she said; she was speaking in short phrases and gasping for breath. "Everyone should have the right to pray as they wish." She lay back on her pillow and closed her eyes. When she opened them again, I offered her some water. She sipped it, and, putting down the glass, she spied the pile of books on her table.

"I am putting aside funds so that you can purchase books from the Grand Bazaar," she said slowly. "I want to leave behind a library, filled with volumes from the West. And anyone from the harem who wishes to read those books will have the right to do so."

I promised to do as she asked. She wanted me by her side, and the least I could do was comfort her, but it pained me to watch. She was the only one in the harem who had shown me love, the only one who treated me as a full human being. I hated to see her suffer: I loved her with all my heart.

After several months of growing weaker, on a night when her son came to visit, she requested a Catholic priest. Good man that he is, the sultan did as she wished. And sadly, as you know, Father, a few hours later, she died. Tomorrow I will lead the procession to bury Valide Sultan Nakshidil in her turbe, and though I will grieve much, I know that nothing can bring her back.

.....

"I hope you understand, Father. She was a good woman. The incident with Aysha . . . I take full responsibility for what happened."

The priest put his arm around the eunuch. "Do not worry," he replied. "You are a good man, Tulip. And Nakshidil has been forgiven for all her sins."

With that, the chief black eunuch rose and put on his ferace. "Thank you, Father," he said. "I bid you farewell, and please know, I will always be grateful to you for giving me this opportunity to remember my dear friend."

Epilogue
· · · · ·

Seven cannons rang out from the palace in the spring of 1830, announcing the birth of a prince, the second son of Sultan Mahmud, and second male heir to the Ottoman throne. Turks thronged the streets in celebration, and from the distant corners of the empire, thousands of honored guests arrived in Istanbul.

In the midst of the festive air, Father Chrysostome filled a suitcase with his robes, his rosaries, and his crucifix, and left the small room where he had lived for thirty years. The bag was heavy, the sidewalk crowded, and as the priest stepped outside onto the cobblestones of Pera, he bumped into a passerby.

"Excuse me, excuse me," he said, anxious to see that the fellow was not hurt. The black man brushed off his woolen trousers, and as he looked up to answer, his eyes met the priest's.

"Father Chrysostome, how nice to see you."

"Why Tulip what a surprise. It's wonderful to see you too."

Noting that the priest had aged a good deal and was now rather frail, the eunuch offered to carry his suitcase. "But where are you off to?"

"Why don't I tell you over a cup of coffee," the Jesuit suggested.

They made their way through the thick crowd to a café, and once they had ordered, they caught up on the dozen years since they had last met.

Since then, the empire had been transformed. Greece had been lost to independence, and Egypt was verging on autonomy, but Arabia was regained, and once more the provinces of Wallachia and Moldavia were held by the Turks.

It had taken years, the two men agreed, but Mahmud had carried out extensive reforms with his mother's words in mind: he had abolished the Janissaries, Westernized the new military, established engineering colleges and medical schools, weakened the ulema, installed ambassadors in Europe, and changed the system of taxation. They concurred that he had had his failures as well as his gains, and his critics had dubbed him the "infidel sultan," but for most of the Ottoman world, his changes improved their lives.

"There is no doubt that Mahmud will go down as one of the great Ottoman emperors," said Father Chrysostome.

"They are calling him the Great Reformer," Tulip said, and as he looked around the coffeehouse he nodded at the men reading. "It is thanks to Sultan Mahmud that we now have our own Turkish newspapers. And I must say," he added, brushing some crumbs off his jacket, "I rather like the way he has us dress."

"Yes, you do look elegant," the priest agreed, observing the fellow's frock coat and trousers and his tasseled fez. "But tell me, what has happened to you since we last met?"

"You must tell me first about yourself," the eunuch said. "Why are you carrying this valise? Where are you off to?"

"As you say, things have changed a great deal. You mentioned the sultan's successes. Without doubt, his policy of equality marks success for us all. I shall never forget his words:

" 'Muslims in the mosque, Christians in the church, and Jews in the synagogue, but there is no difference among them in any other way. My affection and sense of justice for all of them is strong and they are all indeed my children.' "

"They were courageous words for a sultan."

"Indeed. You also spoke of his failures. My friend, what is failure to one is sometimes success to another. My people come from the Morea, and this year, when Greece declared its independence from the Ottomans, I made up my mind to go back. So I am off to the Peloponnese, to live out my last years at home. But what about you? How is life at the palace?"

The eunuch explained that he was no longer at the palace. After the valide sultan died, he was given his freedom.

313

"And are you content?" the priest asked.

"Ah, Father," the eunuch smiled, "I must admit, I was fearful at first, never having lived on my own. But now I am quite content."

"And what has made the difference?"

"I mentioned long ago that we are not always what we seem. I was quite fortunate. I have always been able to enjoy the flowers, even if I was not able to produce any fruit." He paused for a minute. "My visits to the bazaar were not only for buying books," he said with a smile.

"And now?"

"And now I am a happily married man."

"And who is the lucky woman?" asked the astonished priest.

"You remember that Nakshidil insisted her slaves be freed. I am married to one of the girls from the harem."

"I wish you the best, Tulip."

"And I wish you the same, Father."

With that the two embraced. As Father Chrysostome arranged himself to go, Tulip helped him out of the café and into a passing carriage. With a tip of his red fez, he waved goodbye and made his way to the palace. Walking along the cobblestone streets, he heaved a sigh. If only Nakshidil could have been with him now to celebrate the birth of her second grandson, Prince Abdul Aziz.

ACKNOWLEDGMENTS

I am indebted to the following authors: Aksit, Atasoy, Blanche, Bruce, Chase, Coco, Croutier, Davey, Davis, Du Theil, Erickson, Freely, Goodwin, Hanum, Hobhouse, Kinzer, Kinross, Krody, Levy, Lewis, Mansel, McCarthy, Melling, Montagu, Morton, Mossiker, Pardoe, Penzer, Pierce, Schama, Shaw, Thackeray, Ulucay, Wheatcroft, and White.

My gratitude to Talman Halmat, Ertogrul Osman, and Zenob Osman, who are the essence of Turkish charm and provided introductions to some of the most delightful scholars, writers, and historians in Turkey. Dilek Pamir offered her gracious hospitality and answered dozens of questions about Nakshidil.

Professor Nurhan Atasoy filled me with her enthusiasm; Gungor Dilmen showed me the Topkapi harem as no one else could; Murat Bardakci made Selim III come alive, cooked the finest Turkish cuisine, and introduced me to Professors Yildiz Gultekin and Fikret Sarkaoglu, who researched documents for me in the Topkapi archives; Professors Hakan Erdem and Edhem Eldem encouraged me

ACKNOWLEDGMENTS

to continue even when the outlook was unpromising; Harry Ojalvo showed me the world of the kira.

Special thanks to Lenny Golay, who first gave me the idea for this book and then read the manuscript with care. Special appreciation to my agent, Linda Chester, for her unflagging support, generosity, and friendship. Lorna Owen read the manuscript thoughtfully and was always ready to help. Helen Armstrong shared her knowledge of music. Patricia Friedman taught me Turkish dancing. Elizabeth Atkins guided me through eighteenth-century France. Liza Nelligan gave me treasured advice. Bernard Kalb's exuberance spurred on my Turkish pursuits.

Nan Talese, a writer's dream editor, waited patiently for a biography and then encouraged me to write this book as a novel, guiding it in her firm yet gentle way.

As always, my late husband, John Wallach, was my travel partner and my life partner, uncomplaining and understanding through it all.

A NOTE ABOUT THE AUTHOR

JANET WALLACH is the author of *Desert Queen: The Extraordinary Life of Gertrude Bell* and *Chanel: Her Style and Her Life.* She is also coauthor, with her husband, John Wallach, of three previous books on the Middle East: *The New Palestinians, Arafat: In the Eyes of the Beholder,* and *Still Small Voices: The Real Heroes of the Arab–Israeli Conflict.* A frequent contributor to the *Washington Post Magazine* and other periodicals, she lives in New York City and Connecticut.

A NOTE ABOUT THE TYPE

The text of this book is set in Mrs. Eaves,
a historical revival based on the design of Baskerville
and designed in 1995–1996.

*"In translating this classic to today's digital font technology, I focused on capturing
the warmth and softness of letterpress printing that often occurs
due to the 'gain' of impression and ink spread."*

Zuzana Licko (type designer)